Prai...

Wow. Just wow.
FWIW.net

Captivating.
...ure ...

An amazing read Awesome!
BetweenThePages.com

Grabs you from the first sentence. The story is full of
sharp wit and terrifying chills.
RT Book Reviews

Sucked me in and kept me glued to the pages.
Paranormal Book Reviews

Riveting. A tremendous read.
TheBookFairy.com

A definite must buy!
GoodChoiceReading.com

One of the BEST books I have ever read.
EzineofaRandomGirl.blogstop.com

GIRL OF
NIGHTMARES

ORCHARD BOOKS
338 Euston Road, London NW1 3BH
Orchard Books Australia

Level 17/207 Kent Street, Sydney, NSW 2000

First published in 2012 in the United States by Tor Teen
This edition published by Orchard in 2013 by Orchard Books

ISBN 978 1 40832 612 1

Text © Kendare Blake 2012

A CIP catalogue record for this book is
available from the British Library.

3 5 7 9 10 8 6 4 2

Printed in Great Britain

Orchard Books is a division of Hachette Children's Books,
an Hachette UK company.

www.hachette.co.uk

GIRL OF NIGHTMARES

KENDARE BLAKE

ORCHARD

CHAPTER ONE

I think I killed a girl who looked like this once.

Yeah. Her name was Emily Danagger. She'd been murdered in her early teens, by a contractor working on her parents' house. Her body was stuffed into the attic wall and plastered over.

I blink and mutter a vague answer to whatever question the girl next to me just asked. Emily's cheekbones were higher. And the nose is different. But the shape of the face is so similar, it's like I'm staring at the girl I tracked into the upstairs guestroom. It took the better part of an hour, hacking with the athame at wall after wall as she seeped out of it, quietly trying to get behind me.

'I love monster movies,' says the girl in front of me whose name I can't remember. 'Jigsaw and Jason are definitely my favorites. What about you?'

'I don't much care for monster movies,' I reply, and don't mention that neither Jigsaw nor Jason are technically monsters. 'I like explosions, special effects.'

Cait Hecht. That's this girl's name. She's another junior at Winston Churchill. She has hazel eyes, sort of too big for her face, but pretty. I don't know what color Emily Danagger's eyes were. By the time I met her, all the blood had leaked out of them. I remember her face, pale but not sightless, materializing through faded flower-print wallpaper. Now it seems dumb, but at the time it was the most intense game of dead-girl whack-a-mole ever. I was covered in sweat. It was a long time ago, when I was younger and more easily rattled. It would still be years before I'd go up against ghosts of any real strength – ghosts like Anna Korlov, the girl who could have torn out my spine anytime she liked, but wound up saving me instead.

I'm sitting in the corner booth of a coffee shop off Bay Street. Carmel's across from me with two of her friends, Jo and Chad, who I think have been a couple since seventh grade. Gross. Beside me, Cait Hecht is supposed to be my date. We just saw a movie; I don't remember what it was about but I think there were giant dogs in it. She's talking to me with oversized gestures, cocked eyebrows, and teeth made perfect by a childhood full of retainers, trying to keep my attention. But all I can think is how much she looks like Emily Danagger, except far less interesting.

'So,' she says awkwardly, 'how's your coffee?'

'It's good,' I reply. I try to smile. None of this is her fault. Carmel's the one who talked me into this farce, and I'm the one who went along with it to shut her up. I feel like an ass for wasting Cait's time. I feel like a bigger ass for secretly comparing her to a dead girl I killed four years ago.

The conversation stalls. I take a long drink of my coffee, which really is good. Full of sugar and whipped cream and hazelnut. Under the table, Carmel kicks me and I almost spill it down my chin. When I look up she's talking to Jo and Chad, but she meant to do it. I'm not being a proper date. There's a tic starting underneath her left eye.

I briefly contemplate making polite conversation. But I don't want to encourage this, or lead Cait on. It's a mystery why she wanted to go out with me anyway. After what happened to Mike, Will, and Chase last year – Mike getting murdered by Anna, and Will and Chase eaten by the ghost that killed my father – I'm the pariah of Winston Churchill. I was never linked to their murders, but everyone suspects. They know that those guys hated me, and that they ended up dead.

There are actual theories about what might have happened, big, swirling rumors that circulate and grow before finally reaching epically ridiculous proportions and dying off. It was drugs, people whisper. No, no, it was an underground sex ring. Cas was supplying them with amphetamines so they could perform better. He's like a druggie pimp.

People pass me in the halls and avoid my eyes. They whisper in my wake. Sometimes I second-guess my decision to finish high school in Thunder Bay. I can't stand that these idiots have all these theories, most of them outlandish to the extreme, yet none of them have thought to mention the ghost story that they all knew. No one has ever talked about Anna Dressed in Blood. That, at least, would be a rumor worth listening to.

Some days, I open my mouth to tell my mom to get ready, to find us another house in another city where I could be hunting any number of the murderous dead. We'd have packed up months ago had it not been for Thomas and Carmel. Despite all efforts to the contrary, I've come to rely on Thomas Sabin and Carmel Jones. It's weird to think that the girl across the table, giving me secret dagger eyes, started out as just a mark. Just a way to know the town. It's weird to think that I once saw Thomas, my best friend, as an annoying, psychic tagalong.

Carmel nudges me again and I glance at the clock. Barely five minutes have passed since the last time I looked. I think it might be broken. When Cait's fingers slide against my wrist, I pull away and take a drink of my coffee. I don't miss the embarrassed and uncomfortable shift of her body when I do it.

All of a sudden, Carmel says loudly, 'I don't think Cas has even researched colleges yet. Have you, Cas?' She kicks me harder this time. What is she talking about? I'm still a junior. Why would I be thinking about college? Of course, Carmel has probably had her future planned out since preschool.

'I'm thinking about St. Lawrence,' Cait says when I just sit there. 'My dad says St. Clair might be better. But I don't know what he means by *better*.'

'Mm,' I say. Carmel's looking at me like I'm some kind of idiot. I almost laugh. She means well, but I have absolutely zero to say to these people. I wish Thomas were here. When the phone in my pocket starts buzzing, I jump up from the table too fast. They'll start talking about me the minute I'm out the door, wondering what my problem is, and Carmel will tell them I'm just nervous. Whatever.

It's Thomas calling.

'Hey,' I say. 'Are you mindreading again, or is this just good timing?'

'That bad, huh?'

'No worse than I thought it would be. What's up?'

I can almost feel him shrug through the phone.

11

'Nothing. Just thought you might want an escape route. I got the car out of the shop this afternoon. It could probably take us down to Grand Marais now.'

It's on the tip of my tongue to say, 'What do you mean, *probably*?' when the door of the coffee shop opens and Carmel glides out.

'Oh, shit,' I mutter.

'What?'

'Carmel's coming.'

She stops in front of me with her arms crossed over her chest. Thomas's tiny voice is chirping, wanting to know what's going on, whether he should swing by my house and pick me up, or not. Before Carmel can say anything, I put the phone back to my ear and tell him yes.

Carmel makes our excuses for us. In her Audi, she manages to keep up the silent treatment for all of forty seconds as she drives through the Thunder Bay streets. As we go, there's that odd coincidence of the streetlights turning on just ahead of us, like an enchanted escort. The roads are wet, still crunchy with lingering ice patches at the shoulders. Summer vacation starts in two weeks, but the town doesn't seem to know it. Late May and temps still dip below freezing at night. The only indication that winter is ending are the storms:

screaming, wind-driven things that go out over the lake and swing back in again, rinsing away the wreck of winter sludge. I wasn't ready for so many months of cold. It clamps around the city like a fist.

'Why did you even bother to come?' Carmel asks. 'If you were just going to act like that? You made Cait feel really bad.'

'*We* made Cait feel really bad. I never wanted to do this in the first place. You were the one who got her hopes up.'

'She's liked you since chemistry last semester,' Carmel says, scowling.

'Then you should have told her what an ass I am. Made me sound like a moronic jerk.'

'Better to let her see it for herself. You barely said five words to anyone.' She's got this disappointed squint on her face that's hovering close to disgust. Then her expression softens and she pushes her blond hair off of her shoulder. 'I just thought it would be nice if you got out and met some new people.'

'I meet plenty of new people.'

'I mean living people.'

I stare straight ahead. Maybe she meant that as a jibe about Anna, and maybe she didn't. But it pisses me off. Carmel wants me to forget. To forget that Anna saved all of our lives, that she sacrificed herself and dragged the Obeahman down to Hell. Carmel, Thomas, and I have been trying to figure out what happened to her after that night, without much luck. I guess Carmel thinks it's time to stop looking and let her go. But I won't. Whether I'm supposed to or not doesn't matter.

'You didn't have to leave, you know,' I say. 'I could've had Thomas pick me up there. Or I could have walked.'

Carmel chews her pretty lip, used to getting her way. We've been friends for most of the year now, and she still gets this puzzled puppy face when I don't just do what she says. It's strangely endearing.

'It's cold out. And it was boring anyway.' She's unruffled in her camel peacoat and red mittens. The red scarf at her neck is carefully knotted, despite the fact that we left in a hurry. 'I was just doing Cait a favor. I got her the date. It isn't our fault if she couldn't dazzle you with her charm.'

'She has good teeth,' I offer. Carmel grins.

'Maybe it was a bad idea. You shouldn't force it, right?' she says, and I pretend not to notice the hopeful glance she gives me, like I should keep this conversation going. There's nowhere for it to go.

When we get to my house, Thomas's beat-up Tempo is parked in the driveway. I can see his silhouette inside, talking to my mom's. Carmel pulls in right behind it. I expected to be dropped at the curb.

'We'll take my car. I'm going with you,' she says, and gets out. I don't object. Despite my best intentions, Carmel and Thomas have joined the ranks. After what happened with Anna, and the Obeahman, cutting them out wasn't really an option.

Inside the house, Thomas looks like one big wrinkle plopped down on the sofa. He stands up when he sees Carmel, and his eyes do their usual googley routine before he adjusts his glasses and goes back to normal. My mom is sitting in the chair, looking comfortable and motherly in a wrap sweater. I don't know where people get these ideas that witches all wear a metric ton of eyeliner and bounce around in velvet capes. She smiles at us and tactfully asks how the movie was, rather than how the date went.

I shrug. 'I didn't really get it,' I say.

She sighs. 'So, Thomas tells me that you're going to Grand Marais.'

'Seems like as good a night as any,' I say. I look at Thomas. 'Carmel's coming too. So we can take her car.'

'Good,' he replies. 'If we take mine we'll probably wind up on the side of the road before we even cross the border.'

There's a brief moment of awkwardness as we wait for my mom to leave. She's not a civilian by any means, but I try not to bother her with details. After my near death this past fall, her auburn hair has become peppered with white.

Finally she stands and presses three small but very smelly velvet bags into my hand. I know what they are without looking. Fresh, herbal blends of her classic protection spell, one for each of us. She touches my forehead with a fingertip.

'Keep them safe,' she whispers. 'And you too.' She turns back to Thomas. 'And now I should get to work on more candles for your grandfather's shop.'

'The prosperity ones have been going faster than we can get them on shelves.' He grins.

'And they're so simple. Lemon and basil. A lodestone core. I'll stop in with another batch by Tuesday.' She goes up the stairs, to the room she's taken over for spell-work. It's full of block wax and oils and dusty bottles of herbs. I hear that other mothers have entire rooms designated for sewing. That must be weird.

'I'll help you pack the candles when I get back,' I say as she vanishes up the stairs. I wish she'd get another cat. There's a cat-shaped hole where Tybalt used to be, floating in her footsteps. But I suppose it's only been six months since he died. Maybe that's still too soon.

'So, are we ready?' Thomas asks. Under his arm there's a canvas messenger bag. Every scrap of info we get on a particular ghost, a particular job, he stuffs inside that bag. I hate to think how quickly he'd be tied to a stake and burned if anyone ever got hold of it. Without looking into the mess, he reaches in and does his creepy psychic thing, where his fingertips find whatever he's after, every time, like that girl from *Poltergeist*.

'Grand Marais,' Carmel murmurs as he hands the papers to her. Most of it is a letter from a professor of psychology at Rosebridge Graduate School, an old crony of my dad's, who, before buckling down and shaping young minds, expanded his own by participating in trance circles led by my parents in the early 80s. In the letter, he talks about a ghost in Grand Marais, Minnesota, rumored to inhabit an abandoned barn. Six deaths have occurred on the property over the last three decades. Three of them have been deemed as under suspicious circumstances.

So what, six deaths. Stats like that don't make my usual A-list. But now that I'm rooted in Thunder Bay, my options are limited to a few road trips a year, and places I can get to over the weekend.

'So, it kills by making people have accidents?' Carmel says, reading over the letter. Most of the barn's victims appeared to be accidental. A farmer was working on his tractor when the thing slipped off the bricks and pinned him. Four years later, the farmer's wife fell chest-down on a pitchfork. 'How do we know they aren't really accidents? Grand Marais is a long drive for a no-show.'

Carmel always calls the ghosts 'it.' Never 'he' or 'she' and rarely by name.

'Like we have anything better to do?' I say. In my backpack, the athame shifts. The knowledge of it there, tucked into its leather sheath, sharp as a razor without ever needing to be sharpened, makes me uneasy. It almost makes me wish I were back on that damned date.

Ever since the confrontation with the Obeahman, when I found out that the knife had been linked to him, I...I don't know. It's not that I'm afraid of it. It still feels like it's mine. And Gideon assures me that the link between it and the Obeahman has been severed, that the ghosts I kill now no longer go to him, feeding him and increasing his power. Now they go where they were supposed to go. If anyone would know, it would be Gideon, over in London, knee-deep in musty books. He was with my dad since the beginning. But when I needed a second opinion, Thomas and I went to the antique shop and listened to his grandfather Morfran run through a speech about how energy is contained on certain planes, and that the Obeahman and the athame don't exist on the same plane anymore. Whatever that means.

So I'm not afraid of it. But sometimes I feel its power reach out and give me a shove. It's a little bit more than an inanimate thing, and sometimes I wonder what it wants.

'Still,' Carmel says, 'even if it is a ghost, it only kills once every few years? What if it doesn't want to kill us?'

'Well,' Thomas starts sheepishly, 'after the last time we came up empty-handed, I started working on this.' He reaches into the pocket of his Army surplus jacket and pulls out a circular piece of light-colored stone. It's flat and about one inch thick, like a large, fat coin. There's a symbol carved into one side, something that looks like a modified Celtic knot.

'A runestone,' I say.

'It's pretty,' Carmel says, and Thomas hands it to her. It really is well done. The carving is exact, and he's polished it so it shines white.

'It's a lure.'

Carmel passes it to me. A rune to lure them out, sort of like ghostly catnip. Very clever, if it works. I turn it over in my hand. It's cool to the touch and heavy as a hen's egg.

'So,' Thomas says, taking the runestone back and pocketing it. 'Do you want to try it?'

I look at the two of them and nod.

'Let's get going.'

The drive to Grand Marais, Minnesota, is long, and boring in the dark. Boughs of pine trees flicker in and out of the headlights, and watching the dotted line is starting to make me motion-sick. For most of the ride down I try to sleep in the backseat, or at least feign sleep, alternately eavesdropping on and tuning out their conversation. When they whisper, I know they're talking about Anna, but they never use her name. I hear Carmel say it's hopeless, that we'll never find out where she went, and that even if we could, maybe we shouldn't. Thomas doesn't argue much; he never does where Carmel is concerned. That kind of talk used to make me angry. Now it's just commonplace.

'Turn off,' Thomas says. 'I think that might be the road.'

I crane my head over the seat as Carmel tries to navigate the Audi down something that isn't so much a road as a mud-rutted four-by-four trail. The car has all-wheel drive, but this still poses a high risk of getting stuck. They must've had heavy rain here in the last day or so, and the tracks are covered over with puddles. I'm just about to tell Carmel to forget it, and to try to back out, when something black flashes up in the headlights.

We skid to a stop. 'Is that it?' Carmel asks. 'It' is an enormous black barn, standing at the edge of a barren field with dead stalks of plants shooting up like stray hairs. The house that it must have belonged to, along with any other buildings, has long since been torn down. All that remains is the barn, dark and alone, waiting for us in front of a forest of silent trees.

'Matches the description,' I say.

'Description nothing,' Thomas says, rooting around in his messenger bag. 'We got the sketch, remember?' He pulls it out and Carmel flips on the dome light. I wish she hadn't. There's an instant sensation of being watched, like the light just gave away all of our secrets. Carmel's hand jerks to turn it off, but I put my hand on her shoulder.

'Too late.'

Thomas holds the sketch up to the window, comparing it to the shadowy figure of the barn. In my opinion, it isn't much use. It's rough, and done in charcoal so everything is just a different shade of black. It came in the mail along with the tip, and is the product of a psychic trance. Somebody drew out his vision while he was having it. He probably should have opened his eyes and looked down at the paper. The sketch has a definite dreamlike quality, a blurring of the edges and lots of harsh lines. It looks like it was done by a four-year-old. But as I compare them, the barn and the sketch start to look more and more similar, like it isn't really the shape that matters so much as whatever is *behind* the shape.

This is stupid. How many times did my father tell me that *places* can't be bad? I reach into my backpack and grab the athame, then get out of the car. The puddles reach up to my shoelaces, and my feet are soaked by the time I get to the Audi's trunk. Both Carmel's and Thomas's cars have been outfitted and stocked like survival outposts, with flares and blankets and enough first-aid supplies to satisfy the most paranoid hypochondriac. Thomas is beside me, stepping gingerly through the mud. Carmel pops the trunk, and we grab three flashlights and a camping lantern. We walk together in the dark, feeling our feet go numb and listening to our socks squelch inside our shoes. It's wet and cold. Stubborn snow patches still cling to the bases of the trees and around the sides of the barn.

I'm struck again by how ominous the barn looks. Worse even than Anna's falling-down Victorian house. It crouches like a spider, waiting for us to get just close enough, pretending to be inanimate. But that's stupid. It's just the cold and the dark getting under my skin. Still, I wouldn't necessarily give a thumbs-down if someone decided to come out here with gasoline and a match.

'Here.' I hand Thomas and Carmel their fresh protection spells. Thomas puts his in his pants pocket. Carmel holds hers like a rosary. We turn on the lantern and flashlights just outside the door, which creaks back and forth like a come-hither finger. 'Stay close,' I whisper, and they press in on either side.

'I tell myself every time that we're crazy for doing this,' Carmel mutters. 'Every time, I think that I'll just wait in the car.'

'It's not like you to stay on the sidelines,' Thomas whispers, and on my other side, I sense Carmel's smile.

'Get a room,' I mutter, and reach forward to pull open the door.

Thomas has this annoying habit of going in hot, flashing his beam of light every which way at a million miles an hour, like he's expecting to bust a ghost mid-haunt or something. But ghosts are shy. Or if not shy, at least cautious. Never in my life have I opened a door and found myself staring directly into a dead face. I have, however, stepped inside and instantly known I was being watched. Which is what happens now.

It's a strange sensation, that feeling of intense awareness from somewhere behind you. When you're watched by the dead, the sensation is weirder, because you can't pinpoint which direction it's coming from. It's just there. Annoying, but there's nothing you can do about it. Sort of like Thomas's strobe-flashlight.

I walk to the center of the barn and set the camping lantern on the ground. The air smells heavy with dust and old hay, which is scattered across the dirt floor. When I turn a slow circle, my flashlight beam steady and careful, it whispers and crunches beneath my feet. Carmel and Thomas pay close attention and stay right beside me. I know that Thomas at least, witch that he is, can feel that we're being watched too. His flashlight beam zips up and down the walls, seeking out the corners and the places to hide. He's giving too much away, instead of using the light as a decoy and paying attention to the dark. The sounds of clothing are loud; Carmel's hair rustling back and forth over her shoulder as she looks around is like a fricking waterfall.

I put my hands out and step away, letting the light from the camping lantern break through our huddled mass. Our eyes have adjusted, and Carmel and I turn off our flashlights. The barn is empty except for what looks like the skeleton of an old plow in the south corner, and the camping lantern colors the room a muted yellow.

'Is this the place?' Carmel asks.

'Well, it's good enough to stay in for the night,' I say. 'In the morning we'll try to walk somewhere with better reception and call a tow truck.'

Carmel nods. She's caught on. The stranded traveler act works more often than you'd think. Which is why it shows up in so many different horror movies.

'It isn't any warmer in here than it is outside,' Thomas

comments. He shuts his flashlight off too, finally. There's a rustle of commotion overhead, and he jumps a mile, does the quick-draw on his flashlight, and points the beam at the ceiling.

'Sounds like pigeons,' I say. 'Good thing. If we're stuck out here too long we might have to do some yard-bird rotisserie.'

'That's…disgusting,' says Carmel.

'It's low-rent chicken. Let's check it out.' There's a rickety, rotting ladder that leads up to a trapdoor. I assume that all we'll find is a hayloft and a bunch of roosting pigeons and sparrows. But I don't need to tell Thomas and Carmel to be alert. They stay right behind, in constant contact. When Carmel's toe strikes the tines of a pitchfork, half-buried in the hay, she makes a face. We look at each other and she shakes her head. It can't be the same one, the same pitchfork that the farmer's wife fell on. That's what we say to ourselves, though I guess there's no real reason it can't be.

I go up into the hayloft first. A sweep of my flashlight shows a large, flat expanse of hay-covered floor, and a few tall stacks of bales along the south wall. When I cast my light up toward the slanted roof, I see what has to be close to fifty pigeons, none of whom appear to mind the disturbance.

'Come on up,' I say. Thomas climbs up next and we

both help Carmel. 'Watch it; this hay is loaded with bird shit.'

'Nice,' she mutters.

Once we're all up we look around, but there isn't a whole lot to see. It's just a vast, open space, lined with hay and bird turds. There's a pulley system they must've used to move hay suspended from the ceiling, and thick ropes are looped over the rafters.

'You know what I hate about flashlights?' Thomas asks, and I watch his beam move around the room, revealing sudden bird faces and shifting wings, then nothing but cobweb-covered boards. 'They always make you think about the stuff that you're not seeing. The stuff that's still in the dark.'

'It's true,' says Carmel. 'That's the worst shot in a horror movie. When the flashlight finally finds whatever it was looking for, and you realize that you'd rather not know what it looks like.'

They should both shut up. Now is not the time for them to be trying to freak themselves out. I walk off a little way, to hopefully put an end to the conversation and also to test out the quality of the floor. Thomas walks a little in the other direction, staying close to the wall. My flashlight moves over the hay bales, paying close attention to places something might hide. I don't notice anything except how gross they look speckled

26

with brown and white. Behind me, there's a long creaking sound, and when I turn a rush of wind hits my face. Thomas found one of the hay doors and opened it up.

The feeling of being watched is gone. We're just three kids, in an abandoned barn, pretending to be stranded for the benefit of no one. Maybe this wasn't even the right place to begin with, and the feeling I got walking through the door was a fluke.

'I don't think that rune of yours is working too well,' I say. Thomas shrugs. His hand drifts absently to his pocket, where the runestone weighs on the fabric.

'It was never a sure thing. I don't work with runes very often. And I've never carved one myself before.' He bends down and looks through the hay door, out into the night. It's gotten colder; his breath is a foggy cloud. 'Maybe it doesn't matter anyway. I mean, if this is the place, how many people are really in danger? Who comes out here? The ghost of whoever it was probably got bored and went to fake accidental deaths somewhere else.'

Accidental deaths. The words scratch at the surface of my brain.

I'm an idiot.

A rope falls from the rafter. I turn to yell at Thomas but the words don't come out fast enough. All I get out is his name, and I'm running, sprinting toward him because the rope is falling, and the ghost attached to the end of it becomes corporeal half a second before it shoves Thomas through the hay door, headfirst to a forty-foot drop to the cold, hard ground.

I dive. Hay needles into my jacket, slowing me down, but I'm not thinking of anything besides that glimpse of Thomas, and when I vault myself through the hay door I manage to catch hold of his foot. It takes every ounce of strength in my knuckles to hold on to him as he bangs into the side of the barn. In the next moment, Carmel's there with me, hanging half out of the door too.

'Thomas!' she shouts. 'Cas, pull him up!' With each of us holding a foot we jerk him back inside, first to the toes, then to the knees. Thomas is handling all this very well, not screaming or anything. We've almost got him back up when Carmel screams. I don't need to look to know it's the ghost. There's an icy pressure against my back and all of a sudden the air smells like the inside of a meat locker.

I turn and he's right in my face: a young guy in faded overalls and a short-sleeved chambray shirt. He's fat, with a gut paunch and arms like pale, overstuffed sausages. There's something wrong with the shape of his head.

I've got the knife out. It flashes from my back pocket,

ready to go straight into his belly, when she laughs.

She laughs. That laugh that I know so well even though I heard it only a handful of times. It's coming out of this fat hillbilly's gaping mouth. The athame almost falls out of my hand. Then the laugh cuts out, abruptly, and the ghost backs off and roars, something that sounds like English played backward though a bullhorn. Overhead, the fifty or so pigeons erupt off of their roosts and flap down toward us.

In the middle of feathers and musty bird smell, I shout at Carmel to keep pulling, to not let Thomas fall, but I know she won't, even though tiny beaks and claws are getting caught in her hair. As soon as we have Thomas back inside I shove them both toward the ladder.

Our feet tramp down in a panic of flapping wings. I have to remind myself to look back, to make sure the bastard isn't going to try another push.

'Where are we going?' Carmel shouts, disoriented.

'Just get out the door,' Thomas and I shout back. By the time my feet hit the bottom rung of the ladder, Carmel and Thomas are way ahead, running. I sense the ghost materialize to our right, and turn. Now that I have a closer look, I can see that what's wrong with the shape of his head is that the back of it is caved in. I can also see that he's holding the pitchfork.

Just before he throws it, I shout something at Carmel. It must be the right thing, because she whirls to see what it is and jerks her body to the left just before the tines of the pitchfork impale the wall. She finally starts screaming and the sound sharpens me; I draw my arm back and throw the athame in a snapping motion. It flies through the air and finds its home in the farmer's gut. For an instant, he looks my way, at me and right through me, with eyes like tepid pools of water. I don't feel anything this time. I don't wonder where the knife is sending him. I don't wonder whether the Obeahman can still feel it. When he wavers right out of existence like a ripple of heat, I'm just glad he's gone. He almost killed my friends. Screw that guy.

The athame hits the ground with a soft thud and I run to pick it up before going to Carmel, who is still screaming.

'Carmel! Are you hurt? Did it get you?' Thomas asks. He inspects her as she whips her head back and forth in a panic. The pitchfork came just that close. So close that one of the tines stabbed through the shoulder of her coat and pinned her to the wall. I reach up and yank the pitchfork loose, and she jumps away, brushing at her coat like it's dirty. She's equal parts scared and pissed off, and when she screams, 'You stupid asshole!' I can't help but feel like she's screaming at me.

CHAPTER TWO

The athame is resting in its jar of salt, buried up to the hilt in white crystals. The morning sun coming through the window hits the glass of the jar and refracts in every direction, bright gold, almost like a halo. My dad and I used to sit and stare at it, stuffed into this same jar, having been purified by moonlight. He called it Excalibur. I don't call it anything.

Behind me, my mom is frying eggs. A set of her freshest spell candles are stacked on the countertop. There are three different colors, each with a different smell. Green for prosperity, red for passion, white for clarity. Next to them are three small stacks of parchment bearing three different incantations, to be wrapped around the candles and tied with string.

'Toast or no toast?' she asks.

'Toast,' I reply. 'Do we have any more Saskatoon jam?'

She gets it out and I pop four pieces of bread into the

toaster. When they're done, I layer them with butter and jam and take them to the table, where my mom has already set our plates with eggs.

'Get the juice, would you?' she says, and as I'm half-buried in the refrigerator, 'So, are you going to tell me how things went Saturday night?'

I stand up and pour two glasses of orange juice. 'I was on the fence about it.' The ride back from Grand Marais was near silent. By the time we got home, it was Sunday morning, and I immediately passed out, only regaining consciousness to watch one of the Matrix movies on cable before passing back out and sleeping through the night. It was the best avoidance plan I'd ever come up with.

'Well,' my mom says chirpily, 'get off the fence and dive in. You have to be to school in half an hour.'

I sit down at the table and set down the juice. My eyes stay trained on the eggs, which stare back at me with yellow yolk pupils. I jab them with my fork. What am I supposed to say? How am I supposed to make sense of it for her, when I haven't made sense of it myself? That was Anna's laugh. It was clear as a bell, unmistakable, falling out of the farmer's black throat. But that's impossible. Anna is gone. Only I can't let her go. So my mind has started making things up. That's what the daylight tells me. That's what any sane person would tell me.

'I messed up,' I say into my plate. 'I wasn't sharp enough.'

'But you got him, didn't you?'

'Not before he pushed Thomas out a window and almost turned Carmel into shish kebab.' My appetite is suddenly gone. Not even the Saskatoon jam looks tempting. 'They shouldn't come with me anymore. I never should have let them.'

My mom sighs. 'It wasn't so much an issue of 'letting them,' Cas. I don't think you could have stopped them.' Her voice is affectionate, completely lacking in objectivity. She cares about them. Of course she does. But she's also pretty glad I'm not out there by myself anymore.

'They were sucked in by the novelty,' I say. Anger flies to the surface out of nowhere; my teeth clench down on it. 'But it's real, and it can get them killed, and when they figure that out, what do you think is going to happen?'

My mother's face is calm, no more emotion there than a slight furrow of her eyebrows. She forks a piece of egg and chews it, quietly. Then she says, 'I don't think you give them enough credit.'

Maybe I don't. But I wouldn't blame them for running for the hills after what happened on Saturday.

I wouldn't have blamed them for running after Mike, Will, and Chase got murdered. Sometimes I wish I could have.

'I've got to get to school,' I say, and push my chair away from the table, leaving the food untouched. The athame has been purified and is ready to come out of the salt, but I walk right past. For maybe the first time in my life, I don't want it.

The first sight I catch after rounding the corner toward my locker is Thomas yawning. He's leaning against it with his books under his arm, wearing a plain gray t-shirt that is ready to rip through in a few places. His hair points in completely contradictory directions. It makes me smile. So much power contained in a body that looks like it was born in a dirty clothes basket. When he sees me coming, he waves, and this big, open grin spreads across his face. Then he yawns again.

'Sorry,' he says. 'I'm having trouble recovering from Saturday.'

'Epic party, right, Thomas?' snickers a sarcastic voice behind us, and I turn to see a group of people, most of whom I don't know. The comment came from Christy something or other, and I think, who cares, except that Thomas's mouth has pinched together and he's looking at the row of lockers like he wants to melt into it.

I look at Christy casually. 'Keep talking like that and I'll have you killed.' She blinks, trying to decide whether or not I'm serious, which makes me smirk. These rumors are ridiculous. They walk on, silent.

'Forget them. If they'd been there they'd have pissed themselves.'

'Right,' he says, and stands up straighter. 'Listen, I'm sorry about Saturday. I'm such a dope, leaning out the window like that. Thanks for saving my skin.'

For a second, there's this lump in my throat that tastes like gratitude and surprise. Then I swallow it. 'Don't thank me.' Remember who put you there in the first place. 'It was no big deal.'

'Sure.' He shrugs. Thomas and I have first period physics together this semester. With his help I'm pulling an A-minus. All of that shit about fulcrums and mass times velocity might as well be Greek to me, but Thomas drinks it up. It must be the witch in him; he has a definite understanding of forces and how they work. On the way to class, we pass by Cait Hecht, who makes a point of looking as far away from me as she can. I wonder if she'll start to gossip about me now too. I guess I'd understand if she did.

I don't catch anything more than a glimpse of Carmel until our shared fifth period study hall. Despite being the third leg in our strange, ghost-hunting trio, her queen bee status has remained intact. Her social calendar is as full as ever. She's on the student council and a bunch of boring fundraising committees. Watching her straddle both worlds is interesting. She slides into one as easily as the other.

When I get to study hall, I take my usual seat across from Carmel. Thomas isn't here yet. I can tell immediately that she isn't as forgiving as he is. Her eyes barely flicker up from her notebook when I sit down.

'You really need to get a haircut.'

'I like it a little long.'

'But I think it gets into your eyes,' she says, looking right at me. 'Keeps you from seeing things properly.'

There's a brief stare-down, during which I decide that almost getting pinned like a butterfly in a glass case deserves at least an apology. 'I'm sorry about Saturday. I was stupid and off. I know that. It's dangerous—'

'Cut the crap,' Carmel says, snapping her gum. 'What's bothering you? You hesitated in that barn. You could have ended it all, up in the loft. It was a foot away, its guts bared like it was serving them up on a platter.'

I swallow. Of course she would notice. Carmel never misses anything. My mouth opens, but nothing comes out. She slides her hand out and touches my arm.

'The knife isn't bad anymore,' she says softly. 'Morfran

said so. Your friend Gideon said so. But if you have doubts, then maybe you should take a break. Someone's going to get hurt.'

Thomas slides in next to Carmel and looks from one of us to the other.

'What's the what?' he asks. 'You guys look like someone died.' God, Thomas, that's such a risky expression.

'Nothing,' I say. 'Carmel's just concerned about why I hesitated on Saturday.'

'What?'

'He hesitated,' Carmel replies. 'He could have killed it, in the hayloft.' She stops talking as two kids walk by. 'But he didn't, and I wound up staring down the wrong end of a pitchfork.'

'But we're all OK.' Thomas smiles. 'The job got done.'

'He's not over it,' Carmel says. 'He still wonders if the knife is evil.'

All the talking about me as if I'm not here is getting on my nerves. They go back and forth for a minute or so, Thomas defending me feebly and Carmel asserting that I need at least six sessions of paranormal counseling before I return to the job.

'Do you guys mind catching a little detention?' I ask suddenly. When I jerk my head toward the door and stand, they both get up too. The study hall monitor shouts some question about where we think we're going, or what we think we're doing, but we don't stop. Carmel just calls out, 'Uh, I forgot my note cards!' as we go through the door.

We're parked in the lot of a rest stop off 61, sitting in Carmel's silver Audi. I'm in the back, and both of them have twisted in their seats to look at me. They wait, patiently, which makes it worse. A little prodding wouldn't hurt.

'You're right about me hesitating,' I say finally. 'And you're right that I still have questions about the knife. But that's not what happened on Saturday. Questions don't keep me from doing my job.'

'So what was it?' Carmel asks.

What was it. I don't even know. In the instant that I heard her laugh, Anna bloomed red behind my eyes, and I saw everything she had ever been: the clever, pale girl in white, and the black-veined goddess dressed in blood. She was close enough to touch. But the adrenaline is gone now, and there's daylight all around. So maybe it was nothing. Just a wishful hallucination. But I brought them all the way out here to tell them, so I might as well tell them something.

'If I told you that I couldn't let go of Anna,' I say,

looking down at the Audi's black floor-mats, 'that I need to know she's at peace, would you understand that?'

'Yeah, absolutely,' Thomas says. Carmel looks away.

'I'm not ready to give up, Carmel.'

She tucks her blond hair behind her ear and looks down guiltily. 'I know. But you've been looking for answers for months. We all have.'

I smile ruefully. 'And what? You're tired of it?'

'Of course not,' she snaps. 'I liked Anna. And even if I didn't, she saved our lives. But what she did, sacrificing herself – that was for you, Cas. And she did it so that you could live. Not so you could walk around half dead, pining for her.'

I have nothing to say. The words bring me down, far and fast. Not knowing what happened to Anna has driven me close to insane these past months. I've imagined every imaginable hell, the worst possible fates. It would be easy to say that's why letting her go is difficult. It would be true. But it's not all. The fact is, Anna is gone. She was dead when I met her, and I was going to put her back in the dirt, but I didn't want her to go. Maybe the way that she left was supposed to wrap things up. She's deader than dead and I should be glad; instead I'm so pissed off that I can't see straight. It doesn't feel like she left. It feels like she was taken away.

After a minute, I shake my head and words fall out of

my mouth, practiced and calm. 'I know. Listen, maybe we should just cool it for a while. I mean, you're right. It isn't safe, and I'm sorry as hell for what happened on Saturday. I really am.'

They tell me not to worry about it. Thomas says it was nothing and Carmel makes a joke about getting harpooned. They react like best friends should, and all of a sudden I feel like a total dick. I need to get my head straight. I need to get used to the fact that I'm never going to see Anna again, before someone really does get hurt.

CHAPTER THREE

The sound of that laugh. It plays back in my head for about the hundredth time. It was her voice; Anna's voice, but it sounded mad, and shrill. Almost desperate. Or maybe that's just because I heard it coming out of a dead man's mouth. Or maybe I never really heard it at all.

A sharp crack makes me blink and look down. One of my mom's white clarity candles lies in two pieces at my feet, rolled up against my toe. I'd been packing them into a box to take to Morfran's shop.

'What's the matter, son of mine?' She's got this halfway smile on and a cocked eyebrow. 'What's got you so distracted that you're breaking our livelihood?'

I bend down and pick up the two halves of candle, awkwardly shoving the broken ends together like they'll magically merge. Why can't magic work like that?

'Sorry,' I say. She gets up from the table where she

was tying on incantations, takes the candle from me, and sniffs it.

'It's OK. We'll just keep this one. They work just as well broken as not.' She walks over and sets it on the windowsill over the sink. 'Now answer the question, kiddo. What is it? School? Or maybe that date of yours went better than you let on.' The look on her face is half teasing, but there's hope there too.

'No such luck, Mom.' It'd be easy enough to say it was school. Easy enough to say I was daydreaming. And I probably should. My mother is happy here. After we found out that my father's murderer had been renting out the attic of the house and ate her cat, I figured she'd move us. Or burn the house down. But she didn't. Instead she settled and made the place ours, more than any of the rentals we've lived in since my dad died. The whole thing seemed like something she'd almost been waiting for.

I suppose it was something we were both waiting for. Because it's over now. Closed.

'Cas? Are you OK? Did something happen?'

I give her my most reassuring smile. 'It's nothing. Just leftover crap.'

'Mm,' she says. She pulls a box of matches out of the junk drawer. 'Maybe you should light this clarity candle. Get rid of the cobwebs.'

'Sure.' I chuckle, and take the match. 'Shouldn't I say the incantation first?'

She waves her hand. 'The words aren't always necessary. You just have to know what you want.' She pokes me in the chest, and I strike the match.

'You are playing horribly,' Thomas says to me from one couch cushion over.

'So what, it's just Pac-Man,' I reply as my last guy runs smack into a ghost and dies.

'If you're going to look at it that way, you're never going to beat my top score.'

I snort. I'd never be able to beat it anyway. The kid has creepily accurate hand-eye coordination. I can hold my own in a first-person shooter, but he beats me at the old arcade games every time. He takes the controller and the theme music starts over. I watch as Pac-Man eats cherries and dots and sends ghosts back to the start box.

'You've memorized the boards.'

'Maybe,' he grins, then hits pause when his phone starts buzzing. The cell phone is new for Thomas. A gift from Carmel, which she uses to repeatedly text him to try to get us to meet her at the mall. But the mall is a thing that should not be suffered. Except maybe for Cinnabon.

Thomas sighs. 'Want to meet Carmel and Katie at Cinnabon?'

I take a deep breath. He'd come over to give me a book he'd found that had theories about the afterlife. It's sitting next to the Xbox, unopened. I'm tired of reading and coming up with more questions and no answers. I'm tired of chasing down my dad's old associates and getting nothing but best guesses. It's become an exhausting, dead end, and even if it makes me feel guilty to think so, that's the truth.

'Let's go,' I say.

The mall is bright and smells like lotion. Every store we pass by must sell the stuff. Carmel met us at the entrance, alone. Katie bugged out the minute she heard we were coming.

'Does it bother you that your best friend dislikes me so much?' Thomas asks, his mouth stuffed so full of Cinnabon that he's barely understandable.

'She doesn't dislike you. You just never take the chance to get to know her. You both make her feel unwelcome.'

'That's not true,' Thomas objects.

'It's sort of true,' I mutter from just behind them. And it is. When it's just me and Carmel and her friends, it's fine. I can mingle if I have to. But when the three of

44

us are together, it feels like a closed club. I sort of like that, and I don't even feel guilty about it. The three of us together is safe.

'See?' Carmel says. She slows down a step or two so I can catch up and walk beside them. Thomas says something else about Katie and I hear Nat's name come up too, but I'm not really listening. Their couples stuff is none of my business. I drop back to my regular spot just behind. The mall is too crowded to walk three-across without bobbing and weaving through people.

A multitude of voices call Carmel's name, and I look up from my cinnamon roll to see Amanda Schneider, Heidi Trico, and a different Katie something-or-other waving their arms. Derek Pimms and Nate Bergstrom are with them too; guys that Thomas would call the next wave of the Trojan Army. I can almost hear him thinking it now, hear him gritting his teeth as we walk over.

'Hey, Carmel,' Heidi says. 'What's up?'

Carmel shrugs. 'Cinnabon. And wandering around. Dropping hints for birthday gifts that some people are too dense to pick up on.' She nudges Thomas affectionately. I wish she wouldn't have. At least not in present company, because it makes Thomas turn red as a beet, which makes Derek and Nate grin like jackasses. The other girls just glance first his way, then mine, smiling without showing their teeth. Thomas shuffles his feet. He never looks Derek or Nate in the eye, so I compensate by staring them down. I feel like an idiot, but I do it. Carmel just talks and laughs, at ease and seemingly oblivious to the whole thing.

And then something shifts. The athame. It's secure, in its sheath, fastened with two straps around my ankle. But I just felt it move, the way it does sometimes when I'm hunting. And this was no small movement; it was an unmistakable twist.

I pivot in the direction it moved, feeling more than half crazy. There is no dead thing haunting the mall. It's too busy, too bright, and too lotion-ey. But the knife doesn't lie, so I search through the passing faces, faces that stare blankly on their way to American Eagle or laugh and smile with friends. All clearly alive in varying degrees. I pivot again and the knife jerks.

'What?' I mutter, and look ahead, at the window display of the store across from us.

It's Anna's dress.

I blink my eyes hard twice. But it's her dress. White and simple. Beautiful. I walk toward it, and the mall has gone quiet. What am I seeing? Not just a dress that's similar to hers. It's *her* dress. I know it even before the leg of the mannequin steps down off of the pedestal.

She moves jerkily on plastic legs. Her hair is hanging

down her shoulders, limp and loose like a synthetic wig. I don't look at her face. Not even when my fingers are against the glass of the display and her mannequin-legs bend, rustling the white fabric.

'Cas!'

I jerk, and the noise of the mall hits my eardrums like a slamming door. Thomas and Carmel are on either side of me, concerned looks on their faces. My whole head is cloudy, like I just woke up. Blinking up at the glass, the mannequin stands like it always stood, posed and dressed in a white dress that doesn't really look anything like Anna's at all.

I glance back at Amanda, Derek, and the others. They look as shell-shocked as Thomas and Carmel right now. But by tomorrow they'll be laughing hysterically as they tell everyone else they know. I pull my fingers away from the window awkwardly. After what they just saw, I can't say that I blame them.

'Are you OK?' Carmel asks. 'What happened?'

'Nothing,' I say. 'I thought I saw something, but it was nothing.'

She drops her eyes and looks quickly right and left. 'You were shouting.'

I look at Thomas, who nods.

'I guess I got a little loud. The acoustics in here suck; you can't really hear yourself.'

I see the look they give each other, and don't try to convince them. How could I? They see the white dress in the window and they know what it means. They know what it was that I thought I saw.

CHAPTER FOUR

The day after my epic nervous breakdown at the mall I spend my free period outside on the edge of the quad, sitting under a tree and talking to Gideon. There are other students out too, occupying the ground that's not shady, sacked out on the new spring grass with their heads on their backpacks or their friends' laps. Occasionally they look my way, say something, and everybody laughs. It occurs to me that I used to do a better job of blending. Maybe I shouldn't come back next year.

'Theseus, is everything all right? You sound distracted.'

I laugh. 'You sound like my mom.'

'Excuse me?'

'Sorry.' I hesitate, which is stupid. It's the reason I called him in the first place. I wanted to talk about it. I need to hear that Anna is gone. That she can't come back. And I need to hear it in an authoritative British voice.

'Have you ever heard of anyone coming back, after they've crossed over?' I say finally.

Gideon's pause is appropriately thoughtful. 'Never,' he says. 'It simply isn't possible. At least not within the realm of sane probability.'

I squint. Since when do we live in the realm of sane probability? 'But if I can propel them from one plane to another using the athame, couldn't there be some other thing that could get them back?' The pause this time is longer, but he's not really taking it seriously. If he were, I'd hear the jostling of a ladder or the rustle of turning book pages. 'I mean, come on, it's not that far-fetched a thought. A to B to G maybe, but—'

'I'm afraid it's more like A to B to pi.' He takes a breath. 'I know who you're thinking of, Theseus, but it just isn't possible. We can't bring her back.'

My eyes clench shut. 'What if she already is back?'

There's wariness in his voice when he asks, 'What do you mean?'

I hope a laugh will put him at ease, so I twist my mouth into a smile. 'I don't know what I mean. I didn't call to freak you out. I just – I guess I just think about her a lot.'

He sighs. 'I know you must. She was – she was extraordinary. But now she's where she belongs. Listen to me, Theseus,' he says, and I can almost feel his wizened fingers on my shoulders. 'You have to let this go.'

'I know.' And I do. Part of me wants to tell him about the way the athame moved, and about the things I've thought I've seen and heard. But he's right, and I'd only sound nuts.

'Listen, don't worry about me, all right?' I say, and stand up. 'Dammit,' I mutter, feeling the wet backside of my jeans.

'What?' Gideon asks, concerned.

'Oh, nothing. I've got a huge wet spot on my ass from sitting under this tree. I swear the ground around here never dries up.' He laughs, and we hang up. On my way back into the school, Dan Hill hits me in the arm.

'Hey,' he says. 'Did you get the history notes from yesterday? Can I borrow them during study hall?'

'Yeah, I guess,' I say, sort of surprised.

'Thanks, man. Usually I borrow from one of the girls, you know' – he flashes this rake's grin – 'but I'm pulling a low C and you got top score last test, right?'

'Yeah,' I say again. I did get the top score. To my extreme surprise and my mom's utter glee.

'Cool. Hey, I heard you were on acid or something at the mall last night.'

'I saw a dress Carmel wanted and pointed it out to Thomas Sabin.' I shrug. 'People make up some crazy shit at this school.'

'Yeah,' he says. 'That's what I thought. Later, man.' He walks off in another direction. Dan's pretty cool, I guess. If I'm lucky he'll pass my mall alibi on to a few others. Not likely though. Retractions show up in the back of the newspaper. The boring story loses out, truth or not. That's just how it goes.

'How can you not like roasted garlic chicken pizza?' Carmel asks, her phone out to place the order. 'Seriously? Just mushrooms and extra cheese?'

'And tomatoes,' Thomas adds.

'Just regular, cut-up tomatoes?' She looks at me incredulously. 'He's unnatural.'

'I'm with you,' I say from the refrigerator, where I'm grabbing sodas. We're chilling at my house, streaming movies off Netflix. It was Carmel's idea, and I'm choosing to believe it was because she wanted to relax, not because she wanted me away from the public.

'Maybe he's trying to be a gentleman, Carmel,' my mom says, walking through to get a refill of iced tea. 'Keeping away from the garlic for you.'

'Gross,' I say, and Thomas laughs. It's Carmel who blushes this time.

My mom smiles. 'If you order one of each, I'll split the tomato one with Thomas and you and Cas can split the other.'

'OK. But you're going to want the chicken when it gets here.' She orders, and the three of us head into the living room to watch reruns of *Scrubs* until the pizzas arrive and we start the movie. We barely sit down before Carmel jumps back up, her phone between her fingers, texting away.

'What's up?' Thomas asks.

'Sort of a finals studying party-thing,' she says. She heads for the front porch. 'I told Nat and Amanda I'd show up there if the movie didn't get over too late. Be right back.'

After the door closes, I poke Thomas.

'Doesn't it bother you that she goes off like that?' I ask.

'What do you mean?'

'Well,' I start, but I don't quite know. I guess it's just that where Carmel has sometimes tried to mingle me in with her other friends, she doesn't really with Thomas. I'd think it would bother him, but I don't know how to ask that tactfully. And what the hell finals does she still have to study for? I've already taken all of mine but one. Teachers here really like to dial in the last few weeks. Not that I'm complaining. 'Aren't you her boyfriend?'

I blurt finally. 'Shouldn't she be dragging you out with her friends?'

It wasn't the best way to word things, but he doesn't seem offended, or even surprised. He just grins.

'I don't know what we are, technically,' he says quietly. 'But I do know that we don't work like that. We're different.'

'Different,' I mumble, even though the moony look on his face is sort of touching. 'Everybody's got to be different. Did it ever occur to you that 'same' is a classic for a reason?'

'Big talk for somebody whose last girlfriend died in 1958,' Thomas replies, and then hides behind a gulp of soda. I grin and look back toward the TV.

Anna is at the window. She's standing in the bushes outside my house, staring at me.

'Jesus!' I scramble up the back of the couch and barely wince when my shoulder rams into the wall.

'What?' Thomas jumps up too, looking first at the floor like there might've been a rat or something before following my gaze to the window.

Anna's eyes are empty and dead, completely hollow and without any trace of recognition. Watching her blink is like watching an alligator cut through thick, brackish water. As I try to catch my breath, a wormy, dark rivulet of blood runs from her nose.

'Cas, what is it? What's wrong?'

I glance at Thomas. 'You mean you don't see her?' I look back at the window, half expecting her to be gone, half *hoping* that she's gone, but she's still there, immobile.

Thomas scours the window, moving his head to see around the reflections of light. He looks terrified. It doesn't make sense. He should be able to see her. He's a goddamn witch for God's sake.

I can't take it anymore. I bolt off the couch and head for the front door, throwing it open to barge onto the porch.

All I see is Carmel's surprised face, her phone halfway to her ear. In the bushes in front of the window there's nothing but shadows.

'What's going on?' Carmel asks as I plunge down the steps and beat my way through the brush, branches scratching my arms.

'Give me your phone!'

'What?' Carmel's voice is scared. My mom's out here now too, all three of them frightened by they don't know what.

'Just throw it here,' I shout, and she does. I press a button and point it at the ground, using the bluish light to scour the dirt for footprints or disturbances. There's nothing.

'What? What is it?' Thomas squeaks.

'Nothing,' I say loudly, but it isn't nothing. Whether it's all in my head or not, it isn't nothing. And when I reach back for the athame in my pocket, it feels cold as ice.

Ten minutes later, my mom sets a steaming mug down in front of me at the kitchen table. I pick it up and sniff at it.

'It's not a potion; it's just tea,' she says, exasperated. 'Decaffeinated.'

'Thanks,' I say, and sip it. No caffeine and no sugar either. I don't know what about bitter brown water is supposed to be soothing. But I make a show of sighing and settling farther into my chair.

Thomas and Carmel keep exchanging these furtive glances, and my mom picks up on it.

'What?' she asks. 'What do you know?'

Carmel looks at me for permission, and when I don't say anything, she tells my mom what happened at the mall, with Anna's lookalike dress.

'Honestly, Cas, you've been acting sort of weird since Grand Marais last week.'

My mom leans up against the counter. 'Cas? What's going on? And why didn't you tell me about the mall?'

'Because I like to keep my crazy all to myself?' Obviously deflection isn't going to work. They just keep on staring. Waiting and staring. 'It's just – I thought I saw Anna, that's all.' I take another sip of tea. 'And in Grand Marais, in the hay loft – I thought I heard her laugh.' I shake my head. 'It feels like – I don't know what it feels like. Like being haunted, I guess.'

Above the rim of my mug, the expression that ripples through the room is plain. They think I'm hallucinating. They pity me. 'Poor Cas' is written all over their faces, hanging on their cheeks like ten-pound weights.

'The athame sees her too,' I add, and that gets their attention.

'Maybe we should call Gideon in the morning,' my mom suggests. I nod. But he'll probably think the same thing. Still, he is the closest thing I have to an athame expert.

The table falls quiet. They're skeptical and I don't blame them. After all, this is what I've wanted, since Anna's been gone.

How many times have I imagined her, sitting beside me? Her voice has rung around in my head a million times, some lame attempt to have the conversations we missed out on. Sometimes I pretend that we found another way to defeat the Obeahman; one that didn't mess everything up.

'Do you think it's possible?' Thomas asks. 'I mean, is it even possible?'

'Things don't cross over,' I reply. 'Gideon says things don't cross over. They can't. But it feels – like she's calling to me. I just can't hear what she wants.'

'This is so messed up,' Carmel whispers. 'What are you going to do?' She looks at me, then at Thomas and my mom. 'What are we going to do?'

'I have to find out if it's real,' I say. 'Or if I'm officially nuts. And if it's real, I have to find out what she wants. What she needs. We all owe her that.'

'Don't do anything yet,' my mom says. 'Not until we talk to Gideon. Not until we have more time to figure it out. I don't like this.'

'I don't like it either,' Carmel says.

I look at Thomas.

'I don't know whether to like it or not like it.' He shrugs. 'I mean, Anna was our friend, sort of. I can't believe that she'd want to hurt us, or even scare us. It's the athame that bothers me. That the athame responds. We should probably talk to Morfran too.'

They all stare at me. 'OK,' I say. 'OK, we'll wait.' But not for too long.

CHAPTER FIVE

After a night of crappy sleep, I'm sitting at Thomas's kitchen table with Carmel, watching Thomas and Morfran cook breakfast. They move smoothly through their domestic routine, shuffling between the table and stove, still only half-awake. Morfran's wearing a plaid, flannel bathrobe and he looks ridiculous. You'd never guess that underneath that bathrobe is one of the strongest voodoo men in North America. He's sort of like his grandson that way.

There's a sizzle as meat hits a hot skillet. Morfran has this habit of making ring bologna for breakfast. It's sort of weird, yet actually pretty good. This morning I've got no appetite, but Thomas slides a big pile of ring bologna and scrambled eggs in front of me, so I cut it up and push it around to make it look like I ate. Across the table, Carmel is doing pretty much the same thing.

After Morfran dishes up his own plate, he slides a

section of bologna into Stella's dog bowl. The black Lab mix comes barreling into the kitchen like she hasn't eaten in years. Morfran pats her fat rump and leans against the counter with his plate, watching us from behind his specs.

'Mighty early for a junior Ghostbuster meeting,' he says. 'Must be dire.'

'It's not *dire*,' Thomas mutters. Morfran snorts through his eggs.

'You didn't just wake up and come over for the sausage,' he says, and that's another thing. He calls the ring bologna 'sausage.'

'The orange juice is delicious.' Carmel smiles.

'I buy pulp-free. Now spit it out. I've got to get to the shop.' He's looking right at me when he says it.

I had this whole line of questioning worked out in my head. Instead I blurt,

'We need to find out what happened to Anna.' It must be the tenth time I've told him so, and he's as sick of hearing it as I am of saying it. But it has to get through. We need his help, and he hasn't offered any since the night that we fought the Obeahman, when he worked countercurses to keep me alive after I'd been Obeahed and helped Thomas with the protection spells at Anna's house.

'How's the sausage?' he asks.

'Fine. I'm not hungry. And I'm not going to stop asking.'

His eyes drift to my backpack. I never take the athame out when Morfran's around. The way that he looks at it when I do tells me it's unwelcome.

Thomas clears his throat. 'Tell him about Marie La Pointe.'

'Who's Marie La Pointe?' I ask, while Morfran gives Thomas a glare that says he might be grounded later.

'She's,' Thomas hesitates under his grandfather's stare, but I win out this time. 'She's a voodooienne in Jamaica. Morfran's been talking to her about...your situation.'

'What about my situation?'

'About the Obeahman, mostly. The fact that he was an eater of flesh, that he could ingest power and essence even after death; I mean, flesh-eating in itself is rare. What the Obeahman became after he died, by eating your father, linking himself to the athame, feeding off it, that makes him almost a fricking unicorn.'

'Thomas,' Morfran snaps. 'Will you shut your trap?' He shakes his head and mutters 'unicorn' under his breath. 'What that ghost did was take an ancient craft and twist it into something unnatural.'

'I didn't mean – ' Thomas starts, but I cut him off.

'What did you friend say?' I ask. 'Marie La Pointe. Did you ask her about Anna?'

'No,' he says. 'I asked her about Obeah. I asked her if the tie between the Obeahman and the knife was severed, if it could be severed.'

There are prickles on the back of my neck even though we've been over this before. 'What did she say?'

'She said that it could. She said that it was. She said that it will be.'

'Will be?' Carmel says loudly, her fork ringing off her plate. 'What the hell does that mean?'

Morfran shrugs and feeds Stella a piece of bologna off his fork when she paws his knee.

'Did she say anything else?' I ask.

'Yeah,' he replies. 'She said what I've been trying to tell you for months. Stop poking your nose where you shouldn't be poking it. Before you make yourself an enemy that cuts your nose off.'

'She threatened me?'

'It wasn't a threat. It was advice. There are some secrets in this world, kid, that people will kill to keep.'

'What people?'

He turns, rinses his empty plate in the sink, and loads it into the dishwasher. 'Wrong question. You should be asking what secrets. What power.'

At the table, we make frustrated faces and Thomas

mimes a scream and a motion that I guess is him shaking Morfran silly. Always with the cryptic. Always with the riddles. It drives us nuts.

'Something's happening with the athame,' I say, hoping that if I'm direct often enough, it'll start to rub off. 'I don't know what it is. I'm seeing Anna, and hearing her. Maybe because I'm looking, and the athame is seeking her out. Maybe because she's looking for me. Maybe both.'

'Maybe more than that,' Morfran says, turning around. He wipes his hands on the dishtowel and eyeballs me in that way that makes it feel like I'm just a skeleton and a blade. 'That thing in your pocket doesn't answer to the Obeahman anymore. But what does it answer to?'

'Me,' I say. 'It was made to answer to me. To my line.'

'Maybe,' he replies. 'Or was your line made to answer to *it*? The longer I talk to you the more my head fills up with wind. There's more than one thing going on here; I can feel it, like a thunderstorm. And so should you.' He nods his chin toward his grandson. 'And you too, Thomas. I didn't raise you to be off the ball.'

Beside me, Thomas straightens up and looks at me quickly like I'm a page he's been caught not reading.

'Can you not be creepy this early?' Carmel asks. 'I don't like any of this. I mean, what should we do?'

'Melt that knife down to scrap and bury it,' he says, clapping his palm against his knee for the black Lab to follow him back to his bedroom. 'But you're never going to do that.' On his way out of the kitchen he pauses and takes a deep breath. 'Listen, kid,' he says, looking at the floor. 'The Obeahman was the most twisted, hungry thing I've ever had the misfortune to come across. Anna dragged him out of the world. Sometimes your purpose is fulfilled. You need to let her rest.'

'Well that was a bust,' Carmel says on the drive in to school. 'What did Gideon say this morning?'

'He didn't answer. I left a message,' I reply. Carmel goes on a bit behind the wheel, about how she doesn't like what Morfran said and something about having the willies, but I've only got half an ear on her. The other one's on Thomas, who I think is still trying to hone in on the vibe Morfran got off the athame. From the look of near-constipation on his face, I don't think he's having much luck.

'Let's just get through the day,' Carmel says. 'Another day of skating through the end of the year, and we'll figure all this out later. Maybe we can hit up a different ghost this weekend.' She shakes her head. 'Or maybe we should lay off everything for awhile. Until we hear from Gideon at least. Shit. I was supposed to do an inventory of the decorations for the hall before the Graduation Committee meeting.'

'You're not even graduating this year.'

'Doesn't mean I'm not on the committee.' She huffs. 'So. Is that what we're going to do? Lay off and wait for Gideon?'

'Or for Anna to come knocking again,' Thomas says, and Carmel gives him a look.

'Yeah,' I say. 'I guess that's what we should do.'

How did I get here? It wasn't a conscious choice. At least it doesn't feel that way. When Carmel and Thomas dropped me at home after school, the plan was to eat two servings of my mom's spaghetti and meatballs and vegetate in front of the TV. So what am I doing in my mom's car, four hours and I don't know how many miles of highway behind me, staring at dormant smokestacks jutting up against a darkening sky?

This is something from the recesses of my memory, something that Daisy Bristol told me about only a month after Anna's house imploded with her inside it. I'd listened with half an ear. I was in no condition to hunt, no condition to do much of anything but walk around with a hole in my center, wondering. Constantly wondering. The only reason I answered the phone was because it was Daisy, my loyal tipster from New Orleans, and because he had been the one to lead me to Anna in the first place.

'It's a place in Duluth, Minnesota. A factory called Dutch Ironworks. They've been finding the remains of bums on and off for the last decade or so,' Daisy said. 'They find them in batches, but I think that's only because they rarely look. It takes someone reporting a broken window, or a bunch of drunk kids partying in the lot, before anyone does a walkthrough. The factory's been closed down since sometime in the sixties.'

I smiled then. Daisy's tips are sketchy at best, constructed on flimsy and mostly non-specific evidence. When I first met him, I told him to get more of the facts. He looked at me like a dog does after you take the last bite of your cheeseburger. For Daisy, there's magic in not knowing. He gets excited over the possibilities in the spaces in between. New Orleans' love affair with the undead is in his blood. I guess I wouldn't have it any other way.

My eyes roam across the abandoned Dutch Ironworks, where something has been killing the homeless for at least a decade. It's a sprawling set of brick buildings, with two enormously tall smokestacks. The windows are small and covered in dust and grime. Most of them have been boarded up. I might have to break something to get in. The athame flips lightly between my fingers, and I get out of the car.

As I walk around the building, long dead grass whispers against my legs. Looking ahead, there's a glimpse of the black, seething mass of Superior. Four hours of driving and that lake is still with me.

When I round the corner and see the door, hanging ajar with the lock broken, my chest tightens and my whole body starts to hum. I never wanted to be here. It didn't hold any interest. But now that I am here, I can hardly catch my breath. I haven't felt this tuned, this pulled-by-a-string, since I faced down the Obeahman. My fingers tingle around the knife handle and there's the odd, familiar sensation that it is part of me, welded into my skin, down to the bone. I couldn't let it drop if I wanted to.

The air inside the factory is sour but not stagnant. The place is home to countless rodents, and they move the air around. But it's still sour. There's death underneath the dust, death in every corner. Even in the rat shit. They've been feeding on things that are dead. But I don't detect anything fresh; there won't be a stinking bag of meat waiting for me around a corner, nodding a greeting with a falling-off face. What is it that Daisy said? *When the cops find another set of bodies, they're practically mummified. Bones and ash. They mostly just sweep them out the door and straight under the rug. Nobody makes a big fuss over it.*

Of course they don't. They never do.

I've come through the back and there's no telling what part of the factory this used to be. Everything worth taking has been looted, and all that's left is bare scraps of machinery I can't identify. I walk down the hall, the athame out and at my side. There's light enough coming through the windows and reflecting off things so I can see just fine. I pause at every doorway, using my whole body to listen, to smell strong rot, to feel out cold spots. The room on my left must've been an office, or maybe a small employee lounge. There's a table pushed back toward the corner. My eyes zero in on what looks at first like the edge of an old blanket – until I see the foot sticking out of it. I wait, but it doesn't move. It's just a body, used up, nothing much left but raggedy skin. I walk past and let the rest stay hidden behind the table. I don't need to see it.

The hallway opens up on a broad, high-ceilinged space. Ladders and catwalks link through the air, accompanying what look like rusted-out conveyor belts. At one end, a hulking black furnace sits dormant. Most of it has been torn apart, broken down for scrap, but I can still see what it was. So much must've been produced here. The sweat of a thousand laborers' bodies has soaked into the floor. The memory of heat still lingers in the air, god knows how many years later.

The farther I get into the room, the more crowded it feels. Something is here, and its presence is heavy. My grip tightens around the athame. Any minute I expect the decades-dead machinery to jerk back to life. The scent of burning human skin hits my nostrils a fraction of a second before I'm knocked facedown against the dusty floor.

I flip myself over and get to my feet, swinging the athame in a wide arc. I expect the ghost to be right behind me, and for a second I think it fled and I'm in for another game of whack-a-mole or ghost-darts. But I still smell it. And I feel anger moving through the room in dizzying waves.

He's standing at the far end of the room, blocking my way back to the hallway, as if I would try to run. His skin is black as a struck match, cracked and oozing liquid metal heat, like he's covered by a cooling layer of lava. The eyes stand out bright white. I can't make out from this distance whether they're just white or if they have corneas. God I hope they have corneas. I hate that creepy weird-eye shit. But corneas or no corneas, there won't be any sanity in them. All these years spent dead and burning have taken care of that.

'Come on,' I say, and flick my wrist; the athame is

ready to stab or slice. There's a faint pain on my back and shoulders, where he hit me, but I shrug it off. He's coming closer, walking up slow. Maybe because he wonders why I'm not running. Or maybe because every time he moves, more of his skin cracks open and bleeds...whatever that red-orange stuff is that he's bleeding.

This is the moment before the strike. It's the intake of breath and the stretching out of a second. I don't blink. He's close enough that I can see he does have corneas now, bright blue, the pupils constricted in constant pain. His mouth hangs open, the lips mostly gone, cracked and peeled away.

I want to hear her say just one word.

He swings his right fist; it slices the air inches from my right ear, hot enough to sting, and I catch the distinct smell of burnt hair. My burnt hair. There's something Daisy said about the corpses . . . leathery bones and ash. The corpses were fresh. The ghost just burns them up, dries them out and leaves them. His face is a ruin of rage; the nose is gone and the nasal cavity scabbed over. His cheeks are as dry as used charcoal in places and wet with infection in others. I backpedal to stay clear of his blows. With his lips burned away, his teeth seem too big and his expression is a sick, constant grin. How many homeless people woke up to this face, right before they were cooked from the inside out?

I drop to the ground and kick, managing to drop him, but also singeing my shins in the process. My jeans are fused to my skin in one spot. But there's no time to be dainty about it; his fingers reach for me and I roll. The fabric rips loose, taking who knows how much skin with it.

The hell with this. He hasn't made a peep. Who knows if he even has a tongue left, let alone whether Anna feels like speaking through it. I don't know what I was thinking anyway. I was going to wait. I was going to be good.

My elbow cocks back, ready to slam the athame down into his ribs, but I hesitate. The knife could end up bonded to my skin literally if I don't do it right. The hesitation lasts barely a second. Just long enough for the flutter of white to drift through the corner of my eye.

This can't be. It must be someone else, some other spook who died in this godawful factory. But if it is, it didn't die by burning. The girl walking silently across the dust-covered floor is pale as moonlight. Brown hair hangs down her back, falling over the stark white of her dress. I'd know that dress anywhere, whether it was too white to be real or made entirely of blood. It's her. It's

Anna. Her bare feet make a soft, scraping sound as they pad across the concrete.

'Anna,' I say, and scramble up. 'Are you all right?'

She can't hear me. Or if she can, she doesn't turn.

From the floor, the burning man grasps on to my shoe. I kick free and ignore both him and the smell of scorched rubber. Am I going insane? Hallucinating? She can't really be here. It isn't possible.

'Anna, it's me. Can you hear me?' I walk toward her but not too fast. If I go too fast she might disappear. If I go too fast I might see too much; I could pull her around and see that she has no face, that she's a jerking corpse. She could turn to ash in my hands.

There is a gristly sound of meat twisting as the burning man crawls to his feet. I don't care. What is she doing here? Why won't she speak? She just keeps walking, away, ignoring everything around her. Only... not everything. The dormant furnace is in the back of the room. A sudden sense of foreboding clamps down in my chest.

'Anna – ' I scream; the burning man has me by the shoulder and it's like someone just shoved an ember down my shirt. I twist away, and in the corner of my eye I think I see Anna pause, but I'm too busy ducking and slicing with the knife and kicking this ghost's feet out from under him again to really tell.

The athame is hot. I have to toss it back and forth between my hands a second, just from that small, non-lethal slice that is now a narrow fissure of red-orange across his ribcage. I should just put him down now, jab the knife in and pull it out fast, maybe wrap the handle in my shirt first. Only I don't. I just incapacitate him temporarily, and turn back.

Anna stands before the furnace, her fingers slipping lightly across the rough, black metal. I say her name again but she doesn't turn. Instead she curls her fist around the handle and draws the broad door open.

Something in the air shifts. There's a current, a ripple, and the dimensions skew in my vision. The opening of the furnace yawnss wider and Anna crawls in. Soot stains her white dress, streaking across the fabric and across her pale skin like bruises. And there's something wrong with her; something about the way she moves. It's like she's a marionette. When she squeezes through the opening, her arm and leg bend back unnaturally like a spider being sucked into a straw.

My mouth is dry. Behind me, the burning man drags himself onto his feet again. The sear in my shoulder makes me move away; I barely notice the limp brought on by the burns on my shins. *Anna, get out of there. Look at me.*

It's like watching a dream unfold, some nightmare where I'm powerless to do anything, where my legs are made of lead and I can't scream a warning no matter how hard I try. When the decades-dead furnace surges to life, sending flame spewing into its belly, I scream, loud and without words. But it doesn't matter. Anna burns up behind the iron door. One of her pale hands, blistering and turning black, presses against the slats, like she's changed her mind too late.

Heat and smoke drifts up from my shoulder as the burning man grasps my shirt and twists me around. His eyes bulge out of the dark mess of his face and his teeth gnash open and shut. My eyes flicker back to the furnace. There's no feeling in my arms or legs. I can't tell whether my heart is beating. Despite the burns that have to be forming on my shoulders, I'm frozen in place.

'End me,' the burning man hisses. I don't think. I just shove the athame into his guts, letting go immediately but still scorching my palm. I back away as he falls jerking to the floor, and run up against an old conveyor belt, hanging on to it to keep from going down on my knees. For a long second, the room is filled with mingled screams as Anna burns and the ghost at my feet shrivels. He curls in on himself until what's left looks barely human, charred and twisted.

When he stops moving, the air grows immediately cold. I take a deep breath and open my eyes; I don't remember closing them. The room is silent. When I look at the furnace, it's dormant and empty, and if I touched it, it would be cool, like Anna was never there at all.

CHAPTER SIX

They've given me something for the pain. A shot of something or other, and pills to take home for later. It would be nice if it would knock me right on my ass, if it made me sleep through the next week. But I think it's going to be just enough to keep the throbbing down.

My mom is talking to the doctor while the nurse finishes applying ointment to my freshly and insanely painfully cleaned burns. I didn't want to come to the hospital. I tried to convince my mom that a little calendula and a lavender potion would be enough, but she insisted. And now, truthfully, I'm pretty happy about having the shot. It was fun too, listening to her try to come up with the best explanation. Was it a kitchen accident? Maybe a campfire accident. She decided on the campfire, turning me into a klutz and saying I fell into the embers and basically rolled around in a panic. They'll buy it. They always do.

There are second-degree burns on my shin and shoulders. The one on my hand, from the final blow of the athame, is pretty minor, first degree, nothing more serious than a bad sunburn. Still, a bad sunburn on the palm of your hand sucks a whole lot. I expect to be carrying around unopened cans of ice-cold soda for the next few days.

My mom comes back in with the doctor so they can start gauzing me up. She wavers between tears and consternation. I reach out and take her hand. She'll never get used to this. It eats her up, worse than it did when it was my dad. But in none of her lectures, none of her rants about taking precautions and being more careful, has she ever asked me to stop. I thought she'd demand it after what happened with the Obeahman last fall. But she understands. It isn't fair that she has to, but it's better that she does.

Thomas and Carmel show up the next day, right after school, practically peeling into our driveway in their separate cars. They burst in without knocking and find me semi-comfortably drugged on the couch, watching TV and eating microwave popcorn, clutching an ice pack in my right hand.

'See? I told you he was alive,' says Thomas. Carmel looks nonplussed.

'You shut your phone off,' she says.

'I was sick at home. Didn't feel like talking to anybody. And I figured you were at school, where policy says you are not to be frivolously texting and making phone calls.'

Carmel sighs and drops her school bag onto the floor before plopping down in the wingback chair. Thomas perches on the arm of the couch and reaches for the popcorn.

'You weren't 'sick at home,' Cas. I called your mom. She told us everything.'

'I was too 'sick at home.' Just like I'm going to be tomorrow. And the next day. And probably the day after that.' I shake more cheddar into the bowl and offer it to Thomas. My attitude is wearing on Carmel's nerves. To be honest it's wearing on mine. But the pills dull the pain, and they dull my mind enough so that I don't have to be thinking about what happened at the Dutch Ironworks. I don't have to wonder if what I saw was real.

Carmel would like to lecture me. I can see the admonishment dancing around her lips. But she's tired. And she's worried. So instead she reaches for the popcorn and says she'll pick up my homework for the next few days.

'Thanks,' I say. 'I might be out part of next week too.'

'But that's the last week of classes,' says Thomas.

'Exactly. What are they going to do? Flunk me? It'd be too big of a pain. They just want to make it to summer like we do.'

They exchange this look, like they've decided I'm hopeless, and Carmel stands up.

'Are you going to tell us what happened? Why didn't you wait, like we decided to?'

There isn't an answer for that. It was an impulse. More than an impulse, but to them it must seem like a selfish, stupid move. Like I couldn't be patient. Whatever it was, it's done. When I confronted that ghost, it was just like before, in the hayloft. Anna came through, and I saw her suffer. I watched her burn.

'I'll tell you everything,' I tell them. 'But later. When I'm on fewer painkillers.' I smile and rattle the orange bottle. 'Want to stick around and watch a movie?'

Thomas shrugs and plops down, digging his hand into the cheddar corn without a second thought. It takes Carmel an extra minute and a couple of sighs, but she eventually drops her book bag and sits in the rocking chair.

For all their horror at the prospect of missing one of the last days of school, curiosity gets the better of them and they show up the next day around eleven thirty, just before lunch period. I thought I was ready for it but it still takes me a few times to get it right, to tell them everything. I'd already said it once, to my mom, before she left to go shopping and drop spells around town. When I'd finished, she looked like she wanted an apology. An *I'm sorry, Mom, for almost getting myself killed. Again.* But I couldn't quite manage it. It didn't seem like the important thing. So she just told me I should have waited for Gideon, and left without looking me in the eye. Now Carmel's got the same look.

I manage to croak out, 'I'm sorry that I didn't wait for you guys. I didn't know I was going to do it. I didn't plan it.'

'It took you four hours to drive there. Were you in a trance the whole time?'

'Can we just focus?' Thomas interjects. He asks it carefully, with a disarming smile. 'What's done is done. Cas is alive. A little crispier than before, but he's breathing.'

Breathing and craving a Percocet. The pain in my shoulders is like a living thing, all throbbing and heat.

'Thomas is right,' I say. 'We need to figure out what to do now. We need to figure out how to help her.'

'How to help her?' Carmel repeats. 'We need to figure out what's going on first. For all we know, the whole thing might be in your head. Or an illusion.'

'You think I'm making it up? Concocting some kind

of fantasy? If that were true, why would it be like this? Why would I imagine her catatonic, throwing herself into a furnace? If I'm making this up, then I need several hours of intense therapy.'

'I'm not suggesting you're doing it on purpose,' Carmel says apologetically. 'I just wonder if it's real. And remember what Morfran said.'

Thomas and I look at each other. All we remember is Morfran spewing a bunch of crazy. I sigh.

'So what do you want from me? You want me to sit here and wait, when what I saw might be real? What if she's really in trouble?' The image of her hand, flung up against the furnace door, floats behind my eyes. 'I don't know if I can do that. Not after yesterday.'

Carmel's eyes are wide. I wish we hadn't gone to Morfran, because the things he said only scared her worse. All of his posturing, his forces spinning around the athame, something wicked this way comes B.S. My shoulders tighten and I wince.

'OK,' Thomas says. He nods to Carmel and takes her hand. 'I mean, I think we're fooling ourselves thinking we have a choice anyway. Whatever's happening is happening, and I don't think it's going to stop. Unless we really do destroy the athame.'

They leave a little while later, and I spend the afternoon on painkillers, trying not to think about

Anna and what might be happening to her. I keep checking my phone, waiting for Gideon to call back, but he doesn't. And the hours tick by.

When my mom gets home, close to evening, she makes me a mug of decaf tea and spikes it with lavender to heal the burns from the inside. It's not a potion. There are no enchantments. Witchcraft and pharmaceuticals don't mix. But even without the mojo the tea is soothing. Plus, I've taken another Percocet, because my shoulders feel like they're ready to rip clean off. It's kicked in nicely, and I want to crawl under the covers and pass out until Saturday.

When I walk into my bedroom, I half expect Tybalt to be curled up on my navy blanket. Why not? If my dead girlfriend can cross over, then my murdered cat probably can too. But there isn't anything there. I get into bed and try to get comfortable against my pillows. Unfortunately, burned shoulders make that pretty much impossible.

When I close my eyes, a chill creeps up my legs. The temp in the room has plummeted, like one of the windows has come open. If I was to breathe out in a huff, it would be a cloud of vapor. Under my pillow, the athame is practically singing.

'You're not really here,' I say to convince myself. Maybe to will it into truth. 'If it was really you, it

82

wouldn't be like this.'

How would you know, Cassio? You've never even been dead once. I've been dead lots of times.

I let my eyes drift up, just far enough to see her bare feet pressed into the corner beside my dresser. Up just a little farther, to the white hem of her skirt, below her knees. I don't want to see any more. I don't want to see her break her own bones, or throw herself through my window. And her damn blood can stay inside of her nose too, thank you. She's more terrifying this way than she ever was with black veins and drifting hair. Anna Dressed in Blood I knew how to face. The empty shell of Anna Korlov...I don't understand.

The figure in the corner is half encased in shadow, not much more substantial than moonlight.

'You can't be here. Not really. My mom's barrier spell is still up on the house.'

Rules rules rules. No rules anymore.

Oh. Really. Is that how it is? Or are you just a figment, like Carmel says? Maybe you're not even you. Maybe you're a trick.

'Are you just going to stand there all night?' I ask. 'I want to get some sleep, so if there's something mind-numbingly disturbing you want to show me, can we just get it over with?' My intake of breath is sharp, and a tight lump rises in my throat when her feet start to move, taking short, shuffling strides toward my bed. She comes so close, just outside of my reach. Then she lowers herself to sit beside my feet, and I see her face.

Anna's eyes are her own, and the sight of them shakes me out of the drugs like ice water across my back. The expression on her face is the same as it was in all of my imaginings. It's like she knows me. Like she remembers. We stare at each other for a long time. Shudders run through her, and she flickers, like an image from an old film strip.

'I miss you,' I whisper.

Anna blinks. When she looks at me again, her eyes are red with blood. A ripple of pain passes through her jaw as phantom cuts open and close across her chest, grotesque flowers of red blooming and disappearing down her arms.

I can't do anything to help. I can't even hold her hand. She's not really here. The burns sear my shoulders as I sink back into my pillow and for a while we sit silently, passing pain back and forth. I keep my eyes open for as long as I can stand to, because she wants me to see.

CHAPTER SEVEN

I finally get fed up with waiting, and call Gideon again in the morning. For a minute I think it's just going to ring and ring, and I'm starting to wonder if maybe something's happened to him, when he picks up.

'Gideon? Where have you been? Did you get my message?'

'Early this morning. I would have called, but you'd have been asleep. You sound terrible, Theseus.'

'You should see how I look.' My hand drags roughly across my face, muffling the last few words. Ever since I was a kid, Gideon could solve any problem. Whenever I needed answers, he had them. And he's who my dad turned to, if things got rough. He has his own brand of magic, popping in and out of my childhood at the perfect times, coming through our front door in a dapper suit with some weird English food for me to try. Whenever I saw his bespectacled face, I knew everything was going to be OK. But this time I get the feeling that he doesn't want to hear what I have to say.

'Theseus?'

'Yeah, Gideon?'

'Tell me what's happened.'

What's happened. He makes it sound so easy. I must've sat in my bedroom with Anna for four hours, watching her skin peel back and her eyes leak blood. Sometime between then and dawn, I fell asleep, because when I opened my eyes it was morning, and the foot of my bed was empty.

And now it's daytime, full-on sunshine with its ridiculous sense of safety. It drives everything that happens in the dark a million miles away. It makes it seem impossible, and even though the memory of Anna's wounds is fresh and the image of her burning inside that furnace is blasted onto the backs of my eyelids, in the daylight it almost feels like make-believe.

'Theseus?'

I take a breath. I'm standing on my front porch, and the morning is quiet except for the creaking boards beneath my feet. There's no breeze, and the sun is livening the leaves, warming the fabric of my shirt. I'm acutely aware of the empty space in the bushes where I saw Anna standing, staring in.

'Anna's back.'

On the other end of the line, something clatters to the floor.

'Gideon?'

'She can't be. It isn't possible.' His voice has gone low and terse, and somewhere inside me a five-year-old cringes. After all these years, Gideon's anger still has power. One harsh word from him and I'm a puppy with its tail between its legs.

'Possible or not, she's here. She's contacting me, like she's asking for help. I don't know how. I need to know what to do.' The words fall out without a note of hope. All of a sudden it hits – how tired I am. How old I feel. Morfran's words, about destroying the athame, melting it down, and letting it fall into deep water, twist in the back of my head. The thought is disconnected, but comforting, and it has something to do with Thomas and Carmel, and something else, if I let my mind wander a little farther. Something I said to Anna once, about possibilities. And choices.

'I think it's the athame,' I say. 'I think something's happening to it.'

'Don't blame the athame. You're the one who wields it. Don't forget that,' he says, his voice stern.

'I never forget that. Not for a single minute. Not since Dad died.'

Gideon sighs. 'When I met your father,' he says, 'he

wasn't much older than you are now. Of course, he hadn't been using the athame for near so long as you have. But I remember thinking how old he seemed.

'He wanted to give it up once, you know.'

'No,' I say. 'He never told me.'

'Well, I suppose that it didn't matter, afterward. Because he didn't.'

'Why didn't he? It would have been better for everyone if he had. He'd still be here.' I stop suddenly and Gideon lets me finish my own thought. My dad would still be here. But other people wouldn't. He saved who knows how many lives by putting away the dead, and so have I.

'What am I going to do about Anna?' I ask.

'Nothing.'

'Nothing? You can't be serious.'

'I am serious,' he says. 'Quite serious. The girl was tragic. We all know that. But you need to put her away and do your job. Stop looking for things you have no business looking for.' He pauses, and I don't say anything. It's almost exactly what Morfran said, and it makes the hairs stand up on my forearms.

'Theseus, if you've ever trusted me before, trust me now. Just do your job. Do your job, and let the girl go, and none of us have anything to fear.'

*

I go back to school, to the surprise of nearly everyone. Apparently, Carmel had already circulated news of my 'illness'. So I put up with curious questions, and when they ask about my sore and bandaged shoulder, the white edge sticking up from my shirt collar, I grit my teeth and tell them about my camping accident. It was funny at the time but now I wish my mom had picked a less embarrassing cover story.

I suppose I could have just stayed home, like I intended. But rattling around the empty rooms like a lonely, crazy marble while my mom made the rounds to clients and occult suppliers wasn't my idea of a good time. I didn't feel like watching TV all day, waiting for Anna to come crawling through it like that mildew-covered chick from the Ring movies. So I came back, determined to soak up the last of what these junior year teachers had to tell me. It was supposed to be like someone kicking you in the shin to take your mind off your broken arm. But now, at every turn, in every class, Anna is on my mind. None of the end-of-the-year lessons are interesting enough to drive her away. Even Mr Dixon, my favorite teacher, just sort of phones it in talking about the aftermath of the Seven Years' War. My mind wanders, letting her back in, and Gideon's voice explodes between my ears. *Stop looking for something you have no business looking for.*

Let her go. Or is it Morfran's voice? Or Carmel's?

The way that Gideon said it, that as long as I let her go, we have nothing to fear...I don't know what that means. Trust me, he said, and I do. It's not possible, he said, so I believe him.

But what if she needs me?

'So we pretty much just got given to England.'

'Huh?'

I blink. Carmel's friend Nat is turned around in her seat, squinting at me curiously. Then she shrugs.

'You're probably right.' She glances toward Mr Dixon, who has gone to sit at his desk to mess with something on his laptop. 'He probably doesn't care if we talk about the war for real. So.' She sighs, looking like she'd rather be sitting in front of anyone else. 'You going to come with Carmel to the senior party?'

'Isn't that just for seniors?' I ask.

'Come on. It's not like they're going to card you and kick you out if you're not one,' she scoffs. 'Well, maybe if you were a freshman. Thomas could even come. Cas? Cas?'

'Yeah,' I hear myself say. But not really. Because Nat's face isn't her face anymore. It's Anna's. The mouth moves with hers, but not the expression. Like a mask.

'You're acting really weird today,' she says.

'Sorry. My Percocet's wearing off,' I mutter, and slide

out of the desk. Mr Dixon doesn't even notice when I walk out of the classroom.

When Thomas and Carmel find me, I'm sitting on the quiet stage in the middle of the theater, staring up at the rows of blue-covered seats, all empty except for one. My trig text and notebook are beside me in a neat stack, as a reminder of where I'm supposed to be.

'Is he catatonic?' Thomas asks. They came in a few minutes ago but I didn't acknowledge them. If I'm going to ignore one friend I may as well ignore them all.

'Hey guys,' I say. Their movements echo loudly through the empty theater as they drop their books and climb up onto the stage.

'You do a pretty good job of avoiding things,' says Carmel. 'But then again maybe not. Nat says that you were acting weird during discussion questions in history.'

I shrug. 'Anna's face transposed over hers while she was talking. I thought I showed a fair amount of restraint.'

They exchange one of their ever more frequent looks as they sit on either side of me.

'What else have you seen?' Thomas asks.

'She's in pain. Like she's being tortured. She was in my room last night. There were wounds, opening and closing on her arms and shoulders. I couldn't do anything to help her. She wasn't really there.'

He pushes his glasses up on his nose. 'We have to find out what's going on. That's – that's sick. There must be a spell, something to reveal—'

'Maybe mysticism isn't what we need right now,' Carmel interjects. 'What about something else, like maybe a psychologist?'

'They'd just drug him to the gills. Tell him he's got ADD or something. And besides, Cas isn't insane.'

'Not to be a downer, but schizophrenia can strike at any time,' she says. 'It's actually common for it to manifest around our age. And the hallucinations seem just as real as you or me.'

'What are you talking about schizophrenia for?' Thomas blurts.

'I'm not saying that specifically! But he's been through a significant loss. None of it might be real. Have you seen anything? Have you even felt anything weird like your grandpa said?'

'No, but I've sort of been slacking off in my voodoo studies. I've got trigonometry, you know?'

'I'm just saying it doesn't always have to be spirits and magic. Sometimes hauntings are in your mind. It doesn't make them less real.'

Thomas nods and takes a breath. 'OK, that's true. But I still think a shrink is the wrong way to go.'

Carmel makes a growling noise. 'Why do you have to

jump straight to a spell? Why are you so sure it's paranormal?'

This is as close as I've ever heard to a Thomas and Carmel argument. And as special as it is to listen to your friends argue over whether or not you have a mental illness, I'm starting to get the urge to go back to class.

Stop poking your nose around where it doesn't belong, before someone cuts it off. There's something else going on around you, like a storm.

I don't care.

In the sixth row of the theater, in the third chair in, Anna winks at me. Or maybe she just blinks. I can't tell. She's missing half of her face.

'Let's go talk to Morfran,' I say.

The bell over the antique shop door jingles and there's the click-click-clatter of dog toenails on hardwood before Stella collides with my legs. I give her a few scratches and she gazes up at me with huge brown eyes like a seal pup's before moving on to Carmel.

We aren't the only ones in the shop. Morfran's talking to two women, forty-something ladies in sweaters asking questions about one of the china washbasins. Morfran laughs and starts telling them a cozy little historical tale that may or may not be true. It's weird to watch him with customers. He's so *nice*. We try not to make too much of a ruckus on our way to the back room. After a few minutes, we hear the women saying good-bye to Stella and thank you to Morfran, and seconds later, he and the dog walk through the curtain into the back, where he keeps the stranger and more obscure occult supplies. My mom's candles enjoy a table in the front window. She's gone mainstream.

The way Morfran's looking at me, I expect him to produce one of those doctor's flashlights and check my pupil response. His arms are crossed over his chest, bunching up the black leather of his vest and covering the Aerosmith logo on his t-shirt. When Thomas tosses him a freshly packed pipe of tobacco, his hand shoots up and catches it, and his eyes never leave my face. It's hard to believe that the kindly antique shop proprietor and this man of dark magic are one and the same.

'You kids here for an afterschool snack?' he asks as he lights up. Then he checks his watch. 'Can't be. School's not out for another five hours.'

Thomas clears his throat uncomfortably, and Morfran's furry eyebrow lifts in his direction

'You flunk out and you'll be picking crud out of everything I buy up at swap meets this summer.'

'I'm not flunking out. It's the last two weeks. Nobody even cares anymore really.'

'I care. Your mama cares. And don't you forget it.' He

nods at Carmel. 'What about you?'

'Perfect grade-point average,' she replies. 'And it'll stay that way. It's all about results, my dad says.' Her smile is sweet, apologetic but confident. Morfran shakes his head.

'You talk to that Brit friend of yours?' he asks me.

'Yeah.'

'What'd he say?'

'He said to let it go.'

'Good advice.' He draws on his pipe; the smoke obscures his face as he exhales.

'I can't take it.'

'You should.'

Carmel steps forward, her arms crossed over her chest. 'Why should he? Can you stop being so cryptic? Maybe if you'd just tell us what's going on, tell us why we should let it go, then maybe we would.'

He exhales and looks away from her, sets his pipe down on the glass countertop. 'Can't tell you what I don't know. It's not an exact science. Not a news bulletin. It just blinks up, in here,' he says, and points to his chest. 'Or in here' – he points to his temple. 'It says stay away. It says let it go. People are watching you. The kind of people you don't mind just watching, but you hope they never show up. And there's something else.' He draws again on the pipe, looking thoughtful, which is really the only way you can look when smoking a pipe. 'Something is trying to hold this back, while another thing is trying to draw it on. And that's the thing that concerns me most, you want to know the truth. Makes it hard to hold my tongue.'

'Hard to hold your tongue on what?' I ask. 'What do you know?'

Morfran looks at me through the smoke but I don't drop my eyes. I'm not letting this go. I can't. I owe her. And more than that. I can't think that she's suffering.

'Just drop it, all right?' he says, but I hear it. The resolve has gone out of his voice.

'What do you know, Morfran?'

'I know...' He sighs. 'Someone who might know something.'

'Who?'

'Miss Riika.'

'Aunt Riika?' Thomas asks. 'What could she know about it?' He turns to me. 'I used to go over to her house when I was a kid. She's not really my aunt, but you know, more like a friend of the family. I haven't seen her in years.'

'We lost touch.' Morfran shrugs. 'It happens sometimes. But if Thomas takes you to see her, she'll talk to you. She's been a Finnish witch all her life.'

A Finnish witch. The phrase makes me want to bare

my teeth and put my fur up. Anna's mother, Malvina, was a Finnish witch. That's how she was able to curse Anna and bind her to the Victorian. Right after she cut her throat.

'She's not the same,' Thomas whispers. 'She's not like her.'

My breath shakes out of my lungs and I nod at him fondly. It doesn't bother me anymore that he sometimes breaks into my thoughts. He can't help it. And the way I instantly seethed about Malvina must've lit his dendrites up like a Christmas tree.

'Will you take me to her?' I ask.

'I guess so.' He shrugs. 'But we might not get anything besides a plate of gingersnaps. She wasn't exactly 'all there' even when I was little.'

Carmel lingers on the outskirts, quietly petting Stella. Her voice cuts through the smoke.

'If the haunting is real, can this Miss Riika make her go away?'

I look at her sharply. Nobody answers and after a few long seconds, her eyes drop to the floor.

'OK,' she says. 'Let's just get on with it, I guess.'

Morfran puffs his pipe and shakes his head. 'Cas and Thomas only. Not you, girl. Riika wouldn't let you in the front door.'

'What do you mean? Why not?'

'Because the answers they're after, you don't want,' Morfran replies. 'Resistance is coming off of you in waves. If you go with them, they won't get anywhere.' He presses the ash in his pipe down.

I look at Carmel. Her eyes are hurt, but not guilty. 'I won't go then.'

'Carmel,' Thomas starts, but she cuts him off.

'You shouldn't go either. Neither of you.' I'd speak up, but she's looking at Thomas. 'If you're really his friend, if you care about him, then you shouldn't indulge this.' And then she turns on her heel and walks out of the room. She's all the way through the antique shop before I can say that I'm not an infant, I don't need chaperones, or babysitters, or a goddamn counselor.

'What's the matter with her today?' I ask Thomas, but from the way his jaw is hanging open in her wake, it's pretty clear that he doesn't know.

CHAPTER EIGHT

Thomas's Aunt Riika lives in the middle of bumble-fuck nowhere. We've been driving on unmarked dirt roads for at least ten minutes. There are no signs of any kind, just trees and more trees, then a brief clearing leading up to more trees. If he hasn't been out here in years, I have no idea how he seems to be finding his way so easily.

'Are we lost? You'd admit it if we were lost, right?'

Thomas smiles, maybe a bit nervously. 'We're not lost. At least, not yet. They might've changed some of the roads around since the last time.'

'Who the hell are 'they'? Road construction squirrels? It doesn't even look like these things have been driven on in the last ten years.' The trees are thick outside my window. The foliage has come back to fill in the winter spaces. We've taken too many turns now, and my sense of direction is shot. We could be going northsouth for all I know.

'Ha! There it is,' Thomas crows. I sit up straighter in my seat. We're approaching a small white farmhouse. There are early shoots of a flower garden cropping up around the front porch, and a walkway of flagstones leads from the driveway to the front steps. As Thomas pulls the Tempo onto the pale gravel, he beeps the horn. 'I hope she's home,' he mutters, and we step out.

'It's nice,' I say, and mean it. I'm surprised there aren't more neighbors; the surrounding property has to be worth something. Trees have been carefully planted around the yard, shielding it from the eyes of the road but opening up in front to sort of hug the house.

Thomas bounds up the steps like an eager hound. This must've been what he was like as a kid too, coming to see his Aunt Riika. I wonder why she and Morfran lost touch. When he knocks on the door, my heart holds its breath, not only because I want my answers, but also because I don't want to see the disappointed look on Thomas's face if Riika isn't home.

I don't have anything to worry about. She answers on the third knock. She's probably been at the window since we drove up. I can't imagine she gets many visitors way out here.

'Thomas Aldous Sabin! You've doubled in size!' She comes onto the porch and hugs him. While his face is pointed toward me I mouth 'Aldous?' at him and try not to laugh.

'What on earth are you doing here?' Riika asks. She's a lot shorter than I expected, barely over five feet. Her hair is loose and dark blond, shot through with white. Lines crack through the soft skin of her cheeks and pinch in the corners of her eyes. The cable-knit sweater she wears looks about three sizes too big and there's support hose bunched around her shoes. Riika is no spring chicken. But when she claps Thomas on the back, he still jolts forward from the force of it.

'Aunt Riika, this is my friend Cas,' he says, and like he gave her permission, she finally looks at me. I push my hair out of my eyes and flash the Boy Scout smile. 'Morfran sent us for help,' Thomas adds quietly.

Riika clucks her tongue, and as her cheeks pull in, I get the first glimpse of the witch she must be underneath the layers of floral print knit. When her eyes dart to my backpack, where the athame rests in its sheath, I have to fight the urge to back off the porch.

'I should have smelled it,' she says softly. Her voice is like the pages of a very old book. She squints at my face. 'The power coming off of this one.' Her hand snakes into Thomas's and she pats it firmly. 'Come inside.'

The interior of the farmhouse smells like blended incense

and old lady. And I don't think she's updated the décor since the 70s. Brown shag carpet stretches as far as the eye can see, beneath cluttered furniture: a rocking chair and long couch, both in green velour. A glass hurricane light fixture hangs over a yellow Formica table in the dining area. Riika leads us to the table and motions for us to sit down. The table itself is a mess of half-burnt candles and incense sticks. After we sit, she squirts some lotion onto her hands and rubs them together briskly.

'Your grandfather is well?' she asks, leaning forward onto her elbows and smiling at Thomas, one fist curled up against her chin.

'He's great. He says hello.'

'Tell him I say hello too,' she says. Her voice bothers me. The accent and timbre are too close to Malvina's. I can't help thinking it, even though the two women look nothing alike. Malvina, when I saw her, was younger than Riika, and her hair was a black braided bun, not a mass of butterscotch and marshmallows. Still, looking into Riika's face, images of Anna's murder aren't far behind. They flash up in my memory of the séance, Malvina dripping black wax onto Anna's white dress, soaked with blood.

'This is not easy for you,' Riika says to me severely, which doesn't help. She reaches for a tin with cardinals painted on it and pries it open, offering the gingersnaps inside to Thomas, who grabs two handfuls. A wide smile spreads on her face as she watches him stuff a few into his mouth before looking back at me impatiently. Was I supposed to say something? Was that a question?

She clucks her tongue again. 'You are a friend to Thomas?'

I nod.

'He's the best, Aunt Riika,' Thomas affirms over crumbles of gingersnap. She smiles at him briefly.

'Then I will help you, if I can.' She leans forward and lights three of the candles, seemingly at random. 'Ask your questions.'

I take a deep breath. Where do I start? There doesn't seem to be enough air in the room for me to explain the situation with Anna, how she came to be cursed, how she sacrificed herself for us, and now, why she can't possibly be haunting me for real.

Riika slaps me on the hand. Apparently I took too long. 'Give,' she says, and I turn it palm up. Her grip is gentle, but there's steel beneath her fingers as she squeezes my bones together and closes her eyes. I wonder if she was the one who helped Thomas develop his mindreading talent, if such a thing can be taught or developed.

I glance at Thomas. He's paused in mid-chew, his eyes intent on our joined hands, like he might see electricity or smoke passing between us. This is taking forever. And I'm not really comfortable with all this touching. Something about Riika, maybe the power emanating off her, is almost making me sick to my stomach. Just when I'm ready to pull free, she opens her eyes and lets go with a brisk pat on the back of my hand.

'He's a warrior, this one,' she says to Thomas. 'A wielder of a weapon older than all of us.' There's a pointed way that she isn't looking at me and her hands are curled like crabs they skitter across the Formica, fingers tapping the tabletop. 'You want to know about the girl,' she says into her lap. With her chin tucked low her voice takes on a choked, froggy quality.

'The girl,' I whisper. Riika looks at me with a sly smile.

'You were the one who took Anna Dressed in Blood out of the world,' she says. 'I felt it when she passed. It was a storm dying over the lake.'

'She took herself out,' I say. 'To save my life. And Thomas's.'

Riika shrugs to say it doesn't matter. There's a velvet bag resting on a gold plate; she empties out the contents and stirs them around. I try not to look too closely. I'm going to pretend that they're carved runes. But I think they're actually small bones, maybe from a bird, or a lizard, maybe from human fingers. She looks down into the pattern and raises her pale eyebrows.

'The girl is not with you now,' she says, and my heart thumps. I don't know what I'm hoping for. 'But she was. Recently.'

Beside me, Thomas inhales fast and sits up straighter. He adjusts his glasses and nudges me with his elbow, I think to be encouraging.

'Can you tell what she wants?' he asks after a minute of me sitting dumb as a rock.

Riika cocks her head. 'How should I know that? You want I should call the wind and ask it? It would not know either. Only one person to ask because only one person knows. Ask Anna Dressed in Blood to give up her secrets.' Her eyes slant toward me. 'I think she would give up much, for you.'

It's hard to hear anything over the pulse pounding in my ears.

'I can't ask her,' I mutter. 'She can't talk.' My head is starting to come out from underneath the shock; it's starting to think ahead and trip over itself. 'I've been told that it's impossible to come back. That she shouldn't be able to be here.'

Riika leans back in her chair. She motions tensely with her hand, toward my backpack and the athame. 'Show me,' she says, and crosses her arms over her chest.

Thomas nods, giving the OK. I unsnap my bag and pull out the knife still in its sheath. Then I lay it on the table in front of me. Riika jerks her head, and I take it out. The flames of the candles flicker along the blade. Her reaction as her eyes move over it is odd, just an uneasy tic of emotion in the corner of her wrinkled mouth, something that looks like revulsion. Finally, she looks away and spits onto the floor.

'What do you know about this?' she asks.

'I know that it was my father's before it was mine. I know that it sends ghosts who kill to the other side, where they can't hurt the living.'

Riika shoots Thomas a raised brow. It looks a lot like the old-lady version of the 'get a load of this guy' expression.

'Good and bad. Right and wrong.' She shakes her head. 'This athame does not think on these terms.' She sighs. 'You do not know much. So I will tell you. You think this athame creates a door between this world and the next one.' She holds up one hand, and then the other. 'This athame *is* the door. It was opened long ago and since then has swung, back and forth, back and forth.'

I watch Riika's hand sway left and right.

'But it never closes.'

'Wait a minute,' I say. 'That's wrong. Ghosts can't

pass back through the knife.' I look at Thomas. 'It doesn't work like that.' I take the athame from the table and stuff it back into my bag.

Riika leans forward and smacks my shoulder. 'How do you know how it works?' she asks. 'But no. It doesn't work like that.'

I'm starting to see what Thomas meant about her being not quite all there.

'It would take a strong will,' she goes on, 'and a deep connection. You said Anna was not sent away with this knife. But she would have to know it, sense it, in order to find you.'

'She was cut,' Thomas interjects excitedly. 'After the scrying spell, Will took the knife and stabbed her, but she didn't die. Or pass on, or whatever.'

Riika's eyes are on my backpack again. 'She is connected to it. To her it would be like a beacon, a lighthouse. Why the others cannot follow it, I don't know. There are still mysteries, even for me.' There's something strange about the way she's watching the knife. Her eyes are intense, but disconnected. I didn't notice before that they have an odd, yellow tint to the irises.

'But Aunt Riika, even if you're right, how can Cas talk to her? How can he find out what she wants?'

Her smile is broad and warm. Almost joyful. 'You

must make the music come in clearer,' she says. 'You must speak the language of her curse. The same way we Finns have always spoken to the dead. With a Lappish drum. Your grandfather will know where to find one.'

'Can you help us do that?' I ask. 'I'm assuming we need a Finnish witch for this.'

'Thomas is more than witch enough,' she replies, but he doesn't look too sure.

'I've never used one before,' he says. 'I wouldn't know where to start. It would be better if you did it. Please?'

Regret clouds Riika's features as she shakes her head. She can't seem to meet his eyes anymore and her breath sounds heavier, more strained. We should probably go. All these questions have to be taxing. And really, she's given us the answers and a good place to start. I lean back away from the table and catch a draft moving through the room; it makes me realize how cold my fingers and cheeks are.

Thomas is babbling, quietly sputtering reasons why it shouldn't be him to do the ritual, and how he wouldn't know a Lappish drum if it smacked him in the face, and that he'd probably wind up channeling the ghost of Elvis. But Riika keeps shaking her head.

It's getting colder. Or maybe it was cold when we came in. She might not have a good central heating system in such an old place. Or she just keeps the heat turned down to save money.

Finally, I hear Riika sigh. It isn't an exasperated sound. There's sadness in it. And resolve.

'Go and get my drum,' she whispers. 'It is in my bedroom. Hanging on the north wall.' She nods toward the short hallway. I can see a sliver of what looks like the bathroom. The bedroom must be farther down. Something's wrong here. And it has to do with the way she looked at the athame.

'Thanks, Aunt Riika.' Thomas grins and gets up from the table to go after the drum. When I see her pained expression, I suddenly know what it is.

'Thomas, don't,' I say, and push myself away from the table. But I'm too late. When I get to the bedroom, he's already there, standing frozen halfway to the north wall. The drum hangs just where Riika said it would be, an oblong shape a foot wide and twice as long, animal hide stretched taut. Riika herself sits looking at it, motionless in her wooden rocking chair, her skin gray and leathery, her eyes sunken in and lips peeled back from her teeth. She's been dead for at least a year.

'Thomas,' I whisper, and reach out to grab his arm. He jerks away with a cry and bolts. I curse under my breath and grab the drum off the wall, then go after him. On our way out of the house I notice how it has changed, covered in dust and spots of dirt, a corner of the couch gnawed away by rodents. Cobwebs hang in the corners and suspend down from the light fixtures. Thomas doesn't stop running until he's outside, in the yard. He's got his hands pressed against the sides of his head.

'Hey,' I say gently. I have no idea what else to do, or what I should tell him. His hand comes up defensively and I back off. His breath comes in hitches and gasps. I think he's crying, and who can blame him? It's OK that he doesn't want me to see. I look back at the farmhouse. The trees around it are sparse, and there's nothing in the flower garden but hard-packed dirt. The white paint on the siding is so thin that it looks like it was done in a quick wash of watercolor, leaving the black boards to show through.

'I'm sorry, man,' I say. 'I should have known. There were signs.' There were signs. I just missed them. Or misread them.

'It's OK,' he says, and wipes his face with the back of his sleeve. 'Riika would never hurt me. She'd never hurt anyone. I'm just surprised, that's all. I can't believe Morfran didn't tell me that she died.'

'Maybe he didn't know either.'

'Oh, he knew,' Thomas says, nodding. He sniffs and grins at me. His eyes are a little red, but he's got it back together already. The kid is resilient. He starts back toward the Tempo and I follow.

'He knew,' he says loudly. 'He knew and he sent me here anyway. I'm going to kill him! I'm absolutely going to kill him.'

'Take it easy,' I say once we're inside the car, Thomas still muttering about Morfran's impending demise. He starts the engine, and pauses.

'No way. Don't you get it, Cas?' He looks at me disgustedly. 'I ate the gingersnaps.'

CHAPTER NINE

Thomas drops me off in my driveway, still grumbling about Morfran and Riika and the gingersnaps. I'm glad I don't have to bear witness to that confrontation. Personally, I think that eating the cookies is a minor point compared to the part where Morfran sent his grandson to unknowingly visit a dead family member, but hey, everybody has their pet peeves. Apparently Thomas's is dead peoples' snack food.

In between mutterings and spitting out the window, Thomas told me he'd need at least a week to research the Lappish drum and the proper ritual to channel Anna through. I put on my most understanding expression and nodded, the whole time fighting the urge to find the nearest stick and start pounding out a solo on the drum in my lap. It's stupid. Being careful and doing things right the first time is pretty much a requirement. I don't know what's going on in my head. When I get inside my house, I find that I can't sit still. I don't want to eat or watch TV. I don't want to do anything but know more.

My mom comes through the door ten minutes after I do, a gigantic pizza box on her arm, and stops when she sees me pacing.

'What's wrong?'

'Nothing,' I say. 'Had an interesting visit with Thomas's dead aunt this afternoon. She gave us a way to communicate with Anna.'

Aside from a slight widening of her eyes, there's a total non-reaction. She almost shrugs before trundling through the living room into the kitchen. A quick spark of anger tingles in my wrists. I expected more. I expected her to be excited, to be happy that I might get to talk to Anna again, to make sure she's all right.

'You had a conversation with Thomas's dead aunt,' she says, calmly opening the pizza box. 'And I had a conversation with Gideon this afternoon.'

'What's the matter with you? I didn't just tell you that there's a new blue plate special over at Gargoyles restaurant. I didn't just tell you that I stubbed my toe, though I'm sure that would have gotten more attention.'

'He said you should leave it alone.'

'I don't know what's going on with everyone,' I say. 'Telling me to let it go. To move on. Like it's that easy.

Like I can just keep on seeing her like this. I mean, hell! Carmel thinks I'm a psycho!'

'Cas,' she says. 'Calm down. Gideon has his reasons. And I think he's right. I can feel it, that something's happening.'

'But you don't know what, right? I mean, it's something bad, but you don't know exactly? And you think I should just let whatever is happening to Anna keep happening, because of what? Your woman's intuition?'

'Hey,' she snaps, her voice deep.

'Sorry,' I snap right back.

'I'm not just your worrying mother, Theseus Cassio Lowood. I'm a witch. Intuition counts for a lot.' Her jaw is set in that particular way that she has when she'd rather chew through leather than say what she wants to say. 'I know what you really want,' she says carefully. 'You don't just want to make sure she's all right. You want to bring her back.'

I lower my eyes.

'And, my god, Cas, part of me wishes it were possible. She saved your life and avenged my husband's murder. But you can't walk down that road.'

'Why not?' I ask, and my voice sounds bitter.

'Because there are rules,' she replies. 'That shouldn't be broken.'

I raise my eyes and glare at her. 'You didn't say 'can't.''

'Cas—'

Another minute of this and I'm going to flip out. So I put up my hands and head for my bedroom, closing my ears to everything she says as I go up the stairs, choking on a million words I want to yell into all of their faces. Thomas seems like the only person remotely interested in figuring out what's going on.

Anna is waiting in my bedroom. Her head lolls as if on a broken neck; her eyes roll up to mine.

'It's too much, right now,' I whisper, and she mouths something back. I don't try to read her lips. Too much black blood spills through them. Slowly, she moves away, and I try to keep my eyes on the carpet but I can't, not quite, so when she throws herself through my window, I see her dress flutter as she falls and hear the thump of her body when it hits the ground.

'God damn it,' I say in a voice caught somewhere between growl and moan. My fists hit the wall, my dresser; I knock the lamp off my bedside table. My mom's words twitter through my ears, making it sound so easy. She talks like she thinks I'm a schoolboy with fantasies of heroes who get the girl and ride off into the sunset. What kind of world does she think I grew up in?

*

'It's probably going to be blood,' Thomas says in a regretful tone that doesn't match the devious excitement in his eyes. 'It's almost always blood.'

'Yeah? Well if it's going to be more than a pint, let me know now, so I can bank it,' I reply, and he grins. We're at his locker, talking about the ritual, which he still doesn't have nailed down. But to be fair, it's only been a day and a half. The blood he's referring to is the conduit – the link to the other side – or the price. I'm not sure which. He's talked about it both ways, like a bridge, and like a toll. Maybe it's both, and the other side is basically a toll road. He's a little bit nervous while we talk, I think because he senses my eagerness. He can probably tell I haven't slept much either. I look like total shit.

Thomas straightens when Carmel walks up, looking ten times better than we do, as usual. Her hair is up in a clip, bouncing jauntily in a sweep of blond. The sparkle from her silver bracelets hurts my eyes.

'Hey, Thomas,' she says. 'Hey, zombie-Cas.'

'Hey,' I say. 'So I guess you heard what happened.'

'Yeah, Thomas told me. Pretty scary stuff.'

I shrug. 'It wasn't that bad. Riika was actually cool. You should've come.'

'Well. Maybe I would have if I hadn't been kicked out of the club.' She lowers her eyes and Thomas goes immediately on the defensive, apologizing for Morfran, insisting he was out of line, and Carmel nods, keeping her eyes on the floor.

Something's going on behind Carmel's lowered lashes. She doesn't think I'm watching, or maybe she thinks I'm too tired to notice, but even through the exhaustion I can see what it is, and the knowledge makes me hold my breath. Carmel was happy to be kicked out. Sometime in between rune-carving and being tacked to a wall by a pitchfork, it all got to be too much. It's there in her eyes; the way they linger regretfully on Thomas when he isn't looking, and the way they blink and sparkle fake interest when he tells her about the ritual. And the whole time Thomas just keeps on smiling, oblivious to the fact that she is basically already gone. It feels like I've watched the last ten minutes of a movie first.

Spending the entire school year at the same school is something I haven't done since eighth grade, and I have to say, it's sort of obnoxious. It's the Monday of the last week of the year, and if I have to sign one more yearbook I'm going to sign it in the owner's blood. People I've never spoken to are walking up with a pen and a smile, hoping for something more personal than 'have a neat summer' when such hopes are futile. And I can't help but suspect that what they really want is for me to write something cryptic or crazy, some new clue they could use for the rumor mill. It's been tempting, but so far I haven't done it.

When there's a tap on my shoulder and I turn around to see Cait Hecht, my botched date from two weeks ago, I almost back into my locker.

'Hey, Cas,' she smiles. 'Sign my yearbook?'

'Absolutely,' I say, and take it, scrambling to think of something personal but all that goes through my brain is 'have a neat summer.' I write her name and then a comma. What now? 'Sorry about the brush-off, but you reminded me of a girl I killed'? Or maybe, 'It never would have worked. The girl I love would disembowel you.'

'So, are you doing anything cool this summer?' she asks.

'Uh, I don't know. Maybe travel around a bit more.'

'But you'll be back here in the fall?' Her brows are raised politely, but it's just small talk. Carmel says Cait started dating Quentin Davis two days after the coffee shop. I was relieved to hear it, and am relieved now that she doesn't seem upset in the least.

'That is a very good question,' I say, before giving up and scribbling 'have a great summer' into the corner of the page.

CHAPTER TEN

Looking out the window of Carmel's car, there's no light except for stars and the pale glow of the city behind us. Thomas waited for the new moon. He said it was the best time for channeling. He also said that it would help if we were near the place where Anna crossed over, so we're headed for the wreckage of her old Victorian. It fits. It makes sense. But the thought of it makes my mouth dry, and Thomas is going to explain everything once we get there, because I could barely sit still to listen back at the shop.

'You sure you're up for this, Cas?' Carmel asks, peering at me in the rearview mirror.

'I have to be,' I say, and she nods.

When Carmel decided to do the ritual with us, I was surprised. Ever since that day in the hall, when I saw the detachment lurking behind her eyes, I haven't been able to look at her the same way. But maybe I was wrong. Maybe I was hallucinating. Three hours of sleep riddled with dreams of your girlfriend killing herself will do that to you.

'This might not work at all, you know,' Thomas says.

'Hey, it's OK. You're trying, right? That's all we can do.' My words and voice sound reasonable. Sane. But that's because I don't have anything to worry about. It's going to work. Thomas is strung tight as a violin, and you don't need a tuning fork to feel the waves of power coming off of him. Like Aunt Riika said, he's more than witch enough.

'Guys,' he says. 'After this is over, can we go get a burger or something?'

'You're thinking about food now?' Carmel asks.

'Hey, you haven't spent the last three days fasting and doing herbal rue steams and drinking nothing but Morfran's gross chrysanthemum purification potions.' Carmel and I grin at each other in the mirror. 'It isn't easy becoming a vessel. I'm freaking starving.'

I clap him on the shoulder. 'Dude, when this is over, I'll buy you the whole damn menu.'

The car goes quiet as we turn down Anna's road. Part of me expects to round the corner and have the house curl into our vision, still standing, still rotting on its crumbling foundation. Instead there's empty space. Carmel's headlights shine into the driveway, and the driveway leads to nothing.

After the house imploded, the city came out and cleared the debris in an effort to determine the underlying cause of the blast. They never found it, though true to form, they didn't really try. They poked around in the basement and shrugged their shoulders and filled it in with dirt. Now everything that was left is concealed completely. The place where the house stood looks like an undeveloped lot, packed dirt and scrubby, fast-growing weeds. If they had looked any closer, or dug any deeper, they might have found the bodies of Anna's victims. But the current of the dead and unknown was still too close, whispering that they should walk softly and leave it alone.

'Tell me what we're doing, again,' Carmel says. Her voice is steady but her fingers are curled around the steering wheel like she's going to rip it off.

'Should be relatively easy,' Thomas replies, scrounging around in his messenger bag, making sure he's remembered everything. 'Or if not easy, then at least relatively simple. From what Morfran told me, the drum used to be used by Finnish witches on a regular basis, to control the spirit world and talk to the dead.'

'Sounds like what we need,' I say.

'Yeah. The trick of it is to be specific. The witches never cared much who they got. As long as they got someone they figured they were wise. But we want

Anna. And that's where you and the house come in.'

Well, we're not getting any younger. I open the door and step out. The air is mild and there's only a hint of a breeze. When my shoes crunch against the gravel the sound brings a flash of nostalgia, a jolt that takes me back six months, when the Victorian still stood and I used to come at night to talk to the dead girl inside it. Warm, fuzzy memories. Carmel hands me the camping lantern from the trunk. It illuminates her face.

'Hey,' I say. 'You don't have to do this. Thomas and I can handle this one on our own.'

For a second she looks relieved. But then the trademark Carmel squint is back in place.

'Don't say that shit to me. Morfran can ban me from his dead tea party if he wants, but not you. I'm here to find out what happened to Anna. We all owe her that.'

When she walks by, she nudges me with her shoulder, to buck me up, and I smile even though the burns are still sore. After this is over, I'm going to talk to her; we're all going to talk. We'll find out what's on her mind and set it right.

Thomas is already ahead of us. He's got his flashlight out and is strobing it around the lot. It's a good thing that the nearest neighbors are half a mile away and separated by dense forest. They'd probably think a UFO had landed. When he gets to where the house once stood, he doesn't hesitate, just jogs into the center. I know what he's looking for: The space where Malvina poked a hole through worlds. And where Anna blasted through it.

'Come on,' he says after a minute, and waves to us. Carmel goes, moving carefully. I take a deep breath. My feet won't seem to cross the threshold. This is what I wanted, what I've waited for since Anna disappeared. The answers are less than twenty feet away.

'Cas?' Carmel asks.

'Right behind you,' I say, but every platitude I've ever heard about ignorance being bliss or being better off in the dark flies through my brain in an instant. It occurs to me that I shouldn't have wanted this to be real. I should hope that the answers I get tonight tell me that it wasn't Anna at all, that Riika was wrong and Anna is at peace. Let whatever is haunting me be something else, something malevolent that I can fight. It's selfish to want Anna here again. She's got to be better off wherever she is, than being cursed and trapped. But I can't help it.

Just a few seconds more and my feet unfreeze. They carry me across the fresh dirt the city used to fill in the basement, and I don't feel anything. No cosmic zap; not even a chill down my spine. Nothing of Anna or her curse remains. It all probably vanished the second that the house imploded. Mom, Morfran, and Thomas must've checked ten times, standing at the corners of the property and casting runes.

In the center of the dirt patch, Thomas is drawing a large circle in the ground with the tip of an athame. Not mine, but one of Morfran's – a long, theatrical-looking thing, with an engraved handle and a jewel at the end. Most people would say it's far prettier than mine, and far more valuable. But it's all show. Thomas can use it to cast a circle, but it's his power that forms the protection. Without Thomas to wield it, that athame would be best used to cut a good steak.

Carmel stands in the center of the circle, holding a burning stick of incense and whispering the protection incantation Thomas has taught her. Thomas is whispering it too, two beats behind hers so it sounds like a round robin. I set the camping lantern down, inside the circle but off to the side. The chanting stops, and Thomas nods at us to sit.

The ground is cold, but at least it's dry. Thomas kneels and sets the Lappish drum on the dirt in front of him. He's brought a drumstick as well. It looks basically like a regular drumstick with a big, white marshmallow at the end. In the low light, you can hardly see the designs painted across the stretched leather of the drum. When I had it with me in the car ride back from Riika's,

I saw that it was covered in faded, reddish stick figures that looked like a primitive depiction of a hunting scene.

'It looks so old,' Carmel comments. 'What do you think it's made of?' She smirks at me. 'Maybe dinosaur leather?'

I laugh, but Thomas clears his throat.

'The ritual is pretty simple,' he says, 'but it's also powerful. We shouldn't go into it with too light a mood.' He's cleaning the dirt off his athame, wiping it down with alcohol, and I know why he's going to the trouble. He was right when he said we would need blood. And he intends to use that athame to get it from me. 'Since you're curious though, I can tell you that Morfran suspects this drum was made from human skin.'

Carmel gasps.

'Not a murder victim or anything like that,' he goes on. 'But probably from the tribe's last shaman. Of course he doesn't know for sure, but he said the best ones were often made from that, and Riika didn't mess around with second-rate product. It was probably passed down through her own family.'

He talks distractedly, failing to notice the way Carmel swallows and can't quite stop looking at the drum. I know what she's thinking. With this new knowledge, it looks completely different than it did a few seconds ago. It may as well be a human ribcage, dried out and sitting in front of us.

'What exactly is going to happen when we do this?' Carmel asks.

'I don't know,' Thomas replies. 'If we succeed, we'll hear her voice. A few texts have vague references to fog, or smoke. And there might be wind. All I know for sure is that I'll be in a trance when it happens. I may or may not know what's going on. And if something goes wrong, I won't be much use to stop it.'

Even in the sparse light from the camping lantern, I can see most of the blood drain out of Carmel's cheeks.

'Well, that's just great. What are we supposed to do if something happens?'

'Don't panic.' Thomas smiles nervously. He tosses her something that glitters. When she opens her hands, she's holding his Zippo lighter. 'This is sort of hard to explain. The drum is like a tool, to find the way to the other side. Morfran says it's mostly about finding the right beat, like tuning in the right frequency on the radio. Once I find it, the gateway has to be channeled by blood. The blood of the seeker. Cas's blood. You'll have to drip it onto his athame, which we'll place in the center of the circle.'

'What do you mean, *I'll* have to?' Carmel asks.

'Well, he can't do it himself, and I'll be in a trance,' Thomas replies like it should have been obvious.

'You can do it,' I say to Carmel. 'Just think of how I embarrassed you on that date. You'll be dying to stab me.'

She doesn't look reassured, but when Thomas holds out his athame, she takes it.

'When?' she asks.

Thomas gives a lopsided grin. 'I sort of hope you'll just know.' The grin throws me a bit. It's the first sign of 'our' Thomas that we've seen since we got here. Usually, when there's spell-work to be done, he's all business, and it occurs to me now that he really has no idea what he's doing.

'Is this dangerous? For you, I mean,' I ask him.

He shrugs and waves his hand. 'Don't worry about it. We need to know, right? Before you get driven to the nuthatch. So let's get going. Carmel,' he says, and looks at her. 'If anything goes wrong, you have to burn the blood off of Cas's athame. Just pick it up and burn it off the blade. OK?'

'Why does it have to be me? Why can't Cas do it?'

'For the same reason you have to cut him. Because you're technically outside of the ritual. I don't know what's going to happen to Cas, or me, once this starts.'

Carmel is shivering, despite the fact that it isn't that cold. Second thoughts are on the tip of her tongue, so before she can say anything, I take the athame out of my back pocket, pull it from its sheath, and set it on the ground.

'It's a beacon, like Riika said,' Thomas explains. 'Let's hope Anna can follow it to us.' He reaches into his messenger bag and produces a small handful of incense sticks, which he holds out for Carmel to light and then blows them out before pushing them into the soft dirt around him. I count seven. Scented smoke curls up in light gray spirals. He takes a deep breath.

'One more thing,' he says, picking up the drumstick. 'Don't leave the circle until it's over.' He's got this 'here goes nothing' expression, and I'd like to tell him to be careful, but my whole face feels paralyzed. Just blinking is a challenge.

He rolls his wrist and the drum starts; the sound of the beat is low and full. It has a heavy, echo-y quality, and even though I'm pretty certain that Thomas has no formal drumming experience, every beat sounds planned. It sounds written. Even when he changes the tempo and the duration of the strike. Time goes by. I don't know how much. Maybe thirty seconds, maybe ten minutes. The sound of the drum throws off my senses. The air seems thick with incense smoke and there's a swimmy feeling sloshing around my head. I glance at Carmel. She's blinking fast and there are a few beads of sweat on her forehead, but otherwise she looks alert.

Thomas's breathing is slow and shallow. It sounds like part of the rhythm. The beat pauses and strikes. One. Two. Three. Four. Five. Six. Seven. Then it starts fresh, faster this time and lower. The smoke coming from the incense wavers back and forth. It's happening. He's finding the way.

'Carmel,' I whisper, and hold my hand out over my athame, resting in the dirt. She grabs me by the wrist and brings Thomas's knife up to my palm.

'Cas,' she says, and shakes her head.

'Come on, it's OK,' I say, and she swallows hard, then bites her lip. The blade drags across the meat of my palm, first a dull pressure and then a short, hot sting. Blood drips down onto my athame, spattering onto the blade. It almost sizzles. Or maybe it really does. Something's happening to the air; it's moving around us like a snake and over the sound of the drum there's a screeching of wind in my ears, only there isn't any wind. The smoke from the incense isn't blowing away. It just swirls continually upward.

'Is this supposed to be happening?' Carmel asks.

'Don't worry. It's OK,' I reply, but I have no idea. Whatever is happening, it's working but it isn't working. It's happening, but too slowly. Everything inside the circle feels like a thing trying to break from a cage. The air is thick and clogged, and I wish there was a moon so it wasn't so freaking dark. We should have left the camping lantern on.

Blood is still dripping from my hand down onto the athame. I don't know how much I've lost. It can't be that much, but my brain isn't working right. I can hardly see through all the smoke, but I don't remember when that happened, or understand how this much smoke is coming from seven sticks of incense. Carmel says something but I can't hear her, even though I think she's shouting. The athame seems to pulse. The sight of it coated in my blood is strange, almost warped. My blood on the blade. My blood inside it. The drum beats and the sound of Thomas breathing rolls through the air... or maybe it's my breathing, and my own heartbeat, pounding in my ears.

Thick fingers of nausea crawl up my throat. I have to do something, before it takes over, or before Carmel panics and leaves the circle. My hand jerks toward the drum and presses down on the taut skin. I don't know why. Just some strange impulse. The touch leaves behind a wet, red print. For an instant it stands out, bright andtribal. Then it sinks into the drum surface, disappearing like it was never there.

'Thomas, man, I don't know how much longer I can do this,' I whisper. I can barely make out the shine from his eyeglasses through the smoke. He doesn't hear me.

A girl's scream cuts through the air, ripping and brutal. And it wasn't Carmel. This scream is a meat cleaver to the ears, and even before I see the first black strands of snaking hair I know that Thomas has done it. He's found Anna's beat.

When this started, I tried not to think ahead, to keep from expecting anything. Turns out it wasn't necessary. The sight in front of me now, I never could have imagined.

Anna explodes into the circle, as if Thomas's drum has pulled her out of another dimension. She breaks through the air between us like a sonic boom and strikes some unseen surface three feet off the ground. It isn't the quiet girl in white who he's called but the black-veined goddess, monstrous and beautiful, saturated in red. Black hair roils behind her in a cloud, and my head spins. She's right in front of me, streaked with red, and for a second I can't remember why, or what I was supposed to say. Blood drips from her dress but never hits the dirt, because she isn't really where the dirt is. We're just looking through an opened window.

'Anna,' I whisper. For an instant, she bares her teeth and her oil-black eyes go wide. But instead of answering, she shakes her head and squeezes them shut. Her fists pound against some unseen surface.

'Anna.' Louder this time.

'You're not here,' she says, staring down, and relief floods through my chest, leaving my insides wide open and rubbery. She hears me. That's something.

'You're not here either,' I say. The sight of her. The magnitude. I hadn't forgotten, but seeing it again blows me away. She's crouched, on the defensive like a hissing cat.

'You're just my imagination,' she counters. She sounds like me, just like me. I glance at Thomas, holding the beat on the drum, keeping his breathing steady. A dark ring of sweat has spread around the collar of his t-shirt; rivulets are running down his face from the effort. We might not have much time.

'That's what I thought,' I say. 'When you first showed up at my house. That's what I tried to tell myself when you'd put yourself into a furnace or throw yourself out my window.'

Anna's face twitches, I think, with cautious hope. It's sort of hard to tell, hard to read emotions through black veins.

'Was it really you?' I ask.

'I didn't throw,' she mutters to no one in particular. 'I was thrown. Down, onto the stones. I was pulled. Pulled inside to be burned.' She shudders, maybe at the memory, and so do I. But I have to get her on track.

'The girl we're looking at now, is it you?' There isn't

time, but I don't know what to say. She seems so confused. Was it really her? Was she asking for my help?

'You can see me?' she asks, and before I can answer, the dark goddess melts away. Black veins recede into pale skin, and her hair stills and turns brown, hanging limp over her shoulders. When she pushes back onto her knees, the familiar white dress crumples around her legs. It's streaked with black stains. Her hands flutter in her lap, and those eyes, those dark, fierce eyes are still unsure. They flicker back and forth. 'I can't see you. It's just dark.' Regret makes her words halting and quiet. I don't know what to say. There are fresh scabs on her knuckles, and her arms are bruised purple. Narrow scars crisscross her shoulders. This can't be.

'Why can't I see you?'

'I don't know,' I say quickly. Smoke swirls up between us and I'm relieved to look away, to blink. There's a choking feeling in the back of my throat. 'This is only a window that Thomas was able to open,' I say. This is all wrong. Wherever she is, it isn't where she's supposed to be. The scars on her arms. The bruises.

'What happened to you? Where did you get those scars?'

She looks down at herself, sort of surprised, like she's just now realizing they're there. 'I knew you were safe,' she says softly. 'After we crossed over. I knew.' She smiles, but there isn't any real feeling in it. We don't have time for this.

I swallow hard. 'Where are you?'

Her hair hangs across her cheeks and she stares into nothing. I don't even know if she really believes we're having this conversation.

'In Hell,' she whispers like it's a matter of course. 'I'm in Hell.'

No. No, that's not where she belongs. It wasn't where she was supposed to go. She was supposed to be at rest. She was – I stop, because what the hell do I know? These aren't decisions that I make. That's just what I wanted, and what I tried to believe.

'You're asking for my help, is that it? Is that why you showed me these things?'

Her head shakes. 'No. I didn't think you could really see. I didn't think it was real. I just imagined you. It was easier, if I could see your face.' She shakes her head again. 'I'm sorry. I don't want you to see.'

There's a puckered, healing cut along the curve of her shoulder. It isn't right. I don't know who or what decides, but now I'm going to. It can't stand this way.

'Anna, listen. I'm going to bring you back. I'm going to find a way to bring you home. Do you understand?'

Her head jerks to the right, and she goes still and tense like a prey animal hiding from a wolf. Instinctually I stay silent and watch the rapid rise and fall of her ribcage. After a few long seconds, she relaxes.

'You should go,' she says. 'He'll find me here. He'll hear you.'

'Who?' I ask. 'Who will find you?'

'He always finds me,' she goes on like she hasn't heard. 'And then he burns. And cuts. And kills. I can't fight him here. I can't win.' Black tendrils of hair are beginning to shoot through the brown. There's a faraway tone in her voice. She's hanging by a thread.

'You can fight anyone,' I whisper.

'This is his world. His rules.' She's talking to no one now, crouched back down. Blood is starting to seep through the white fabric. Her hair twitches and turns black.

What the hell was I thinking, doing this? It's a million times worse, seeing her in front of me and still a world away. My hands curl into fists to keep from reaching out to her. The energy rolling in the smoke between us is running at a hundred thousand volts. She's not really close enough to touch. It's only magic. An illusion made somehow possible by a drum of human skin, by my blood sliding over my athame. Somewhere to my right, Carmel says something, but I can't hear and it's impossible to see through the smoke.

The ground shakes beneath Anna's body. She steadies

herself with her hands and cowers as something somewhere not far away bellows. The sound is inhuman, echoing off a million walls. Sweat prickles down my spine and my legs move on their own; her fear drives me halfway to my feet.

'Anna, tell me how to find you. Do you know?'

Her hands cover her ears and her head whips back and forth. The window between us is thinning, or widening, I can't tell which; a foul smell of rot and wet rocks floats past my nose. The window can't close. I'm going to rip it wide open. Let it burn me up. I don't care. When she sacrificed herself for us, when she dragged him down—

And all at once I know who it is that's there with her.

'It's him, isn't it?' I shout. 'It's the Obeahman. Are you trapped with him?!' She shakes her head harshly, unconvincingly. 'Anna, don't lie!' I stop. It doesn't matter what she says. I know it. Something in my chest curls like a snake. Her scars. The way she crouches like a dog that's been kicked. He's breaking her bones. Murderer. Murderer.

My eyes burn. The smoke is thick; I can feel it against my cheeks. Somewhere the drum is still drumming, louder and louder, but I don't know if it's coming from the left anymore, or from the right, or behind. I've stood up without realizing it.

'I'm coming for you,' I shout over the drum. 'And I'm coming for him. Tell me how. Tell me how to get there!' She cringes. There's smoke, and wind, and screaming, and it's impossible to tell which side it's all coming from. I lower my voice. 'Anna. What do you want me to do?'

For a second I think she'll stonewall. She takes quaking, deep breaths and with every exhale bites down on her words. But then she looks at me, straight at me, into my eyes, and I don't care what she said earlier. She sees me. I know she does.

'Cassio,' she whispers. '*Get me out of here.*'

CHAPTER ELEVEN

What I'm aware of before anything else is Carmel slapping me. Then the real pain starts. My head may very well be in three or four pieces; it hurts that bad. Blood is everywhere in my mouth, all over my tongue. It tastes like old pennies, and my body has that vibration-tinged numbness that tells me I've just recently flown through the air and come down hard. My world is pain and dim yellow light. There are familiar voices. Carmel and Thomas.

'What happened?' I ask. 'Where's Anna?' A few blinks clear the fog from my eyeballs. The light from the camping lantern shines yellow. Carmel is kneeling beside me with dirt smudges on her face and a runner of blood leaking from her nose. Thomas is by her side. He looks dazed and knocked around, positively soaked with sweat, but there's no blood on him.

'I didn't know what else to do,' Carmel says. 'You were going to reach through. You didn't answer me.

I don't think you could even hear me.'

'I couldn't,' I say, and push myself up onto my elbows, careful not to jar my head too much. 'The spell was strong. The smoke and the drum – Thomas, are you OK?' He nods and gives a weak ten-four salute. 'Did I try to reach through? Is that what caused the blast?'

'No,' Carmel replies. 'I grabbed the athame and burned your blood off of it, like Thomas told me. I didn't know that it would be so – I didn't know it was going to go off like a fricking block of C4. I hardly held on to it.'

'I didn't know either,' Thomas mutters. 'I never should have asked you to do that.' He presses his hand to her cheek and she lets it linger for a moment before brushing it away.

'I thought you were going to try to go through,' she says. Something presses into my palm: the athame. Thomas and Carmel each take an arm and help me to my feet. 'I didn't know what else to do.'

'You did the right thing,' Thomas tells her. 'If he'd tried, he'd have probably been turned inside out. It was just a window. Not a doorway. Or a gate.'

I look around the dirt lot that used to be Anna's Victorian. The ground that was beneath the circle is darker than the rest, and there are swirling wind patterns cut into it, like desert dunes. The spot where I landed is about ten feet from where I was sitting.

'Is there a doorway?' I ask loudly. 'Is there a gate?'

Thomas looks at me with a jolt. He'd been walking around the remains of the circle on shaky legs, picking up his scattered supplies: the drum, the drumstick, the ornamental athame.

'What are you talking about?' they both ask.

My brain feels like scrambled eggs, and my back must be bruised like a hippo's trampoline, but I remember everything that happened. I remember what Anna said, and how she looked.

'I'm talking about a gate,' I say again. 'Big enough to walk through. I'm talking about opening a gate and bringing her back.' I listen for a few minutes while they sputter and tell me it's impossible. They say things like, 'That wasn't what the ritual was about.' They tell me I'm going to get myself killed. They might be right. I guess they probably are. But it doesn't matter.

'Listen to me,' I say carefully, dusting off my jeans and putting the athame back in its sheath. 'Anna can't stay there.'

'Cas,' Carmel starts. 'There's no way. It's crazy.'

'You saw her, didn't you?' I ask, and they exchange a guilty glance.

'Cas, you knew that's how it might be. She – ' Carmel swallows. 'She killed a lot of people.'

When I spin on her, Thomas takes half a step in between.

'But she saved us,' he says, and Carmel mutters, 'I know.'

'He's there too. The Obeahman. The bastard that murdered my father. And I'm not going to let him spend eternity feeding on her.' I squeeze the handle of the athame so hard my knuckles crack. 'I'm going to walk through a gate. And I'm going to shove this so far down his throat that he chokes on it.'

When I say that, they both take a breath. I look at them, beaten and scuffed up as a pair of old shoes. They're brave; they've been braver than I gave them credit for or had any right to expect. 'If I have to do this alone, I understand. But I'm getting her out.' When I'm halfway to the car, the argument starts. I hear 'suicide mission' and 'doomed quest for closure,' both in Carmel's voice. Then I'm too far down the drive to hear what they're saying.

It's true what they say about answers only leading to more questions. There will always be more to find out, more to learn, more to do. So now I know that Anna's in Hell. And now I have to find a way to get her out. Sitting at my kitchen table, poking a fork at one of my mom's mushroom omelets, it feels like I've been stuffed into a cannon. There's so much to do. What the hell am I doing here prodding a cheesy egg pouch?

'Do you want toast?'

'Not really.'

'What's the matter with you?' My mom sits down in her bathrobe, looking worn around the edges. Last night I added a few more grays to her head, coming in with a bruised skull. She stayed awake while I slept, and shook me to consciousness every hour and a half, to make sure I didn't have a concussion and die. Last night she didn't ask questions. I suppose the relief of seeing me alive was enough. And maybe part of her doesn't want to know.

'The drum worked,' I say quietly. 'I saw Anna. She's in Hell.'

Her eyes light up and burn out in the space of a blink.

'Hell?' she asks. 'Fire and brimstone? Little red guy with a big fork and a pointy tail?'

'Is this funny to you?'

'Of course not,' she replies. 'I just never thought it actually existed.' And she doesn't know what to say either.

'For the record, I didn't see any pointy tail. But she's in Hell. Or someplace like it. I guess it doesn't matter if it's *the* Hell or not.'

My mom sighs. 'I suppose that decades of murder is a

lot to atone for. It doesn't feel fair to me, but—there's nothing we can do about it, sweetheart.'

Atonement. The word makes me glare so hard that heat rays might shoot out of my eyeballs.

'As far as I'm concerned,' I say, 'it was all one big screw-up.'

'Cas.'

'And I'm going to get her out.'

Mom's eyes fall to her plate. 'You know that isn't possible. You know that you can't.'

'I think I can. My friends and I just opened a window between here and Hell, and I'm willing to bet that we can open a door.'

There's a long, simmering silence. 'It's an impossible thing to do and just trying it is probably enough to kill you.'

I try to remember that she's my mother, and it's her job to talk to me about impossible, so I sort of nod. But she sees through it, and her feathers are up. In one breath she threatens to move my ass out of Thunder Bay, to take me far away from Thomas and his witchy ways. She even says she's going to take the athame and send it to Gideon.

'Don't you listen? When Gideon or I tell you something, do you listen?' Her lips form a tight, thin line. 'What happened to Anna, I hate it. It's not fair. It might be the worst case of unfair I've ever heard. But you're not trying this, Cas. You're absolutely not.'

'Yes, I will,' I growl. 'And it's not just her either. It's him. The bastard that killed Dad. He's there too. So I'm going to go after him and I'm going to kill him again. I'm going to kill him a thousand times.' She starts to cry, and I'm dangerously close to it myself. 'You didn't see her, Mom.' She has to get it. I can't sit at this table and try to eat eggs when I know that she's trapped over there. There is only one thing I should be doing and I have no idea where to start.

I love her, I almost say. *What would you do if it were Dad?* I almost say. But I'm wrung out. She's wiping tears from her cheeks and I know she's thinking about the cost, how much this has cost us. I can't think about that anymore. I'm sorry as hell, but I can't. Not even for her. Not when I have work to do.

My fork clatters down on my plate. Food is out. And school is out too. There are only four days left, and most of them are pep rallies. I took my last test last Thursday, and passed with a B+ average. It's not like they're going to expel me.

Black Labs probably shouldn't eat peanut butter cookies. Maybe they shouldn't drink milk either. But they sure do like both of those things. Stella's head is lodged into my lap, and she's heaved most of her body onto the burgundy cushions of the sofa I'm sitting on. Her seal pup eyes flicker from my face to my glass of milk, so I tip it to the side to let her big pink tongue go to work. When she's finished, she slurps a thank-you into my palm.

'You're welcome,' I say, and give her a scratch. I didn't want to eat anyway. I came to the shop right after my non-breakfast to see Morfran. Apparently he and Thomas sat up most of the night talking over the ritual, because he had this broody, sympathetic expression behind his glasses, and instantly plunked me onto this couch and served me a snack. Why do people keep trying to feed me?

'Here, drink this,' Morfran says, appearing out of nowhere. He stuffs a mug of some foul, herbal blend into my face, and I recoil.

'What is it?'

'Angelica root rejuvenation potion. With a little thistle tossed in. After what that Obeah did to your liver last fall, you've got to take care of it.'

I look at it skeptically. It's hot, and it smells like it was brewed with ditchwater.

'Is it safe?'

'As long as you're not pregnant,' he snorts. 'I called Thomas. He's on his way. He went in to school this

morning, thinking you'd be there. Some psychic, eh?'
We sort of smile and say, 'It only works some of the
time,' together in Thomas's voice. I sip at the potion
tentatively. It tastes worse than it smells, bitter and for
some reason almost salty.

'This is disgusting.'

'Well, the milk was supposed to coat your stomach
and the cookies would've taken the taste out of your
mouth. But you gave it all to the dog, you idiot.' He pats
Stella's rear and she lumbers off of the couch. 'Listen,
kid,' Morfran says, and I stop sipping at his grave tone.
'Thomas told me what you're going to try to do. I don't
think I need to tell you that you're probably going to get
yourself killed.'

I look down into the brown green liquid. A smart
remark is creeping up on my tongue, something about
how his potions are going to kill me first, and I swallow
hard to keep quiet.

'But,' he sighs. 'I'm also not going to tell you that you
don't have a chance. You've got the stuff, power rolling
off you in waves I've never heard before. And they're not
just coming from that backpack.' He jerks a finger
toward my bag, next to me on the sofa. Then he sits
down, on the arm of the chair opposite, and runs his
hand across his beard. Whatever it is he needs to say
isn't easy. 'Thomas is going to go with you on this

thing,' he says. 'I couldn't stop him if I tried.'

'I won't let anything happen to him, Morfran.'

'That's a promise you can't make,' he says, his voice harsh. 'You think you're just up against the forces of the other side? That shadowy, dreadlocked dude who wants to finish digesting you from the inside out? You should be so lucky.'

I sip the potion. He's talking about the storm again. The thinghat he senses, coming at me, or pulling me, or tripping me, or whatever the hell he said in that vague, useless way of his.

'But you're not going to tell me to stop,' I say.

'I don't know if it can be stopped. I think maybe you've got to go through it. Maybe you'll come out the other side. Maybe you'll come out the other side looking like a spit-up owl pellet.' He rubs his beard, having gotten off track. 'Look. I don't want anything to happen to you, either. But if my grandson gets hurt, or worse – ' He looks me in the eye. 'You'll have made an enemy of me. Do you understand?'

Over these months, Morfran has become sort of a grandfather to me too. Becoming his enemy is the last thing I want.

'I understand.'

He grabs me, his hand striking like a snake and holding mine fast. In the quarter second before a shot of energy makes my blood jump under my skin, I notice his ring: a small circle of carved skulls. I've never seen it on his hand before, but I know what it is, and what it means. It means that I won't just have made an enemy of Morfran, but of voodoo itself.

'Be sure that you do,' he says, and lets go. Whatever it was that ran through me made sweat stand out on my forehead. Even on my palms.

The door to the shop jingles and Stella trots over to meet Thomas, her toenails clicking. At his entrance, the tension dissipates and Morfran and I take a deep breath. I hope Thomas's psychic thing isn't working right now, and that he isn't particularly observant, or he's going to ask why we look so uncomfortable and embarrassed.

'No Carmel today?' I ask.

'She stayed home with a headache,' he replies. 'How are you feeling?'

'Like I was thrown twelve feet through the air and landed on second-degree burns. You?'

'Groggy, and weak as a wet noodle. Plus, I think I may have forgotten a letter from the alphabet. If I hadn't asked to leave, Mrs Snyder would have sent me home anyway. Said I looked pale. Thought I might have mono.' He grins. I grin back, and we sit in silence. It's strange and filled with tension, but it's also kind of nice. It's nice to linger here, to hold ourselves back and not barrel through this moment. Because whatever we say next is going to catapult us into something dangerous, and I don't think either one of us really knows where it might lead.

'So, I guess you're really going to try this,' he says. I wish he wouldn't sound so hesitant, so skeptical. The quest might be doomed, but there's no reason to paint it that way from the get-go.

'I guess I am.'

He smiles, lopsided. 'Want some help?'

Thomas. He's my best friend and sometimes he still makes it sound like he's a tag-along. Of course I want his help. More than that: I need it.

'You don't have to,' I say.

'But I will,' he replies. 'Do you have any idea where to start?'

I run my hand through my hair. 'Not really. There's just an urge to get moving, like there's a clock ticking somewhere that I can barely hear.'

Thomas shrugs. 'It's possible that there is. Figuratively speaking. The longer that Anna stays where she is, the harder it might be for her to cross over to somewhere else. She might become embedded in it. Of course that's just conjecture.'

Conjecture. Honestly, half-cocked guesses about worst-case scenarios aren't what I need right now.

'Let's just hope it's not a real clock,' I say. ' She's already been there too long, Thomas. One second is too long, after what she did for us.'

Thoughts about what she did to all of the runaways in her basement – all the teens who wound up in the wrong place and the wanderers stuck in her web – flutter over his features. Other people might judge Anna's fate as a proper punishment. Maybe lots of people. But not me. Anna's hands were tied by the curse put on her when she was murdered. Every one of her victims was a casualty of the curse, not the girl. That's what I say. I'm well aware that none of the people she tore apart would be likely to say the same thing.

'We can't rush this, Cas,' Thomas says, and I agree. But we can't keep treading water, either.

CHAPTER TWELVE

Morfran writes Thomas a note to get him out of the last days of school, saying he's come down with a bad case of mono. We've spent every moment we've been awake poring over books – old, musty tomes that have been translated from older, mustier tomes. I was grateful to have something to do, to feel like we were moving forward. But after three days of minimal sleep and living off sandwiches and frozen pizza, we have virtually nothing to show for our efforts. Every book is a dead end, going on and on about contacting the other side, but never even addressing the possibility of punching through, let alone pulling something back. I've called every contact I know who might have information, and I got jack squat.

We're sitting at Thomas and Morfran's kitchen table, surrounded by more useless books, while Morfran adds potatoes to a pot of beef stew on the stove. On the other side of the windows, birds flit from tree to tree, and a few large squirrels are fighting for control of the birdfeeder. I haven't seen Anna since the night we contacted her. I don't know why. I tell myself that she's afraid for me, that she regrets telling me to come for her, and is staying away deliberately. It's a nice delusion. Maybe it's even true.

'Heard from Carmel lately?' I ask Thomas.

'Yeah. She says we're not missing much at school. That it's mostly a bunch of back-to-back pep rallies and friendship circles.'

I snort. I remember thinking the same thing. Thomas doesn't seem worried, but I wonder why Carmel hasn't called me. We shouldn't have left her alone for so many days. The ritual had to have shaken her up.

'Why hasn't she come by?' I ask.

'You know how she feels about this,' Thomas says without looking up from the book he's reading. I tap a pen against the open page in front of me. There's nothing useful there.

'Morfran,' I say. 'Tell me about zombies. Tell me how voodooists and obeahmen raise the dead.'

A flicker of motion catches my eye: Thomas is flapping his hand toward his throat, giving me the cut-it signal.

'What?' I ask. 'They bring people back from the dead, right? That's crossing over, if I ever heard it.

152

There's got to be something there we can use.'

Morfran sets the spoon down on the counter with a sharp crack. He turns toward me with an irritated expression.

'For a professional ghost killer, you sure ask a lot of numb-nut questions.'

'What?'

Thomas nudges me. 'Morfran gets offended when people say voodoo can bring you back from the dead. It's sort of a stereotype, you know?'

'It's utter Hollywood bullshit,' Morfran grumbles. 'Those "zombies" aren't anything more than poor, drugged souls who got sedated, buried, and dug up. They shuffle around afterward because the drug was poison from a puffer fish and it boiled their brains tender.'

I narrow my eyes. 'So there was never even one real zombie? Not even one? It's what the religion is famous for.' I shouldn't have said that last part. Morfran's eyes bug out momentarily, and he sets his jaw.

'No real voodooist ever tried to raise a zombie. You can't put life back into something once it's gone.' He turns back to his stew. I guess that's the end of that subject.

'We're not coming up with anything,' I mutter. 'I don't think these people even knew what the other side really was. I think they're just talking about contacting ghosts that were still trapped here, on this plane.'

'Why don't you call Gideon?' Thomas asks. 'He's the one who knows the most about the athame, right? And according to Carmel, the athame was seriously pulsing the night of the ritual. That's why she thought you were going to try to cross over. She thought you could.'

'I've tried to call Gideon about a dozen times. Something's going on with him. He's not calling back.'

'Is he OK?'

'I think so. I feel like he is. And I think someone would have heard and passed the news along if he wasn't.'

The room goes quiet. Morfran is even stirring more quietly while he pretends not to listen. They would both like to know more about the knife. Inside, Morfran is dying to know, I'm sure of it. But Gideon has told me everything. He's sung me that stupid riddle – *The blood of your ancestors forged this athame. Men of power, bled their warrior, to put the spirits down* – and the rest has been lost in time. I say the riddle out loud now, absently.

'Aunt Riika said something about it too,' Thomas says softly, his eyes unfocused but looking in the general direction of the athame in my backpack. He starts to smile. 'God, we're idiots. The knife is the door? It swings back and forth? It's just like Riika said. It's never really closed.' His voice grows in intensity, his eyes swelling behind his glasses. 'That's why the drum ritual wasn't just wind and voices like it was supposed to be! That's why we could open the window to Anna's Hell. That's probably why Anna's able to communicate with you from over there in the first place. The cut she took from the athame that didn't send her away. She's got her foot in the proverbial door.'

'Wait,' I say. The athame is a blade of steel and a handle of dark oiled wood. It isn't something you can crack open and walk through. Unless...my head is starting to hurt. I'm no good at this metaphysical crap. A knife is a knife, it's not also a door. 'Are you saying I can use the knife to cut a gateway?'

'I'm saying the knife *is* the gateway.'

He's killing me here. 'What are you talking about? I can't walk through the knife. We can't pull Anna back through the knife.'

'Cas, you're thinking in solid states,' Thomas explains, and smiles at Morfran, who I must say looks damned impressed by his grandson. 'Remember what Riika said. I don't know why I didn't catch on sooner. Don't think about the knife. Think about the shape behind the knife, about what the athame is, at its core. It isn't really a knife at all. It's a door, disguised as a knife.'

'You're weirding me out.'

'We just have to find the people who can tell us how to really use it,' Thomas says, not even looking at me anymore, but at Morfran. 'We have to find out how to blow it wide open.'

My backpack feels heavy, now that I'm carrying an entire gateway inside it. Thomas's excitement is enough to lift him off the floor, but I can't wrap my head around what he wants to do. He wants to open the knife. He's saying that on the other side of the athame is Anna's Hell? No. The knife is the knife. It fits in my hand. On the other side of the knife is...the other side of the knife. But this hunch is all we have to go on, and every time I question him about feasibility, he smiles at me like he's Yoda and I'm just a dumbass without the Force.

'We're going to need Gideon, that's for certain. We need to know more about where the knife comes from, and how it's been used in the past.'

'Sure,' I say. Thomas is driving a bit too fast, and paying a bit too little attention. When he brakes at the stop sign before the high school, it's sudden and jerks me forward, almost onto the dash.

'Carmel's still not picking up,' he mutters. 'I hope we don't have to go in and find her.'

It's doubtful. As we crest the hill it looks like most of

the school is hanging out around the quad and parking lot. Of course they would be. It's the last day of the year. I hadn't even noticed.

It doesn't take long for Thomas to zero in on Carmel; her blond hair shines a few shades brighter than everyone else's. She's in the middle of a crowd, laughing, with her backpack on the ground, resting against her lower leg. When she hears the Tempo's distinctive sputter, her eyes flash our way and her face tenses. Then the smile is back like it never left.

'Maybe we should wait and call her later,' I say, without knowing why. Despite her queen bee status, Carmel is our friend first. Or at least she used to be.

'What for?' Thomas asks. 'She's going to want to know this.' I don't say anything while he pulls into the first open space and puts the Tempo into park. Maybe he's right. After all, she's always wanted to know before.

When we get out, Carmel's back is to us. She's in a circle of people, but somehow manages to still be perceived as the center of it. Everyone's body is slightly turned toward hers, even when she's not the one talking. Something's wrong here, and all of a sudden I want to grab Thomas by the shoulder and wrench him around. *We don't belong*, is what my blood is screaming, but I don't know why. The people surrounding Carmel are people I've seen before. People I've talked to in passing and they've always been friendly enough. Natalie and Katie are both there. So are Sarah Sullivan and Heidi Trico. The guys in the group are the leftovers of The Trojan Army: Jordan Driscoll, Nate Bergstrom, and Derek Pimms. They know we're coming, but none of them acknowledges us. And there's something frozen about the smiles on their faces. They look triumphant. Like cats who've swallowed a flock of canaries.

'Carmel,' Thomas calls, and jogs the last few steps to her.

'Hey, Thomas,' she says, and smiles. She doesn't say anything to me, and none of the others pay much attention to me either. They all have predatory expressions locked on Thomas, who doesn't notice a thing.

'Hey,' he says, and when she doesn't say anything in return, but just stands there looking at him expectantly, he starts to trip up. 'Um, you weren't answering your phone.'

'Yeah, I've just been hanging out,' she replies with a shrug.

'I thought you had mono or something,' Derek interrupts with a smirk. 'But I don't know how you'd have gotten it.'

Thomas shrinks a few inches. I want to say something, but it's Carmel who should do the talking. These are her friends, and on any normal day they would know better than to say anything off-sides to Thomas. On any normal day, Carmel would rip them a new one just for looking at him funny.

'So, uh, can we talk to you a minute?' Thomas has his hands shoved into his pockets; he couldn't look more awkward if he started kicking the dirt. And Carmel just stands there, disaffected.

'Sure,' she says with another half smile. 'I'll give you a call, later on.'

Thomas doesn't know what to do. It's on the tip of his tongue to ask what's the matter, what's going on, and it's all I can do to keep my own mouth shut, to keep from telling him to be quiet, not to give them anything else. They don't deserve the satisfaction of seeing this look on his face.

'Or maybe tomorrow,' Derek says, stepping closer to Carmel. His eyes are on her in a way that makes my stomach turn. 'Tonight we're going out, right?' He touches her, snakes an arm around her waist, and Thomas goes pale.

'Maybe I'll call you tomorrow,' Carmel says. She doesn't move out of Derek's grip and her face barely twitches while Thomas's crumples.

'Come on,' I say finally, and grab his shoulder. The minute I touch him he turns and heads back for the car, half running, humiliated and broken in ways I don't want to think about.

'This was a real pile of shit, Carmel,' I say, and she crosses her arms over her chest. For an instant, it looks like she might cry. But in the end she doesn't do anything but look down at the ground.

There's pure silence on the drive from the school to my house. I can't think of a single thing to say and I feel useless. My lack of experience at friendship is showing. Thomas looks brittle as a brown leaf. Someone else would know something, some anecdote or story. Someone else would know what to do besides sit in the passenger seat and be uncomfortable.

I don't know whether Thomas and Carmel were actually dating. She might get out of the cheating title on a technicality. But that's all it is. A technicality. Because she and I and everyone else know that Thomas is in love with her. And for the past six months, she's done a pretty good job of acting like she was in love with him too.

'I, uh, just need to be alone for awhile, OK, Cas?' He talks without looking at me. 'I'm not going to drive my car off the falls or anything,' he says, and tries to smile. 'I just need to be alone.'

'Thomas,' I say. When I put my hand on his shoulder,

he lifts his arm and gently knocks it away. I get it. 'OK, man,' I say, and open my door. 'Just give a shout if you need anything.' I step out.

There should be more to say, something better that I could do. But the best I've got is to keep my eyes straight ahead and not look back.

CHAPTER THIRTEEN

The house is a sad sort of quiet. That's what I notice when I walk in. There's nothing inside of it with me, nothing living and nothing dead, and somehow that doesn't make it feel safe so much as insubstantial. The sounds it makes, the whisper and click of the front door closing and the creaks of the floorboards are hollow and ordinary. Or maybe it just seems that way because I feel like I'm suspended mid train-wreck. Things are being crushed around me and there doesn't seem to be any action to take. Thomas and Carmel are collapsing. Anna is being torn to shreds. And I can't do a damn thing about any of it.

I haven't said more than five words to my mom since we had our last argument about me tracking Anna into Hell, so when I pass by the kitchen window and see her in the backyard, seated cross-legged in front of the bedraggled choke cherry, tree I almost jump. She's in a breezy summer dress, and there are a few white candles lit around her, three that I can see. Smoke from something, maybe incense, drifts up above her head and disappears. I don't recognize this spell, so I go out the back door. Mom's spell work these days is mostly commercial. Only under special circumstances does she take the time to do anything personal. So help me, if she's trying to bind me to the house, or bind me from doing harm to myself, I'm moving out.

She doesn't say anything as I approach, doesn't even turn as my shadow falls over her. A photo of Anna rests against the base of the tree. It's the one from the newspaper that I tore out this fall. I always have it with me.

'Where did you get that?' I ask.

'I took it from your wallet this morning, before you left with Thomas,' she replies. Her voice is sad and serene, still tinged with the spell she was just performing. At my sides, my hands go slack. I was ready to snatch the picture back, but all of the will just leaked out of my arms.

'What are you doing?'

'Praying,' she says simply, and I sink down beside her in the grass. The flames sitting atop the candlewicks are small and so motionless they could be solid. The smoke that I saw rising above my mom's head came from a piece of amber resin, set on a flat stone, burning a quiet blue and green.

'Will it work?' I ask. 'Will she feel it?'

'I don't know,' she answers. 'Maybe. Probably not, but I hope so. She's so far away. Past the limit.'

I don't say anything. She's close enough to me, linked to me strongly enough to find her way back.

'We've got a lead,' I say. 'The athame. We might be able to use it.'

'Use it how?' Her voice is clipped; she'd still rather not know.

'It might be able to open a door. Or it is the door. We might be able to open *it*.' I shake my head. 'Thomas explains it better. Well, actually, he doesn't.'

My mom sighs, staring down at Anna's photo. In it she was a girl of sixteen, with dark brown hair and a white blouse, wearing a smile that isn't quite there.

'I know why you have to do this,' Mom says finally. 'But I can't bring myself to want you to. Do you understand?'

I nod. It's as good as I'm going to get, and really, more than I should ask for. She takes a deep breath and blows out all the candles at once without turning her head, which makes me smile. It's an old witch's parlor trick she did all the time when I was a kid. Then she snuffs out the amber resin and reaches for Anna's photo. She hands it back to me. As I put it back into my wallet, she pulls out a thin, white envelope that

164

was tucked under her knee.

'This came for you in the mail today,' she says. 'From Gideon.'

'Gideon?' I say absently, and take the envelope. It's a little bit weird. Usually when he sends us mail it's an enormous care package of books and the chocolate-covered flapjacks my mom likes. But when I rip it open and tip the contents into my palm, all that falls out is an old, blurry photograph.

Around me I hear the clicking of wax on wax as my mom gathers up candles. She says something to me, some vague question as she moves around the tree, smearing the ash of the amber resin against the rock. I don't really hear what she says. All I can do is stare at the photo in my hand.

In it, a robed and hooded figure stands before an altar. Behind him are other figures, dressed similarly in robes of red. It's a picture of Gideon, performing a ritual, with my athame in his hand. But that's not the part that stops my brain. It's the fact that the rest of the figures in the photo appear to be holding my athame as well. There are at least five identical knives in the picture.

'What is this?' I ask, and show it to my mom.

'It's Gideon,' she replies absently, and then stops when she sees the athames.

'I know it's Gideon,' I say. 'But who are they? And what the hell are *those*?' I point to the knives. Dummy knives is what I want to believe they are. Knockoffs. But why? And what if they're not? Are there others, out there, doing what I do? How have I not known? Those are my first thoughts. My second is that I'm looking at the people who created the athame. But that can't be right. According to my dad, and Gideon too, the athame might literally be older than dirt.

My mom is still staring at the picture.

'Can you explain that?' I ask, even though it's plain that she can't. 'Why would he send me this? With no explanation?'

She bends and picks up the torn envelope. 'I don't think he did,' she says. 'It's his address, but not his handwriting.'

'When is the last time you heard from him?' I ask, wondering again if something's happened.

'Just yesterday. He's fine. He didn't mention it.' She looks toward the house. 'I'll call and ask him about it.'

'No,' I say suddenly. 'Don't do that.' I clear my throat, wondering how to explain what I'm thinking, but when she sighs, I know that she already knows what I'm thinking. 'I think I should go there.'

There's a slight pause. 'You just want to pack up and go to London?' She blinks. It wasn't the outright no

I expected. In fact, there is more curiosity in my mother's eyes than I've seen in maybe ever. It's the picture. She feels it too. Whoever sent it, sent it as bait, and it's working on both of us.

'I'm going with you,' she says. 'I'll book the flights in the morning.'

'No, Mom.' I put my hand on her arm and pray that I can make her understand. She can't come along. Because someone, or something, wants me to go there. All of that mojo that Morfran was talking about, that thunderstorm of push and pull; I'm finally catching its scent. This photo isn't a photo at all. It's a big fat breadcrumb. And if I follow it, it'll lead me to Anna. I can feel it in my gut.

'Look,' I say. 'I'll go to Gideon. He'll explain this and keep me out of trouble. You know he will.'

She glances at the picture with doubt flickering through her features. She's not ready to let one image change everything about a man we've known most of our lives. Truthfully I'm not ready to either. Gideon will explain everything when I get there.

'Whoever is in that picture,' she says. 'Do you think they know about the athame? About where it came from?'

'Yes,' I say. And I think Gideon knows too. I think he's known all along.

'And you think they'll know how to open it, like Thomas said?'

'Yes,' I say. And more than that. It all feels connected. Mom is looking down at the tree, at the black smudge of ash left over from her prayer.

'I want you to do something for me, Cas,' she says in a faraway voice. 'I know you want to save her. I know you think you have to. But when the time comes, if the price is too high, I want you to remember that you're my son. Do you promise?'

I try to smile. 'What makes you think there's going to be a price?'

'There's always a price. Now do you promise?'

'I promise.'

She shakes her head, and brushes the grass and dirt off her dress, effectively brushing off the gravity of the previous moment. 'Take Thomas and Carmel with you,' she says. 'I can pitch in for their tickets.'

'Might be a problem there,' I say, and tell her what happened. For a minute, it seems like she might have a suggestion – something I should do, or how to get them back together – but then she shakes her head.

'I'm sorry, Cas,' she says, and pats my arm like I'm the one who got broken up with.

A day and a half passes without so much as a text from

Thomas. I find myself checking my phone every five minutes like a lovesick schoolgirl, wondering if I should call him, or if he's better left alone. Maybe he and Carmel have managed to talk it over. If that's the case, I don't want to interrupt it. Still, my head's going to explode if I don't tell him about the photograph soon. And about the trip to London. He might not even want to go.

Mom and I are in the kitchen, keeping ourselves busy. She's taken the day off from being witchy and has decided to experiment with a new casserole. Some six-bean chicken thing that I'm not too excited about, but she looks happily distracted and daring in her rooster-print apron, so I'll do my part and be daring enough to eat it when it comes out of the oven. So far, we've avoided talking about anything related to Anna, or the athame, or Hell or Gideon. It's actually sort of comforting, that we do have other things to talk about.

When someone knocks at the door, I come half out of my chair. But it isn't Thomas. Standing in our entry way is Carmel. She looks guilty and a little lost, but her clothes still match and her hair is still perfect. Conversely, somewhere else in Thunder Bay, Thomas is a complete wreck.

'Hey,' she says. My mom and I glance at each other. We don't play casual very well; we just stand sort of frozen, me half in and half out of my chair, and my mom half bent over the stove, with her oven mitts on.

'Can I talk to you?' Carmel asks.

'Have you talked to Thomas?'

She looks away.

'Maybe you'd better talk to him first,' I say.

The way she's standing, I can't help but give in. I've never seen Carmel Jones look out of place before. She's fidgeting, trying to decide whether to stay or go, one hand on the doorknob and the other clutching the strap of her shoulder bag so hard it might snap. My mom nods her head toward the door, up toward my room, and gives me the eyes. I sigh.

'You're welcome to stay for lunch, Carmel,' Mom says.

Carmel smiles shakily. 'Thanks, Mrs Lowood. What are you having?'

'I don't know. I made it up.'

'We'll be down in a few minutes, Mom,' I say, and brush past Carmel on my way to the stairs. Questions flash through my mind while we head for my room. What is she doing here? What does she want? Why isn't she fixing things with Thomas?

'So how was your big date with Derek?' I ask as I close the door.

She shrugs. 'It was OK.'

'Not worth breaking Thomas's heart, then?' I spit.

170

I don't know why I feel so betrayed. Part of me thought the date with Derek was just a cover and she'd never actually go. It pisses me off, and I want her to say what she came here to say, to ask me if we'll still be friends, so I can tell her no, and to get the hell out of my house.

'Derek's not that bad,' she says, unbelievably. 'But he's not the reason. For any of it.'

Halfway to slinging my next insult, my mouth closes. She's looking at me evenly, and the apology on her face isn't just for Thomas. Carmel didn't come here to explain. She didn't come to ask if we were still going to be friends. She came here to tell me that we weren't.

'My mom was right,' I mutter. I am getting broken up with.

'What?'

'Nothing. What's going on, Carmel?'

Her hip shifts. She had something planned, some big speech, but now that she's here it's failing her. The phrases 'I never' and 'It's just' fall out of her mouth, and I lean on my dresser. There are going to be a few false starts before she gets it right. To her credit, she doesn't pout, or try to lead me with questions so I'll make it easier. Carmel is always tougher than I think she's going to be, which is why what's happening doesn't make sense. Finally, she looks me straight in the eyes.

'There's no way to say this that isn't going to sound

selfish,' she says. 'It is selfish. And I'm OK with it.'

'OK,' I say.

'I'm still glad to know you, and Thomas. And aside from all the murders' – she scrunches her face – 'I don't regret anything that's happened.'

I stay quiet, waiting for the *but*. It's coming.

'But, I guess the bottom line is that I don't want to do it anymore. I have this whole life of plans and goals and things that don't mesh well with death and the dead. I thought I could do both. That I could have both. But I can't. So I'm choosing the other way.' Her chin is raised, ready for a fight, waiting for me to attack her. The funny thing is, I don't want to. Carmel's not tied to this like I am, or even like Thomas is. Nobody raised her to be a witch, or forged her blood with steel who knows how many hundreds of years ago. She can choose. And despite my friendship with Thomas, I can't be angry about that.

'I suppose I have really bad timing,' she says. 'With everything that's happening with Anna.'

'It's OK,' I say. 'And it isn't selfish. I mean, it is, but...it's good. What's less good is you throwing Derek in Thomas's face like that.'

She shakes her head guiltily. 'It was the only way I could think of that would make him let go.'

'It was cold, Carmel. The kid loves you. You know

172

that, right? If you talked to him, he'd—'

'Give it all up?' She smiles. 'I'd never ask him to do that.'

'Why not?'

'Because I love him too.' She bites her lip and fidgets. Her arms are crossed over her chest to the point of hugging herself. Whatever it looked like on that last day of school, the decision Carmel made didn't come easy. She's still wavering on it. I can see it swirling around in her head. She wants to ask whether she's making a mistake, whether she'll regret it, but she's scared of what I'd say.

'You'll take care of him, won't you?' she asks.

'I'll be here if he needs me. I'll watch his back.'

Carmel smiles. 'Better watch all sides. He can be downright clumsy sometimes.' Her face sort of crumples and she wipes at her cheek quickly, maybe wicking away a tear. 'I'm going to miss him, Cas. You have no idea how much I'm going to miss him.'

That's my cue to walk over and deliver the most awkward hug she's ever received. But she takes it, and leans what feels like her whole weight onto my shoulder.

'We're going to miss you too, Carmel,' I say.

CHAPTER FOURTEEN

'Thomas, you home?'

I knock a few times, but the door's open when I try it. Poking my head into the house, I don't see anything out of place. Morfran and Thomas keep things pretty clean, for a pair of bachelors. The only complaint anyone could have is that they're always killing the houseplants. I whistle for Stella, but I'm not surprised when she doesn't come. Morfran's car is gone and she's always with him at the shop. I close the door behind me and walk farther in, through the kitchen. There's muffled music coming from Thomas's closed bedroom door. I knock briefly and then twist the knob.

'Thomas?'

'Hey, Cas.'

The scene isn't what I expected. He's up, dressed, and on the move, walking from his cluttered desk to his even more cluttered bed. There are books open everywhere, and loose-leaf papers strewn around. He's got his laptop up too, sitting in the middle of about three filled ashtrays. Gross. There's a lit cigarette between his fingers and smoke follows him in a languid, lifting tail.

'I tried to call,' I say, stepping farther in.

'I shut my phone off,' he says, and puffs on the cigarette. His hands are shaking and he's not looking at me. He just keeps on turning pages. This is what Thomas looks like on a bender, chain-smoking and drowning in research. How long has it been since he's eaten? Or slept?

'You should ease up on those.' I gesture to the cigarette, and he looks at it like he forgot it was there before snuffing it out into an already full ashtray. The action seems to jar him a bit and he stops and scratches his head like someone waking up from a dream.

'I guess I have been smoking a lot,' he says, and licks his lips. When he swallows, his face is disgusted and he pushes the ashtray away. 'Yuck. Maybe now I'll finally quit.'

'Maybe.'

'So, what are you doing here?'

I give him an incredulous look. 'Checking up on you,' I say. 'It's been four days. I thought at the very least I'd come over here and find you with your hair dyed black, listening to Staind.'

He smiles. 'Well, it was touch and go there for a few days.'

'Do you want to talk about it?'

His *no* is so abrupt that I almost take a step backward. But then he shrugs and shakes his head.

'Sorry. I was going to call you today. Honest. I've just been up to my eyeballs in paper, trying to come up with something useful. Not having much luck.'

I almost say something about how he didn't need to do that at a time like this, but the twitchy way he scratches his head is practically pleading with me not to. Distraction is good, that gesture says. Distraction is necessary. So I pull the photograph of a young, robed Gideon out of my pocket.

'I guess I had a little,' I say. Thomas takes it and studies it. 'It's Gideon,' I add, because he probably couldn't tell. He's only seen one or two pictures of Gideon when he's really old.

'The knives,' Thomas says. 'They all look exactly like yours.'

'For all I know, one of them is mine. I think what we're looking at are the people who created the athame. That's what my gut tells me.'

'You *think*? Where did you get this?'

'Someone sent it to me under Gideon's address.'

Thomas scans the photo again. When he does, he

notices something that makes his eyebrow arch up two inches.

'What is it?' I ask as he starts sifting through his bedroom, shuffling piles of papers and stacks of books.

'I don't know if it's anything,' he replies. 'Just that I feel like I saw this somewhere.' He flips through a stack of photocopies, black ink smudging his fingers. 'Here!' He pulls out a paper-clipped bundle and folds back pages until his eyes light up.

'Look at the robes,' he says, showing me. 'The Celtic knot design on the ends of the rope belt, and again at the collar. The same as the photograph.'

What I'm looking at is a photocopy of a photocopy, but he's right. The robes are the same. And I can't believe that just anyone can buy them at a renaissance fair. They're custom. Worn by only a specific and select group of people that apparently call themselves the Order of the Biodag Dubh.

'Where did you get this?' I ask.

'One of my grandpa's old friends has an amazing occult library. He's been copying everything he's got and faxing it to me. This one's collected from an old issue of the *Fortean Times*.' He takes the pages back and starts to read, pronouncing the Gaelic phonetically, which is more than likely extremely wrong. 'The Order of the Biodag Dubh. The Order of the Black Dagger. Supposedly they were a group that controlled something they called 'the concealed weapon." He pauses and eyeballs my backpack, where the athame sits. 'It's unknown exactly what the weapon was, but it is believed that the Order forged it themselves around the time of their creation, estimated to be between the third and first century BC. The exact power of the weapon is also unknown; however, several documents allude to the use of a black dagger in the slaying of Loch monsters, similar to the modern-day Nessie.' He makes a face and rolls his eyes. 'It is unknown whether the black dagger and the concealed weapon refer to the same artifact.' He flips through the remaining pages, looking for more of the article, but comes up empty.

'That's the vaguest thing I've ever heard.'

'It's pretty bad. They're usually much better. Must've been a fly-by-night contributor.' He tosses the fax down on the bed. 'But you have to admit, if you take out the part about the Loch Ness monster, there's a shadow of something there. The references to an unknown weapon, a concealed dagger maybe, and the two matching photographs – I mean, come on. These are dots that need connecting.'

The Order of the Biodag Dubh. Is that right? Are they the ones who created the athame? And why do these things always have to call themselves the Order of Something?

'How much do you know, anyway, about Gideon Palmer?' Thomas asks.

'He's a friend of my father's. He's like a grandfather to me,' I say, and shrug. I don't like the tone in Thomas's voice. It's too suspicious, and after seeing the photo, I'm suspicious enough for everyone. 'Look, let's not jump to conclusions. This picture could be from anything. Gideon's been involved in the occult since he was a kid.'

'But that is your athame, isn't it?' Thomas asks, checking the photo again to make sure he wasn't mistaken.

'I don't know. It's hard to tell,' I say, even though it isn't.

'You don't really think that,' he says, breaking into my head. 'You're trying to talk yourself out of it.'

Maybe I am. Maybe Gideon's involvement in all this is the one thing I'd rather not know. 'Look,' I say. 'It doesn't matter. We can ask him in person.' Thomas looks up. 'My mom's springing for two tickets to London. Want to go?'

'Face down an ancient secret druidic order that obviously wants you to know they exist?' Thomas scoffs. His eyes drift to his pack of cigarettes, but after a second he just runs his hand across his face, roughly. When his eyes are visible again, they look tired, like the distraction mask is wearing off and he doesn't care much one way or the other. 'Why not?' he says. 'I'm sure we can take 'em.'

'I don't know why you don't want me to tell him you're coming,' my mom says as she tucks another pair of socks into my suitcase. The thing is stuffed to the gills already but she keeps adding more. It took me ten minutes to convince her to take out the rosemary herb packs because the reek would set off the security dogs.

'I want it to be a surprise.' It's the truth. I want to get the drop on him, because ever since I saw that photo I feel like he's had one on me. I trust Gideon with my life. I always have, and so did my dad. He'd never do anything to harm me, or put me in harm's way. I know that. Or am I just being stupid?

'A surprise,' my mom says in that way moms have of repeating things just to have the last word. She's worried. She's got that crease between her brows, and the meals these past few days have been stupendous. She's feeding me all of my favorites, like it's my last chance to eat them. Her hands wring the life out of my socks, and she sighs before closing my suitcase and zipping it up.

Our flight leaves in four hours. We've got a connection in Toronto, and should touch down at Heathrow at 10

PM, London time. Thomas has been texting for the last hour and a half, asking what he should pack, like I should know. I haven't been to London, or to see Gideon, since I was four. The entire experience is a fuzzy, patchy memory.

'Oh,' Mom says suddenly. 'Almost forgot.' She unzips the suitcase again and looks at me, her hand out expectantly.

'What?'

She smiles. 'Theseus Cassio, you can't fly with that in your pocket.'

'Right,' I say, and reach for the athame. It seems like a dumb mistake, one that my mind was making on purpose. The thought of putting my knife into checked baggage, risking the loss of it, makes me more than a little queasy. 'You sure you can't just put some mojo on it?' I ask, only half joking. 'Make it invisible to metal detectors?'

'No such luck,' she replies. I hand it over and watch with gritted teeth as she tucks it in deep, right in the center, and covers it with clothes.

'Gideon will keep you safe,' she whispers, and then again, 'Gideon will keep you safe,' like a chant. Second thoughts hover around her like slow insects, but her arms are still and tight by her side. It occurs to me that I've bound her to this act as surely as if I'd tied her with

181

rope, through my stubbornness, my refusal to let go of Anna.

'Mom,' I say, and stop.

'What is it, Cas?'

I am coming back, is what I was going to say. But this isn't a game, and that isn't a promise I should make.

Chapter Fifteen

Thomas does OK on the flight to Toronto, but spends the first hour and a half of the London flight clutching the business end of a barf bag. He doesn't actually throw up, but he's definitely green. A couple of ginger ales later, though, he's settled in, comfortable enough to try reading the Joe Hill hardback he's brought with him.

'The words won't hold still,' he mutters after a minute, and closes the book. He looks out the window (I let him have the window seat) at bleak darkness.

'We should try to get some sleep anyway,' I say, 'so we won't be dogging it when we land.'

'But it'll be ten PM there. Shouldn't we try to stay up so we can fall asleep?'

'No. Who knows how long it'll be before we have a chance. Rest up while you can.'

'That's the problem,' he grumbles, and punches the inadequate in-flight pillow. Poor kid. He has to have a million things on his mind, the least of which is a fear of flying. I haven't worked up the nerve to ask whether he's talked to Carmel, and he hasn't mentioned it. And he hasn't asked me much about what we're doing going to London, which is very un-Thomas-like. It might. be that this trip is a convenient escape. But he's fully aware of the danger. The lingering handshake he exchanged with Morfran at the airport spoke volumes.

He rolls over as far as he can in the cramped coach seat. Thomas is polite to a fault, and hasn't reclined his chair back. His neck is going to feel like a trampled pretzel when he wakes up, if he manages to sleep at all. I close my eyes and do my best to get comfortable. It's close to impossible. I can't stop thinking about the athame, buried inside my luggage in the belly of the plane, or at least it goddamn better be. I can't stop thinking about Anna, and the sound of her voice, asking me to get her out. We're traveling at over 500 miles per hour, but it's nowhere near fast enough.

By the time we touch down at Heathrow, I've officially entered zombie mode. Sleep was fleeting: a half hour here, fifteen minutes there, and all of it with a kink in my neck. Thomas didn't fare much better. Our eyes are red and scratchy and the air on the plane was so dry that we're about ready to flake off and fall into a pair of

Thomas- and Cas-colored piles of sand. Everything is surreal, the colors too bright and the floor not quite solid beneath my feet. The terminal is quiet at ten thirty at night, and that at least makes things easier. We don't have to swim through a torrent of people.

Still, our brains are slow, and after collecting our luggage (which was a nerve-wracking chore – waiting around the carousel on the balls of my feet, paranoid that the athame didn't make it onto the connecting flight from Toronto, or that someone else would grab it before I did) we find ourselves milling around, unsure of where to go next.

'I thought you'd been here before,' Thomas says crankily.

'Yeah, when I was four,' I reply, equally crankily.

'We should just take a cab. You've got his address, right?'

I look around the terminal, reading the overhead signs. I'd been planning on getting travel cards and taking the Tube. Now it just seems complicated. But I don't want to start this trip with compromise, so I haul my suitcase through the terminal, following the arrows toward the trains.

'Wasn't so hard, was it?' I ask Thomas a half hour later, as we sit, exhausted, on the bench seat of the Tube train.

He gives me an eyebrow, and I smile. After one more only mildly disconcerting line change, we get off at Highbury and Islington station and drag ourselves up to ground level.

'Anything familiar yet?' Thomas asks, peering down the street, lights illuminating the sidewalk and the shop fronts. It looks vaguely familiar, but I suspect that all of London would look vaguely familiar. I breathe in. The air is clear and cool. A second breath brings in a whiff of garbage. That seems familiar too, but probably only because it isn't any different from other large, urban cities.

'Relax, man,' I say. 'We'll get there.' I flip my suitcase onto its side and unzip it. The minute the athame is tucked into my back pocket, my blood pumps easier. It's like a second wind, but I'd better not dawdle; Thomas looks tired enough to kill me, hollow me out, and use me for a hammock. Luckily, I Google-mapped Gideon's address from this station, and his house isn't more than a mile away.

'Come on,' I say, and he groans. We walk quickly, our suitcases wobbling on the uneven pavement, passing by Indian-owned diners with neon signs and pubs with wooden doors. Four blocks down, I head right on my best guess. The roads aren't labeled well, or maybe they are and I just can't make them out in the dark. On the side streets, the lamps are dimmer, and the area we're in looks nothing like Gideon's neighborhood. Chain-link fences border us on one side, and there's a high brick wall on the other. Beer cans and garbage litter the gutter, and everything seems damp. But maybe this is the way things always were, and I was too young to remember. Or maybe this is just how things have become since then.

'OK stop,' Thomas breathes. He pulls up and leans on his suitcase.

'What?'

'You're lost.'

'I'm not lost.'

'Don't bullshit me.' He taps his index finger to his temple. 'You're going round and round, in here.'

His smug face sets me off, and I think very loudly, *this mindreading shit is annoying,* and he grins.

'Be that as it may, you're still lost.'

'I'm turned around, that's all,' I say. But he's right. We'll have to find a phone, or get directions in a pub. The last pub that we passed was inviting; the doors were propped open and yellow light streamed onto our faces. Inside, people were laughing. I glance back the way we came and see one of the shadows move on its own.

'What is it?' Thomas asks.

'Nothing,' I reply, blinking. 'Just tired eyes.' But my

feet won't carry me back in that direction. 'Let's keep going.'

'OK,' Thomas says, and glances over his shoulder.

We walk on in silence and my ears are tuned behind us, editing out the grumble of our suitcase wheels. There's nothing back there. It's the exhaustion, playing tricks with my vision, and my nerves. Only I don't believe that. The sound of my footsteps seems heavy and too loud, like something is using the noise to hide in. Thomas has quickened his pace to walk by my side rather than behind. His radar has been tripped too, but he might just be getting it from me. We couldn't be in a worse place than this deserted, dark side street, lined with alleys cut between buildings and black spaces between parked cars. I wish we hadn't stopped talking, that something would break the eerie silence that amplifies every noise. The silence is getting the better of us. There's nothing following. There's nothing back there.

Thomas is walking faster. The panic pulse is setting in, and given the option of fight or flight I know which way he's leaning. But fly to where? We have no idea where we're going. How far would we get? And how much of this is the product of a lack of sleep and an overactive imagination?

Ten feet ahead, the sidewalk disappears into a long

shadow. We'll be in the dark for at least twenty yards. I stop and glance behind me, scanning the spaces beneath parked cars and watching for movement. There isn't any.

'You're not wrong,' Thomas whispers. 'Something's back there. I think it's been following us since we left the station.'

'Maybe it's just a pickpocket,' I mutter. My whole body tenses like a coil at the sound of movement ahead of us, in the shadow. Thomas pushes into me, hearing it too. It got ahead of us somehow. Or maybe there's more than one. I pull the athame out of my back pocket, out of its sheath, and let the streetlight shine on the blade. It's sort of silly, but maybe it'll scare them off. Exhausted as I am, I don't have the energy to deal with more than one alley cat, let alone anything else.

'What do we do?' Thomas asks. Why's he asking me? All I know is we can't stay under the streetlight until sunrise. No choice but to go ahead, into the shadow.

When I'm shoved onto one knee I think it's Thomas at first, until he shouts, 'Watch out!' about three seconds too late. My knuckles skid against the concrete and I push myself back up. Tired eyes blink in the dark as I slide the athame back into my pocket. Whatever it was that hit me wasn't dead, and the knife can't be used on the living. A round object flies my way; I duck and it clatters off the building behind me.

'What is it?' Thomas asks, and then he's knocked back, or I think he is. The street is so dark and the quarters are close. Thomas is thrown out into the lamplight, where he bounces off a parked car by the curb and reels back to hit the bricks of the wall like he's in a pinball machine. A figure spins into my adjusting vision and plants a foot solidly against my chest. My ass hits the pavement. He strikes again and I get my arm up to defend, but all I manage is a rough shove. It's disorienting, the way he's moving; in fast and slow spurts. It throws off my equilibrium.

Snap out of it. It's exhaustion; it's not a drug. *Focus and recover.* When he strikes again, I duck and block, and land a shot to his head that sends him spinning.

'Get out of here,' I shout, and barely avoid a clumsy attempt at a leg sweep. For a second I think he'll just bug out and run. Instead he stands straight and grows a foot taller. Words hit my ears, spoken in what I think is Gaelic, and the air around me presses in tight.

It's a curse. To do what, I don't know, but pressure builds in my ears ten times worse than on the plane.

'Thomas, what is he doing?' I shout. It's a mistake. I shouldn't have let the air go. My lungs are too tight to take any more in. The chant takes over everything. My eyes are burning. I can't breathe. I can't exhale, or inhale. Everything's frozen. The sidewalk is pressing against my knees. I've fallen.

My mind screams out for Thomas, for help, but I can already hear him, whispering a chant to counteract the other. The attacker's is all lyric and glottal stop; Thomas's is deep and full of melody. Thomas grows gradually louder, his voice pushing over the top of the other voice until the other voice falters and gasps. My lungs let loose. The sudden rush of air to my throat and blood to my brain makes me shake.

Thomas doesn't quit, even though the figure that attacked us is doubled over. An arm waves a feeble defense, and the sound of air being dragged into his lungs is sharp and thin.

'Stop!'

I put my hand out and Thomas pauses his chant. It wasn't me who spoke.

'Stop, stop!' The figure cries, and waves for us to get away. 'You win, right? You win.'

'Win what?' I bark. 'What were you trying to do?'

The figure backs away slowly, down the sidewalk. In between the gasps for breath is what sounds like shreds of laughter. The figure backs into the streetlight, clutching hischest, and pulls down the hood of his sweatshirt.

'It's a girl,' Thomas blurts, and I sort of elbow him. But he's right. It's a girl, standing in front of us in a plaid cap and looking innocent enough. She's even smiling.

'This is the wrong street,' she says. Her accent sounds like Gideon's, but looser and less precise. 'If you're looking for Gideon Palmer, you'd better follow me.'

CHAPTER SIXTEEN

The girl turns on her heel and promptly walks off. Just walks off, like two minutes ago she hadn't ambushed us on the street and tried to kill me. She expects us to follow, figures that we have to, if we want to make it to Gideon's before our legs give out underneath us. And we do follow, with reservation. This behavior, plus the attack, probably qualifies her as ballsy, or cheeky at the very least. Isn't that what Gideon would say?

'You were only off by two streets,' she says. 'But around here, two streets can make quite a bit of difference.' Her hand points right and we turn together. 'These are real proper houses this way.'

I stare into her back. Beneath the plaid cap, blond hair trails down in a tight braid. There's a confidence in her strides and in the way she's not paying any attention to us, right behind her. Back on the sidewalk, beneath the streetlamp, she hadn't apologized. She hadn't been embarrassed in the slightest. Not about attacking us, not even about losing.

'Who are you?' I ask.

'Gideon sent me to collect you from the station.' Not exactly an answer. Half of one. Something I might say.

'My mom told him we were coming.'

She shrugs. 'Maybe. Maybe not. Wouldn't have mattered. Gideon would've known. He has a way of knowing just about everything. Don't you think so?'

'Why did you attack us?' Thomas asks. The question comes through clenched teeth. He keeps shooting me these dagger eyes. He doesn't think we should trust her. I *don't* trust her. I'm just following her because we're lost.

She laughs; the sound is lilting and girlish but not high. 'I wasn't going to. But then you brandished that knife, all Crocodile Dundee. I couldn't resist a little tangle.' She half turns, flashes an imp's grin. 'I wanted to see what the ghost killer was made of.'

Ridiculously, part of me wants to explain, to say I had jet lag and was running on an hour's sleep. But I shouldn't care about impressing her. I don't. It's just her cocky smile that makes me think so.

The street we're on now is more familiar than the others. We're passing by houses with brick fences and low, iron gates, well-pruned shrub borders and nice cars parked in the driveway. White and yellow light sneaks

194

out from between drawn curtains, and around the foundations are flower beds, the petals not yet pulled closed for the night.

'Here we are,' she says, stopping so abruptly that I almost run up against her back. The curve of her cheek tells me she did it on purpose. This girl is quickly wearing on my last nerve. But when she smiles at me, I have to force the corners of my mouth down. She unlatches the gate and holds it open with an exaggerated gesture of welcome. I pause for a second, just long enough to register that Gideon's house has barely changed, or maybe it hasn't changed at all. Then the girl jogs around to the front to get the door. She opens it and goes through without knocking.

We squeeze into Gideon's entryway, making enough noise to make water buffalo blush, our suitcases knocking into the walls and our shoes squeaking against the wood floor. Ahead of us, through a narrow passage, is the kitchen. I catch a glimpse of a kettle on the stove, spewing steam. He's been waiting. His voice reaches me before I see his face.

'Finally found them, my dear? I was about to call down to Heathrow to inquire about the flight.'

'They got a bit turned around,' the girl replies. 'But they're in one piece.'

No thanks to you, I think, but Gideon comes around

the corner and the sight of him, in the flesh for the first time in something like ten years, stops me cold.

'Theseus Cassio Lowood.'

'Gideon.'

'You shouldn't have come.'

I swallow. His advancing years haven't taken any of the gravity out of his voice, or any of the steel out of his spine.

'How did you know that I was?' I ask.

'The same way I know everything,' he replies. 'I have spies everywhere. Didn't you see the eyes moving in the paintings around your house?'

I don't know whether or not to smile. It was a joke but it didn't sound like one. I haven't been here in more than ten years, and it feels like I'm going to be kicked out.

'Uh, I'm Thomas Sabin,' Thomas says. Good thinking. Gideon can only stand in the kitchen for a few seconds before his English manners overtake him. He walks over to shake hands.

'That's a dangerous one, there,' the girl says from the kitchen, where she stands with her hands crossed over her chest. Now that the light is better I can see that she's about our age or slightly younger. Her eyes are quick and dark green. 'Thought he was going to explode my heart. I thought you said he didn't hold with black mages.'

'I'm no black mage, or whatever,' Thomas says. He blushes, but at least he doesn't shuffle his feet.

Gideon finally looks at me again, and I can't keep my eyes from flicking to the ground. After what feels like hours and a tired sigh, he pulls me into a hug. The years haven't taken any strength out of his grip, either. But it's weird, being tall enough so that my head is over his shoulder rather than pressed into his stomach. It's sad, but I don't quite know why. Maybe because so much time has passed.

When he lets go, there's fondness in his eyes that the hard set of his jaw can't quite mask. But it tries.

'You look just the same,' he says. 'Only stretched a bit. You'll have to forgive Jessy.' He half turns and gestures for the girl to come over. 'She has a tendency to run in fists first.' When Gideon holds his arm out, she moves lightly into the embrace. 'Since I imagine she was far too rude to do so herself, I'll introduce her. Theseus, this is Jestine Rearden. My niece.'

The only thing I can think to say is, 'I didn't even know you had a niece.'

'We haven't been close.' Jestine shrugs. 'Until recently.' Gideon smiles at her, but the smile is like an ice pick. It's real but it's not real, and the thought crosses my mind that this Jestine person isn't Gideon's niece at all, but his girlfriend or something. But that's not right.

That actually makes me want to throw up a little.

'Give us a minute, won't you, my dear? I'm sure Thomas and Theseus are in need of some rest.'

Jestine nods and smiles without showing her teeth. Her eyes linger on me, amused and appraising. What is she looking at? Everybody looks this crappy after an international flight. When she leaves without saying good-bye, Thomas says, 'Good night,' very loudly in her wake, and rolls his eyes. Whoever she is, she's successfully made it on his shit list.

After taking a few minutes to call my mom and Morfran to reassure them we made it safely, Gideon leads us upstairs, toward the guest room where I stayed when I was a kid and Mom and Dad and I spent the summer with him.

'That's it?' I ask. 'Aren't you going to ask me why I'm here?'

'I know why you're here,' Gideon says darkly. 'You can sleep in the guest room. And in the morning, you're going home.'

'Some goddamn welcome wagon,' Thomas grumbles after we've hauled our suitcases to the second floor guestroom, and I stifle a grin. When he's upset, he sounds just like Morfran. 'I didn't even know he had a niece.'

'I didn't know either,' I reply.

'Well, she's a real ball of sunshine.' He's placed his suitcase at the foot of the better bed. The guestroom, oddly enough, seems like it was outfitted just for us, with two twin beds rather than one double like one might expect in a guestroom. But then, Gideon did know we were coming. Thomas pulls the quilt back and sits down, prying his shoes off with the opposing set of toes.

'What was that, anyway, that she was doing to me?' I ask.

'Some kind of curse. I don't know. You don't see it very often.'

'Would it have killed me?'

He wants to say yes, but he's honest even when he's cranky. 'Not as long as she stopped after you blacked out,' he says finally. 'But who knows if she would have stopped.'

She would have stopped. Something in the way she jumped us, the way she threw her punches; it was all just practice, just a test. It was there in the tone of her voice and the way she gave up. It amused her to have lost.

'We'll get our answers in the morning,' I say, pulling back my quilt.

'I just don't like it. And I don't feel safe in this house.

I'm not going to be able to get any sleep. Maybe we should sleep in shifts.'

'Thomas, nobody's going to hurt us here,' I say, pulling off my own shoes and getting into bed. 'Besides, I'm sure you could stop her if she tried. Where did you learn that spell, anyway?'

He shrugs into his pillow. 'Morfran's taught me my share of the black.' His mouth sets in a firm line. 'But I don't like to use it. It makes me feel pissed off and slimy.' He looks at me accusingly. 'But *she* didn't seem to have a problem with it.'

'Let's talk about it in the morning, Thomas,' I say. He grumbles a bit more, but regardless of what he said about not feeling safe, he starts to snore thirty seconds after the lights go out. Quietly, I slide the athame under my pillow and try to do the same thing.

Jestine is in the kitchen the next morning when I go downstairs. Her back is to me as she washes dishes and she doesn't turn, but she senses I'm here. She doesn't have her cap on today, and about two feet of dark gold hair falls down her back. Streaks of red cut through it like ribbons.

'Can I make you something for breakfast?' she asks.

'No, thanks,' I say. There are croissants in a basket on the table. I take one and tear off a corner.

'Would you like some butter?' she asks, and turns around. There's a large, dark bruise shadowing her jaw. I did that. I remember doing it, doubling her over. When it happened I didn't know who she was. Now the bruise is staring at me like an accusation. But what do I have to feel bad about? She attacked me, and she got what she got.

She walks to the cupboard and gets a saucer and butter knife, then sets a pot of butter on the table before ducking into the refrigerator for jam.

'Sorry about your face,' I say, and motion vaguely toward the bruise.

She smiles. 'No you're not. Not any more than I'm sorry about pulling the air out of your lungs. I had to test you. And frankly, I wasn't that impressed.'

'I was jet-lagged.'

'Excuses, excuses.' She leans on the counter and slides a finger through the loop of her jeans. 'I've been hearing stories about you since I was old enough to listen. Theseus Cassio, the great ghost hunter. Theseus Cassio, the wielder of the weapon. And the moment I meet you, I kick your ass in an alley.' She smiles. 'But I suppose if I was dead it'd be another story.'

'Who told you the stories?' I ask.

'The Order of the Biodag Dubh,' she says, her eyes flashing green. 'Of course, of all the current members, Gideon has the best stories.'

She tears off a piece of croissant and pushes it into her cheek like a squirrel. The Order of the Biodag Dubh. Until a few days ago I'd never heard of it. Now here it is again, and pronounced correctly. It's a struggle to keep my voice from rattling.

'The order of the what?' I say, reaching for the butter. 'The Beedak Dube?'

She smirks. 'Are you making fun of my accent?'

'A little.'

'Oh. Or are you just playing dumb?'

'A little of that too.' Giving away too much would be a mistake. Especially since what I'd be giving away is that I know approximately jack squat.

Jestine turns back to the sink and plunges her hands into the water, finishing off the last of the plates. 'Gideon's gone out for some things for lunch. He wanted to be back before you woke.' She drains the sink and dries her hands on a towel. 'Listen, I'm sorry if I gave your friend a scare. To be honest, I didn't think I'd be able to get one over on you.' She shrugs. 'It's like Gideon says. I'm always running in with my fists first.'

I nod, but Thomas is going to need more of an apology than that.

'Who taught you magic?' I ask. 'Was it the Order?'

'Yes. And my parents.'

'Who taught you to fight?'

She lifts her chin. 'Didn't need much teaching. Some people just have a knack for it, isn't that right?'

There's a knot in my gut about this girl, pulling in different directions. One side tells me that she's Gideon's niece, and that I can trust her for that reason alone. The other side takes one look at her and tells me that niece or not, Gideon couldn't control her. No one could. She's got agenda written over every inch of her body.

Thomas is moving around on the second floor. His footsteps creak and we hear the rush of water as the shower turns on. It feels strange, being here. Almost like an out-of-body experience, or a waking dream. Most of the things are just how I remember them, right down to the organization of the furniture. But others are glaringly different. The presence of Jestine, for instance. She moves through the kitchen, cleaning up, wiping things down with a cloth. She looks at home; she looks like Gideon's family. I don't know why, but that essence of belonging makes me miss my father in a way that I haven't missed him in years.

The door opens, and seconds later Gideon tramps through the kitchen. Jestine takes his grocery bag and starts to unload it.

'Theseus,' Gideon says, turning. 'How did you sleep?'

'Great,' I reply, which is a polite lie. Despite the jet lag and overall exhaustion, there was too much unease in the air. I lay awake until time didn't exist, listening to Thomas's gentle snore. When sleep did come, it was light and laced with menace.

Gideon studies me. He still looks so young. I mean, he looks old, but he doesn't look much older than he did ten years ago, so that's young in my book. He's got the sleeves of his gray shirt rolled up to the elbow above his khaki trousers. It's a rakish sort of look, a retirement-age Indiana Jones. Makes me wish I wasn't about to accuse him of being a lying, backstabbing member of a secret society.

'I suppose we should talk,' he says, and motions out of the kitchen.

When we reach the study, he pulls the doors shut behind us, and I take a deep breath. They say that smell is the strongest memory. I believe it. Your brain never forgets a distinctive smell, and the odor of the ancient, leather-bound pages that populate this room is definitely distinctive. I glance through the shelves, built into the wall and stuffed full with not only occult books, but also copies of the classics: there's *Alice's Adventures in Wonderland*, *A Tale of Two Cities*, and *Anna Karenina* standing out amid the stacks. The old rolling ladder is still there too, resting dormant in the corner, just waiting for someone to ride it. Or use it, I suppose.

I turn around with a big grin on my face, feeling all of about four, but the feeling fades quickly when I see just how far Gideon's glasses have slid down his nose. This is going to be one of those conversations where things get said that won't ever go away, and I'm surprised to find that I don't want to have it yet. It would be nice to relive things here, to listen to Gideon's old stories of my father, and to let him show me around. It would be nice.

'You knew that I was coming,' I say. 'Do you know why I'm here?'

'I imagine most of the paranormal world knows why you're here. Your search has been as subtle as an elephant stampede.' He pauses and adjusts his glasses. 'But that doesn't quite answer the question. I suppose you could say I know what you're after. But not exactly why you're here.'

'I'm here for your help.'

He flashes a smile. 'Just what kind of help do you think I could give you?'

'The kind of help that lets Thomas and me open a door to the other side.'

Gideon's eyes flicker back toward the hall. 'I told you before, Theseus,' he says carefully. 'That it isn't possible. That you need to let the girl go.'

'I can't let her go. That cut that Anna took after the first ritual at her house. It's tied her to the athame somehow. She's breaking through. Just tell me how to get her out, and everything goes back to normal.' Or at least as normal as it ever was.

'Are you even listening to what I'm saying?' he snaps. 'What makes you think I even know how to do such a thing?'

'I don't think that you do,' I say. I reach into my back pocket and pull out the photograph of him and the rest of the Order. Even looking at it in my hand, it doesn't seem real. That he could have been involved with something like this the whole time, and never spoken of it. 'I think that they do.'

Gideon looks at the photo. He doesn't try to take it. He doesn't try to do anything. I expected something different. Outrage, or at least backpedaling. Instead he takes a deep breath and slips his glasses off to rub the bridge of his nose between his thumb and forefinger.

'Who are they?' I ask when I'm sick of his silence.

'They,' he says ruefully, 'are members of the Order of the Biodag Dubh.'

'The creators of the athame,' I say.

Gideon puts his glasses back on and walks wearily to sit behind his desk. 'Yes,' he says. 'The creators of the athame.'

It's what I thought. But I still can't believe it. 'Why didn't you tell me?' I ask. 'All these years?'

'Your father forbade it. He broke with the Order before you were born. When he grew a conscience. When he started to decide which ghosts would be killed and which to spare.' Fire briefly blooms in Gideon's voice. Then it's gone again, and he just looks beaten. 'The Order of the Biodag Dubh believe that the athame is pure of purpose. It is not an instrument to be wielded according to someone else's will. In their eyes, you and your father have corrupted it.'

My father corrupted it? That's ridiculous. The athame and its purpose have driven me my whole life. It cost my father his. The damned thing can serve my purposes for once. I'm owed. We're owed.

'I can see into your head, Theseus. Not as well as your psychic friend upstairs perhaps, but I can see. My words aren't swaying you. None of it is getting through. The Order created the athame to send the dead. Now you want to use it to pull a dead girl back. Even if there was a way, they'd rather destroy the knife than see it happen.'

'I have to do this. I can't let her suffer there, without trying.' I swallow hard and grit my teeth. 'I love her.'

'She's dead.'

'That doesn't mean to me what it does to other people.'

A blankness washes over his face that bothers me. He looks like someone facing down a firing squad.

'When you were here last, you were so small,' he says. 'The only thing regularly on your mind was whether or not your mother would allow you two servings of apple cake.' His eyes drift to the rolling ladder in the corner. He's picturing me there, laughing while he pushed it along the shelves.

'Gideon. I'm not a kid anymore. Treat me like you would have treated my father.' But that's the wrong thing to say, and he squints like I struck him across the face.

'I can't do this now,' he says, to himself as much as me. His hand waves dismissively, and the way his shoulders hunch as he lowers into his armchair, part of me wants to let him rest. But Anna's scream is forever in my ears.

'I don't have time for this,' I say, but he closes his eyes. 'She's waiting for me.'

'She's in Hell, Theseus. Time has no meaning for her, long or short. The pain and fear are constant, and any minutes or hours that you spare her, you will find, will prove irrelevant.'

'Gideon—'

'Let me rest,' he says. 'What I have to say is of little consequence. Don't you understand? I didn't send you that photograph. The Order did. They want you here.'

CHAPTER SEVENTEEN

The door slides shut softly behind me. I'm surprised, because I want to slam it, rattle it around on its track. But Gideon is still in the study, thinking quietly, or maybe even napping, and his voice in my head says that throwing such a fit just won't do.

'How'd that go?' Thomas asks, poking his head out of the kitchen.

'He's napping,' I reply. 'So what does that tell you?'

Walking into the kitchen, I find Thomas and Jestine seated together at the table, sharing a pomegranate.

'He's old, Cas,' she says. 'He was old the last time you were here. Napping is nothing out of the ordinary.' She spoons up a load of the purple fruit and chews carefully past the seeds.

To my right, Thomas crunches through his pomegranate and spits seeds into a mug.

'We didn't cross an ocean to cool our heels and ride the Eye,' he snaps. At first I think he says it for my

210

benefit, but no. He looks irritated and surly; the shower-wetness of his hair gives him the air of an almost-drowned cat.

'Hey,' I say. 'Don't bite Jestine's head off. It's not her fault.' Thomas curls his lip, and Jestine smiles.

'What you two need is a distraction,' she says, and gets up from the table. 'Come on. By the time we get back, Gideon will be up.'

Someone should tell Jestine that distractions only work if you don't know you're being distracted. Someone should tell Thomas too, because he seems oblivious to everything but her; they're talking animatedly about astral projection or something. I'm not sure really. The conversation's taken at least six turns since we got off the Tube at London Bridge Station and I haven't bothered to keep up. Jestine has won him over with witch talk. The fact that she's an attractive girl didn't hurt either. Who knows, maybe she'll help him get over Carmel.

'Cas, come on.' She reaches back and pulls me up alongside by my shirt. 'We're nearly there.'

The 'there' that she's referring to is the Tower of London, the castle-like fortress that sits on the north bank of the Thames. It's touristy and historical, the site of numerous tortures and executions, from Lady Jane

Grey to Guy Fawkes. Looking at it as we cross the Tower Bridge, I wonder how many screams have bounced off the stone walls. I wonder how much blood the ground remembers. They used to put severed heads up on pikes and display them on the bridge until they fell into the river. I glance down at the brown water. Somewhere underneath, old bones might still be fighting their way out of the silt.

Jestine buys our tickets and we go inside. She says we don't need to wait for the tour guide; she's been here often enough that she remembers all the interesting parts. We follow her as she leads us through the grounds, telling stories about the fat, black ravens toddling across the lawn. Thomas listens, smiles, and asks a few polite questions, but the history doesn't quite hold him. About ten minutes in, I catch him gazing wistfully at Jestine's long blond hair, a hangdog look on his face. It reminds him of Carmel, but it shouldn't; Jestine's is shot through with those streaks of fierce red. She doesn't look anything like Carmel, really. Carmel's eyes are warm and brown. Jestine's look like green glass. Carmel's beauty is classic, where Jestine is mostly just striking.

'Cas, are you even listening?' She smiles and I clear my throat. I'd been staring.

'Not really.'

'You've been here before?'

'Once. That summer when I was visiting, Gideon brought me and my mom. Don't feel bad. It was pretty boring then too.' Wasting time like this, my mind turns to Anna. She suffers in my imagination and I suffer with her. I picture the worst, every pain I can conceive of, to torture myself. It's the only penance I can do, until I get her out.

Behind us, one of the Beefeater tour guides is leading a group of visitors, making wry comments that lift good-natured laughter from their throats, telling the same jokes he tells a dozen times a day. Jestine watches me quietly. After a few seconds, she leads us on, up into the White Tower.

'Wasn't there anywhere to go that has fewer stairs?' Thomas asks after touring the third floor. It's full of shields and statues of horses and knights in chain mail and armor. Kids ooh and aah and point their fingers. Their parents do it too. The whole tower vibrates with footsteps and chatter. It's warm from the June heat and too many bodies, and the buzzing of flies is audible.

'Do you hear that buzzing?' Thomas asks.

'Flies,' I reply, and he gives me a look.

'Yeah, but what flies?'

I look around. The buzzing is loud enough to be the inside of a barn, but there aren't any actual flies. And no one else seems to notice. There's a smell too, cloying and metallic. I'd know it anywhere. Old blood.

'Cas,' Thomas says in a low voice. 'Turn around.'

When I turn I'm looking at a display case of used weapons. They haven't been cleaned or polished, and are caked with drying red and bits of tissue. One half of a long spiked mace has a piece of scalp and hair hanging off of it. It was used to cave in someone's head. The buzzing of phantom flies makes Thomas swat at the air even though they aren't real. Looking around, the rest of the exhibit is the same. Case after case filled with relics of war, splashed and streaked with red. Beneath one of the knight's armor, a curl of intestine shows a rubbery pink. My hand strays to my pocket, to the athame, and I feel Jestine touch my back.

'Don't go pulling that out again,' she says.

'What's going on here?' I ask. 'It wasn't like this when we came in.'

'Is it the way they were used?' Thomas asks. 'Did this really happen?'

Jestine looks around at the gory display and shrugs. 'I don't know. It's quite possible. But maybe not. It might just be a show, impotent anger from the dozens of dead things running through this place like a current. There are so many that they don't have separate voices. They have no idea who they are, anymore. They just manifest, like this.'

'Do you remember this from when you were here, Cas?' Thomas asks. I shake my head.

'I thought you'd have been tuned to it right away,' says Jestine. 'But maybe they didn't show you. Most people can't see it of course, but the last time I was here, a little girl walked in and started to cry. No one could make her stop. She wouldn't say why she was upset, but I knew. She walked around this room with her family, crying, while they tried to get her to look at the disemboweled knight, like he would cheer her up.'

Thomas swallows. 'That's disturbing.'

'When did you first see it?' I ask.

'My parents brought me here when I was eight.'

'Did you cry?'

'Never,' she says, and lifts her chin. 'But then, I understood.' She tilts her head toward the door. 'So, do you want to go meet the queen?'

The queen is in the chapel. She sits in the first row, silent, far off to the left. Dark brown hair hangs down her back, and her posture is straight, strapped into a bodice. Even standing in the back, thirty feet away, there's no mistaking that she's dead.

The chapel is in between tours at the moment, and a young couple was just finishing taking a picture of the stained glass as we came in. Now we're alone.

'I don't know which queen she is,' Jestine says. 'Most say that she's the ghost of Anne Boleyn, the second wife of Henry VIII. But she might be Lady Jane Grey. She doesn't speak. And she doesn't resemble any of the portraits.'

This is weird. There's a dead woman in front of me like dozens of other dead women I've seen. But this one is a queen, and a famous one. If it's possible to be star-struck by the dead, then I guess that's what's happening.

Jestine moves to the back of the chapel, near the door.

'Does she respond?' I ask. It's unlikely. She isn't corporeal; if she were, she'd be visible to everyone, and the couple in here snapping photos had no idea they had company. I wonder, though, if she'll show up in a few of their developed shots and give them a good story to tell their friends and neighbors.

'Not to me,' Jestine replies in a whisper, as the queen turns, in a slow rotation, to face me. The movement is regal, or careful. Maybe both. She is balancing her severed head on her neck. Below the cut, she's nothing but blood, and there's something else. I can hear the rustle of her dress against the bench. She's not just vapor anymore.

I've never seen the portraits Jestine mentioned, so I can't speak to any resemblance. But the woman facing me looks not much more than a girl. She's tiny, thin-lipped, and pale. Only the eyes are beautiful, dark and clear. There's a delicate dignity about her, and a little bit of shock. It's how any queen would react, if she were suddenly presented with a kid with hair hanging in his eyes and wrinkly clothes.

'Should I bow or something?' I ask out of the corner of my mouth.

'You should hurry up, is what you should do,' Jestine says, peering out the door. 'The next tour group is going to be popping in here in two minutes.'

Thomas and I exchange a look. 'Hurry up and do what?' I ask.

'Send her,' Jestine whispers, and arches her brow. 'Use the athame.'

'Has she killed people?' Thomas asks. 'Has she even harmed people?'

I doubt it. I doubt if she's even scared people. I can't imagine this girl, this one-time queen, has ever implied a threat to anyone. She's somber, and oddly at peace. It's hard to explain, but I think she'd find the whole concept rude and inappropriate. The thought of stabbing her, or 'sending' her, as Jestine apparently calls it, makes me blush.

'Let's get out of here,' I mumble, and walk toward the door. In the corner of my eye, I catch Thomas sketching an awkward curtsy as he follows. I glance back one more time. The queen is no longer facing us. She resides in her church with no care for the living, balancing her head on her ragged neck.

'Am I missing something?' Jestine asks once we're back in the open air. I lead them quickly toward the exit. Gideon's got to be up by now, and I've had enough of this place.

'Hey,' she says, and takes my arm. 'Did I offend you? Do something out of order?'

'No,' I say. Deep breath in, and out. She's brash, and sort of pushy. But I'm trying to remember what she already apologized for; her habit of running in fists first, without thinking. 'It's just that...I don't 'send' ghosts unless they're a threat to the living.'

The look on her face is genuine surprise. 'But that's not your purpose.'

'What?'

'You're the instrument. The wielder of the weapon. It's the weapon's will that's important. Not yours. And the athame doesn't make distinctions.'

We're stopped before the steps near the exit gate, facing each other. She said the words with conviction. With belief. She's been indoctrinated with that law probably for as long as she can remember. The way she's looking at me, right into my eyes, it's a challenge to tell her different. Even if it won't change her mind.

'Well, I'm the wielder, as you say. It's my blood in the blade. So I guess now that it's in my hand, the athame does make distinctions.'

'Wait a minute,' says Thomas. 'Is she a member of the—'

'A member of the Order of the Blah Blah Blah. Yes, I think she is.'

Jestine lifts her chin. She hasn't done anything to cover up the bruise across her jaw. No makeup, no nothing. But she doesn't wear it like a badge either.

'Well, of course I am,' she says with a grin. 'Who do you think sent you the photograph?'

Thomas's mouth drops slightly open.

'Weren't you worried that your uncle might be pissed about that?' I ask. Jestine shrugs. I think she shrugs even more than I do.

'The Order thought it was time for you to know,' she says. 'But don't be too cross with Gideon. He hasn't been a true member for decades.'

He must've broken away with my dad.

'If he's not a member anymore, then what are we going to do?' Thomas asks.

'Oh, I wouldn't worry about that,' Jestine answers. 'We've been waiting for you.'

*

Standing in the study, Gideon stares at the three of us for a long time. When his eyes finally settle, they rest on Jestine.

'What have you told them?' he asks.

'Nothing that they didn't really know already,' she replies.

I feel Thomas give me a look but don't return it. It would only add to the sense of Hitchcockian vertigo that's been slowly creeping up my throat ever since we left the Tower of London. It's the feeling that none of this is our show. Everyone seems to know more than I do, and being on the shallow end of the information pool is starting to piss me off.

Gideon takes a deep breath. 'This is the turn-back point, Theseus,' he says, staring down at his desk. And he's right, as usual. I can feel that. I've felt it since I decided to come here. But here we are. This is the last moment, the last second, that I could turn away, and Thomas and I could return to Thunder Bay, and nothing would change. We would remain as we are, and Anna would stay where she is.

I glance at Jestine. Her eyes are downcast, but there's this odd, knowing look on her face. Like she knows full well that we passed the turn-back point a few countries ago.

'Just tell me,' I say. 'What exactly is the Order of

– the Black Dagger?' Jestine scrunches her nose at the Anglicizing, but I'm in no mood to tie my tongue up and butcher the Gaelic.

'They're the descendants of the ones who created the knife,' replies Gideon.

'Like me,' I say.

'No,' Jestine says. 'You're the descendant of the warrior they bonded with it.'

'These are the descendants of those who harnessed the power. Magicians. They used to be called Druids and Seers. Now they have no real name.'

'And you were one of them,' I say, but he shakes his head.

'Not traditionally. They brought me in after I befriended your father. My family has ties to it, of course. Most old families do; just about everything is diluted and bastardized by thousands of years of time.' He shakes his head, drifts off. He makes it sound like you can't swing a dead cat without hitting one, but it took me seventeen years.

I feel like I've been spun around blindfolded, then had my eyes uncovered and shoved into daylight. I never figured that I was an outsider to this ancient club. I thought I *was* the club. Me. My blood. My knife. The end.

'What about the athames in the picture, Gideon?

221

Are they just props? Or are there others out there like mine?'

Gideon holds out his hand. 'May I have it, Theseus? Just for a moment.'

Thomas shakes his head, but it's all right. I've always known that Gideon has secrets. He must have lots more than even this. It doesn't mean I don't trust him.

Reaching into my back pocket, my fingers slide the athame out of its sheath, and I flip it gently to place it handle out into Gideon's palm. He accepts it solemnly and turns, toward a dark oak shelf. Drawers open and close. He's working close to the vest, but I still glimpse a flash of steel. When he turns back to us, he's holding a tray, and on it are four knives, all of them identical. Exact replicas of my athame.

'The traditional athames of the Order,' Gideon says. 'A bit more valuable than a dime a dozen, as you'd say, but – no. They're not like yours. There are no others like yours.' He motions to Jestine, and curls his fingers for her to step closer. When she does, there's a look of reverence on her face that almost makes me snort snarky laughter. But at the same time I feel sort of ashamed. She looks so…respectful. I don't know if I've ever looked at the athame that way.

Gideon sets the tray on the edge of his desk and rearranges the knives once, shuffling them like a three-card monty dealer. When Jestine stands before the tray, he straightens and commands her to select the real one.

Even though my athame has never been damaged, and there are no knicks or scars to identify it from the others, I know immediately. It's the third from the left. I feel it so strongly that it may as well be waving at me. Jestine has no idea, but her green eyes glitter at the challenge. After a few deep breaths, she extends her hand over the tray and passes it slowly back and forth. My pulse quickens as she hesitates over the wrong one. I don't want her to choose correctly. It's petty, but I don't.

She closes her eyes. Gideon's holding his breath. After thirty tense seconds, her eyes fly open, and she smiles before reaching down to the tray and picking up my knife.

'Well done,' Gideon says, but he doesn't sound pleased. Jestine nods and hands the knife back to me. I slide it into its sheath, and try not to look like a kid with a broken toy while I do it.

'This is all fun,' I say, 'but what does that have to do with anything? Listen, does the Order know how to cross over to the other side, or not?'

'Of course they do,' Jestine replies. Her face is flushed from whatever parlor trick she just used to identify my knife. 'They've done it before. They'll do it again for you, if you're willing to pay the price.'

'What price?' Thomas and I ask together, but the two of them are tight-lipped, ignoring the question like it wasn't even asked.

'I'll contact them,' Gideon says, and when Jestine looks at him he says it again, more firmly. He never once looks at me, instead focusing on the dummy knives, wiping them with a soft cloth like they're important before placing them back in their drawers. 'Get some rest, Theseus,' he says, implying heavily that I'm going to need it.

Upstairs in the guest room, Thomas and I sit silently on our respective bunks. He's uneasy about all this. I don't blame him. But I haven't come this far to do nothing. She's still waiting for me. I can still hear her voice, and her screams.

'What do you think the Order is going to do?' he asks.

'Help us open a door to Hell, if we're lucky,' I reply. Lucky. Ha ha. The irony.

'She said there would be a price. Is she sure? Do you have any idea what it's going to be?'

'I don't. But there's always a price; you know that. Isn't it what you witches are always going on about? Give and take, balancing things, three chickens for a pound of butter?'

'I've never said anything about bartering farm goods,' he says, but I can hear that he's smiling. Maybe tomorrow I should send him home. Before I get him hurt, or tangled up in something that after tonight feels like only my business.

'Cas?'

'Yeah?'

'I don't think you should trust Jestine.'

'Why not?' I ask.

'Because,' he says quietly, 'when she was doing the athame line-up downstairs, she was thinking about how much she wanted it. She was thinking it was hers.'

I blink. *So what?* is my kneejerk response. It's an unattainable wish. A fantasy. The athame is mine, and it always will be.

'Thomas?'

'Yeah?'

'Could you have identified the athame off of that tray?'

'Never,' he says. 'Not in a million years.'

CHAPTER EIGHTEEN

Anna and I sit at a round wooden table, staring out at an expanse of long, green grass, untouched by the blades of a mower. The white and yellow blossoms of weeds and wildflowers wave in a breeze I can't feel, clustered together in spotty patches. We're on a porch, maybe the porch of her old Victorian.

'I love the sun,' she says, and it is definitely beautiful, a bright, sharp white that strikes the grass and turns it into silver razors. But there's no heat. No sensation in my body, no awareness of the chair or bench I must be sitting on, and if I turned my head to look any farther than her face, there would be nothing there. Behind us there is no house. There is only the impression of a house, in my mind. This is all in my mind.

'It's so rare,' she says, and I can finally see her. My perspective shifts and she's there, her face in shadow. Dark hair lies still on her shoulders, except for a few stray strands near her throat, twisting in the breeze.

I reach my hand across the table, certain that it won't stretch enough, or that the damn table will lose its spatial dimensions, but my palm runs up against her shoulder, and her hair is black and cold between my fingers. The relief when I touch her is so strong. She's safe. Unharmed. The sun is on her cheeks.

'Anna.'

'Look,' she says, and smiles. There are trees now, bordering the clearing. Between the trunks is the shape of a stag. It blinks in and out, a dark shape, and I think of charcoal being rubbed out of a drawing. Then it's gone and Anna is beside me. Too close to be across a table. The length of her is pressed against my side.

'Is this what we were supposed to have?' I ask.

'This is what we do have,' she replies.

I look down at her hand and brush away a crawling beetle. It lands on its back, legs wriggling. My arms wrap around her. I kiss her shoulder, the curve of her neck. On the floorboards, the beetle has become a flaking, empty shell. Six jointed legs lay disconnected beside it. Her skin against my cheek is cool comfort. I want to stay here forever.

'Forever,' Anna whispers. 'But what will it take?'

'What?'

'What will they take,' she repeats.

'They?' I ask, and shift her in my arms. Her flesh is hard and the joints relaxed and dangling. As she clatters to the ground I see that she was just a wooden marionette, in a dress of gray paper. The face is uncarved and blank, except for one word, burnt in deep, cracking black.

ORDER.

I wake up dangling most of the way off of the bed, with Thomas's hand on my shoulder.

'You OK, man?'

'Nightmare,' I mutter. 'Disquieting.'

'Disquieting?' Thomas grasps the edge of my blankets. 'I didn't even know it was possible to sweat this much. I'm going to get you a glass of water.'

I sit up and switch on the table lamp. 'No, I'm OK.' But I'm not, and from the look on his face, that much is clear. I feel like I might throw up, or scream, or do both simultaneously.

'Was it Anna?'

'These days it's always Anna.' Thomas doesn't say anything, and I stare down at the floor. It was just a dream. Just a nightmare like I've had my whole life. It doesn't mean anything. It can't. Anna doesn't know anything about the Order; she doesn't know anything about anything. Everything she sees and feels is pain.

Thinking of her there, locked there with the ruin of the Obeahman, makes me want to hit something until there are no more bones in my hands. She suffered decades under a curse and somehow remained herself, but this will break her. What if she doesn't know who I am, or who she is by the time I get there? What if she isn't human?

What will it take? A trade? I'd do it. I would, I—

'Hey,' Thomas says abruptly. 'That's not going to happen. But we'll get her out. I promise.' He reaches out and physically shakes me. 'Don't think that shit.' He sort of smiles. 'And don't think it so loud. It gives me a headache.'

I look at him. The left half of his hair is smooth. The right half is sticking straight up. He looks like a Sabretooth movie. But he's completely serious when he promises that we'll see it through. He's scared, practically piss-his-pants scared. But Thomas is always scared. The important thing is that his kind of fear doesn't run deep. It doesn't stop him from doing what he has to do. It doesn't mean he's not brave.

'You're the only one who was really behind me on this,' I say. 'Why is that?'

He shrugs. 'I can't speak for the rest of them. But... she's your Anna.' He shrugs again. 'You care about her, you know? She's important. Look.' He runs his hand roughly across his face and into his standing-up hair. 'If it was – if it was Carmel, I'd want to do the same thing. And I'd expect you to help me.'

'I'm sorry about Carmel,' I say, and he still sort of waves it off.

'I didn't see it coming, I guess. It seems like I should have. Like I should have realized that she didn't really…' He trails off and smiles sadly. I could tell him, that it had nothing to do with him. I could tell him that Carmel loves him. But it wouldn't make things any easier, and he might not believe me.

'Anyway, so that's why I'm helping,' he says, and straightens. 'What? Did you think it was all about you? That you just make me so emotional?'

I laugh. The traces of the nightmare are fading from my blood. But the wooden face, and the burnt letters scrawled across it, are going to hang around for a long time.

I think the only thing Jestine does in this house is make breakfast. The smell of buttery eggs pervades the entire lower level, and when I round the corner into the kitchen there's a smorgasbord of food laid out across the table: a pot of oatmeal, eggs done two ways (scrambled and over-easy), sausage and bacon, a basket of fruit, a small stack of toast, and Gideon's entire stock of jellies (which includes the vegetable jelly they call Marmite. Disgusting).

'Are you and Gideon running a secret B&B?' I ask, and she smiles lopsidedly.

'Like he would allow so many strangers through his door. No, I just like to cook, and I like to keep him fed. But don't you sit down just yet,' she says, and points a spatula at my chest. 'He's in the study getting ready to leave. You should probably wish him well.'

'Why? Is he in danger?'

Jestine's eyes don't give me any clues, and nothing about her flinches. My head says that I'm not supposed to like her. But I do anyway.

'OK,' I say after a second.

The study is quiet but when the door slides open he's there, behind his desk, softly opening a drawer and walking his fingers through the contents inside. He spares me only one glance, and it doesn't interrupt the deliberate and focused movement of his hands.

'You'll be leaving tomorrow,' Gideon says. 'I'm leaving today.'

'Leaving for where?'

'The Order, of course,' he replies tersely. But I knew that. I meant where, like, where on a map. But then again, he probably knew that too.

Gideon opens a drawer, and gathers up the dummy

231

athames from their case of red velvet. He slides each one into a leather sheath, then into a silk pouch, which is tied off and tucked into his open suitcase. I hadn't even noticed it, propped up in his chair.

A weird kind of relief is unknotting muscles that had been weaving together for weeks. For months. It's the relief of having a chance, catching a glimpse of even a tiny shred of light down the pipe.

'Jestine's made breakfast,' I say. 'You've got time to eat before you go, don't you?'

'Not especially.' His hands are shaking as he places a few folded shirts onto the top of his suitcase.

'Well – ' I don't know what to say. The shaking makes me nervous. It shows his age, and the way he's leaned down over his chair while he packs isn't helping; it gives the impression of a stooped back.

'I promised your father,' he whispers. 'But you would have kept pressing. You don't give up. You get that from him. From both of your parents, actually.'

I start to smile, but he didn't mean it as a compliment.

'Why aren't we going together?' I ask, and he looks at me from under his brows. *You started this,* says that look. So I won't buckle, or fidget around. I won't let him see that I'm nervous about what I'm going to step in.

'So how do we get there? Is it far?' Once they're out,

the questions sound ridiculous. Like I'm expecting to get on the Tube and ride through four stations to arrive at the doorstep of an ancient Druidic order. Then again, maybe that's what it is. It's the 21st Century. Arriving to find a bunch of old dudes in brown robes would be equally weird.

'Jestine will take you,' Gideon replies. 'She knows the way.'

Questions are ripping through my mind and racing quickly toward daydream and conjecture. I'm imagining the Order as I might find them. I'm imagining Anna, reaching for her, through a gate torn between dimensions. The wooden face of the puppet flashes in between, the carved black letters springing toward my eyes like the rip-off squeal-shot in a horror movie.

'Theseus.'

I look up. Gideon's back is straight now, and the suitcase is clipped closed.

'This would never have been my choice,' he says. 'The moment you came here, you tied my hands.'

'It's a test, isn't it?' I ask, and Gideon lowers his eyes. 'How bad is it? What's going to be waiting for us, while you're in some private train car, or in the back seat of a Rolls, ordering around a chauffeur?'

He doesn't make a big show of caring. He actually winds his pocket watch.

'Aren't you even worried about Jestine?'

Gideon picks up his suitcase. 'Jestine,' he humphs, moving past me. 'Jestine can take care of herself.'

'She's not really your niece, is she,' I say quietly. He pauses just before opening the sliding door. 'Then who is she? Who is she really?'

'Haven't you figured that out yet?' he asks. 'She's the girl they've trained to replace you.'

'This sausage is unbelievable,' Thomas says around a mouthful.

'Bangers,' Jestine corrects. 'We call them bangers.'

'Why the hell would you call them that?' Thomas asks, looking disgusted even as he inhales the rest.

'I don't know,' Jestine laughs. 'We just do.'

I'm barely listening. I'm just robotically shoving things into my mouth, trying not to stare at Jestine. The way she smiles, the easy laugh, how she's managed to win Thomas over despite his suspicions, all of these things juxtapose with Gideon's words. I mean, she's... nice. She hasn't held any information back, hasn't lied to us. She hasn't even acted like we're worth bothering to lie to. And she seems to care about Gideon, even if it's obvious that her loyalty is with the Order.

'I'm stuffed,' Thomas declares. 'I'm going to go take a shower.' He pushes away from the table and hesitates with a mortified expression. 'But I'll help you clean up first.'

Jestine laughs. 'Go,' she says, and slaps his hand away from his plate. 'Cas and I can do the washing up.' After making sure she's serious, he shrugs at me and bounds up the stairs.

'He doesn't seem too concerned about any of this,' Jestine observes as she picks up plates and carries them to the sink. And she's right. He doesn't. 'Is he always so...reckless? How long has he been with you?'

Reckless? I'd never think of Thomas as reckless. 'A while,' I reply. 'Maybe he's just getting used to it.'

'Have you gotten used to it?'

I sigh and get up to put the jams and jellies back into the refrigerator. 'No. You don't really get used to it.'

'What's it like? I mean, are you always afraid?' Her back is to me as she asks. My replacement is pumping me for information. Like I'm going to mentor her or something, train her in before my two weeks are up. She looks at me over her shoulder, expectant.

I take a breath. 'No. Not afraid exactly. It keeps you on your toes. I guess it's sort of like crime-scene cleanup. Just interactive.'

She chuckles. She's tied her hair back to keep it out of the sink, and it hangs down her spine in a long, red-gold rope. It makes me remember how she looked the night we got here, when she jumped us. I might have to take this girl down.

'What's that smile about?' she asks.

'Nothing,' I say. 'Don't you know about ghosts already? The Order must've taught you.'

'I've seen my share, I suppose. And I'm ready to tangle, if they come at me.' She rinses a coffee cup and sets it in the strainer. 'But not like you are.' Her hands plunge back into the sudsy water, and she yelps.

'What?'

'I cut my finger,' she mutters, and lifts it up. There's a slice running between her first and second knuckle, and bright red blood mixes with the water, lacing its way down her palm. 'There was a chip out of the butter dish. It's not bad; the water makes it look worse.'

I know that, but I still grab a towel and wrap it around her finger, pressing down. I can feel her pulse through the thin cloth as the cut throbs.

'Where are the Band-Aids?'

'It's not as bad as all that,' she says. 'It should stop in a minute. Still, you should probably finish up with the dishes.' She grins. 'I don't want it to sting.'

'Sure,' I say, and grin back. Her head dips, to dab and blow at the cut, and I can smell her perfume. I'm still half holding her hand.

The doorbell buzzes shrill and sudden; I jerk away

and almost pull the towel with me. I don't know why, but for a second, my brain was sure that it would be Anna, that she'd be pounding the door down off its hinges with black-veined fists, ready to catch me with my pants down. But we were just doing dishes. My pants are firmly affixed.

Jestine goes to answer the door and I put my hands in the soapy water, fishing around carefully for the broken butter dish. I'm not interested at all in who's at the door. The only thing that matters is it isn't Anna, and even if it were, I am completely innocent, just scrubbing the egg pan. But Jestine's voice is rising about something, and the voice that answers is a girl's voice. Hairs that I never knew I had stand up on the back of my neck. I crane back to peer around the corner, just in time to see Carmel burst into the entryway.

CHAPTER NINETEEN

'You just drag him off halfway around the world?' Carmel says, her toe tapping with indignation. 'Where he has no contacts or advantages? Into who the hell knows what?' She narrows her eyes. 'You said you'd take care of him.'

'Actually, Carmel, I said—'

'Oh, I don't care what you said!'

'How did you find us, anyway?' I ask, and she finally inhales. She crashed into the house, a disaster in knee-high boots, and brought everything to a skidding stop. Upstairs, I hear the shower abruptly shut off. I hope Thomas doesn't slip and crack his head open in his rush to get down here. And I hope he remembers to put on a towel.

'Morfran told me,' Carmel says. 'Your mother told me.' The heat is suspended in her voice, neither rising nor cooling. Her eyes linger on my hands, studying my rolled-up sleeves and the clinging patches of soap bubbles that drip onto the floor. It must make for a quaint, domestic little scene. Nothing like the torrent of danger she expected. I wipe the suds off against the sides of my jeans.

Jestine slides through from behind, careful to keep from turning her back on Carmel, someone she doesn't know. There's tautness to her movements too, like she's ready to spring. Whoever it was who taught her, taught her well. She moves like me and she's twice as suspicious. I catch her eye and shake my head. Carmel doesn't need to be welcomed the same way we were, with Jestine chanting curses and sucking the air from her lungs.

'She said she knew you,' she says. 'I guess she was telling the truth.'

'Of course I was,' Carmel says, giving Jestine the once-over as she stands beside me. She extends her hand. 'I'm Carmel Jones. I'm Thomas and Cas's friend.' When they shake hands, my stomach relaxes. Jestine's only curious and Carmel's hostility is aimed at me. It's strange, but my instincts told me they'd get along pretty much like a snake and a mongoose.

'Can I take your bag?' Jestine asks, gesturing to Carmel's oversized duffel, some white designer thing with blinged-out zipper clasps.

'Sure,' Carmel says, and hands it off. 'Thanks.'

We stare at each other with restraint until Jestine is

upstairs and safely out of earshot. It's really hard to maintain a serious expression. Carmel's got on her best angry-frustrated face, but she really wants to hug me, I can tell. Instead, she shoves me so hard I stumble and catch myself against the arm of the sofa.

'Why didn't you tell me you were coming over here?' she asks.

'I was sort of under the impression that you didn't want to know.'

Her face scrunches. 'I didn't want to know.'

'So what are you doing here?'

We both look up. Thomas is standing in the middle of the stairs. He was so quiet, coming down. I expected a bunch of stomping. I half expected him to fall and wind up at our feet, shampoo in his hair and naked as a jaybird. I watch Carmel's expression carefully when she sees him. It's as happy as someone can possibly look when they know they have no right to be so happy.

'Can we talk?' she asks. The pulse in her neck speeds up when he purses his lips, but we both know Thomas. He wouldn't let her come across an ocean just to be turned away.

'Outside,' he says, and pushes through us to the door. Carmel follows, and I crane my neck around to different windows, following their progress as they walk around the side of the house.

'Something complicated there,' Jestine says into my ear, and I jump. This place lets people creep too easily. 'Will she be coming with us?'

'I think so. I hope so.'

'Then I hope they get everything sorted. The last thing we need is drama and angst and people making stupid decisions.' She crosses her arms and walks back into the kitchen to finish cleaning the remains of breakfast.

I should probably ask Jestine why that is, what we're going up against, but Thomas and Carmel have disappeared from view. Carmel being here is spinning my head around. She's almost surreal, an unexpected piece of Thunder Bay pasted into the picture. After what she said to me that day in my room, I thought she was gone for good. She'd made a choice, to have the life Thomas and I weren't going to get. I was happy for her. But following Jestine back to the kitchen, there's a big ball of relief in my chest, and gladness too, that this thing I can't get away from isn't that easy to walk away from either.

Checking the windows, I can catch a glimpse of them through the westernmost one that looks into the back garden if I lean far enough to the left. The scene is pretty intense; all direct eye contact and open hands. But damn it. I can't read lips.

'You're like an old woman,' Jestine quips. 'Wipe your nose print off the glass and help with the dishes.' She puts the sponge in my hand. 'You wash. I'll dry.'

We scrub in silence for a minute and the smirk grows deeper around her mouth. I suppose she thinks I'm trying to listen to what they're saying.

'We should leave in the morning,' Jestine says. 'It's a long train ride and a long hike on foot. It'll take two solid days of traveling.'

'Traveling to where, exactly?'

She holds her hand out for a plate. 'There is no *exactly*. The Order doesn't keep a dot on a map. It's somewhere in the Scottish Highlands. The western Highlands, north of Loch Etive.'

'So you've been there before?' I take her silence as a yes. 'Fill me in. What are we in for?'

'I don't know. A lot of pines and maybe a couple of woodpeckers.'

Now she gets dodgy? Irritation creeps up my arms, starting in the hot dishwater and ending in my clenched jaw.

'I hate doing dishes,' I say. 'And I hate the idea of being pulled around Scotland by someone I barely know. They're going to test me. You can at least tell me how.'

Her face is a blend of surprised and impressed.

'Come on,' I say. 'It's pretty clear. Why else wouldn't we just go with Gideon? So what is it? Are you not supposed to tell me?'

'You'd like that, wouldn't you,' she says, and tosses the towel onto the countertop. 'You're so transparent.' She leans in close, scrutinizing. 'The challenge excites you. And so does the confidence of knowing you're going to pass.'

'Cut the crap, Jestine.'

'There is no crap, *Theseus Cassio*. I can't tell you, because I don't know.' She turns away. 'You're not the only one being tested. We're alike, you and me. I knew that we would be. I just didn't know how much.'

Thomas and Carmel come back inside after an hour and find me slumped on the sofa in Gideon's living room, flipping between the BBC 1 and BBC 2. They shuffle in and sit, Carmel beside me and Thomas in the chair. They look awkwardly, uncomfortably reconciled, a kind of made-up that hasn't quite stuck. Carmel looks the most wrung out, but that could just be jet lag.

'So?' I ask. 'Are we all one big happy family again?' They look at me sourly. It didn't come out how I wanted.

'I think I'm on probation,' Carmel says. I glance at Thomas. He seems happy, but guarded. And that's just about right. His trust was shaken. In my brain too, weird phrases whirl around. I want to cross my arms and say things like, 'Don't come back if you're not going to stay!' and 'If you think that nothing's changed, you're wrong.' But she's probably heard all this stuff from Thomas already. I wasn't the boyfriend. I don't know why I feel like I should get the chance to yell at her too.

Jesus. I have become the thing they call the third wheel.

'Cas? Something wrong?' Thomas's brow is knit.

'We're leaving tomorrow,' I say. 'To meet the Order of the Blah Blah Blah.'

'The Order of the what?' Carmel asks, and when I don't, Thomas explains. I listen with half an ear, chuckle at his pronunciation, and supply factoids when asked.

'The journey is going to be a test,' I say 'And I don't think it'll be the last one.' Jestine's comment about enjoying the thrill of the challenge is still bubbling in my stomach. Enjoy it. Why would I enjoy it? Except that I do, sort of, and for exactly the reasons she described. And that's pretty sick when you think about it.

'Listen,' I say. 'Let's take a walk.'

They get up and exchange a glance, catching the ominous vibe.

'Just make it a short walk, OK?' Carmel mumbles.

'I don't know what I was thinking flying in these boots.'

Outside, the sun is out and the sky is cloudless. We head for the cover of trees so we can talk without squinting.

'What's going on?' Thomas asks when we stop.

'Gideon told me something before he left. Something about the Order and Jestine.' I shuffle. It still sounds so impossible. 'He said they were training her to take my place.'

'I knew you shouldn't trust her,' Thomas exclaims, and turns to Carmel. 'I knew it the minute she cursed him in the alley.'

'Look, just because they groomed her for the position doesn't mean that she's going to try to steal it. Jestine isn't the problem. We can trust her.' Thomas clearly thinks I'm a dope. Carmel reserves judgment. 'I think we can. And you'd better hope we can. She's taking us through the Scottish Highlands tomorrow.'

Carmel cocks her head. 'You don't have to use that accent when you say 'Scottish Highlands.' You know as well as we do that this isn't a joke. Who are these people? What are we walking into?'

'I don't know. That's the problem. But don't expect them to be happy to see me.' It's an understatement. I keep thinking of the way Jestine spoke outside the chapel at the Tower of London, and the reverent way she looks at the athame. To these people, I've committed sacrilege.

'If they want Jestine to take over, what does that mean for you?' Carmel asks.

'I don't know. I'm banking on the idea that their respect for the athame extends at least partway to the original bloodline of the warrior.' I glance at Thomas. 'But when they find out what I want to do with Anna, they're going to fight it. It wouldn't hurt to have Morfran's voodoo network up my sleeve.'

He nods. 'I'll tell him.'

'And after you do, you should both stay here. Wait for me here, at Gideon's. He'll watch my back. I don't want you guys getting into it.'

Their faces are pale. When Carmel slides her hand into Thomas's, I can see it shake.

'Cas,' she says gently, and looks me right in the eyes. 'Shut up.'

CHAPTER TWENTY

The train ride feels long. Which doesn't make sense. It should feel short and too soon, my nerves should be shot, wondering what I'm going to find on the other end of the track. The cautionary speeches of my mom, and Morfran, and Gideon, roll back and forth between my ears. I hear my dad too, telling me the way he always used to, that there's never an excuse to not be afraid. He said the fear kept you sharp, that it kept you steadfastly holding on to your life. Rapid heartbeats to keep that heartbeat fresh in your mind. It's maybe the one piece of his advice that I threw away. I had my share of fear in the years after his murder. And besides, when I think of his death, I don't like to think that he died afraid.

Outside, there's nothing but stretches of green, lined with trees. The countryside is still pastoral, and if I saw a carriage roll through one of the fields I wouldn't blink. There's so much of it that it may as well go on forever. It didn't take long for the city to fade out behind us after we left the station at King's Cross.

I'm sitting with Jestine, who has clammed up and is strung tight as a bow. This is what she's been waiting for her whole life, I suppose. My replacement. The thought of it sticks in my throat. But if that's what it takes, will I do it? If that's the price of saving Anna, if we get there and all they ask me to do in exchange is politely hand over my father's athame, will I do it? I'm not sure. I never thought that I wouldn't be sure.

Across the compartment, Carmel and Thomas sit side by side. They're talking a little, but mostly staring out the window. Since Carmel got here, what we're doing feels mostly like playacting, trying to get our old dynamic back when it's obviously been altered. But we'll keep trying, until we get it right.

My mind strays to Anna, and the image of her blooms up so strong in my senses that I can almost see her reflection in the window. It takes everything I've got to blink and stop seeing it.

'Why don't you want to think about her?' Thomas asks, and I jump. He's sitting behind me now, leaned over the partition of the seats. Stupid train noise. Carmel is stretched out across the seats, and beside me Jestine is out cold too, curled up against her duffel bag.

'She's the reason for all this,' he says. 'So what's with the guilt?'

I squint at him. He finds his way in my head at the most inopportune times. 'Carmel's going to have a very annoying life.'

'Carmel's figured out how to block me, for the most part.' He shrugs. 'You, not so much. So?'

'I don't know.' I sigh. 'Because when I do, there's a lot of stuff I'm forgetting.'

'Like what?'

He knows that I don't really want to talk about this. I can barely get it straight in my own head.

'Can I just think the random crap that's going through my head and you can figure it out?'

'Only if you want me to get an unstoppable nosebleed.' He grins. 'Just...talk.'

Like that's the simplest thing in the world. The words have built up in my throat, and if I open my mouth I'm going to heave for who knows how long.

'Fine. The Obeahman, for one. If I'm right, then he's there too. And we all remember how well he kicked my ass last time. Now he's even kicking hers. For two, what kind of Machiavellian shit am I going to step in with the Order? Jestine said there would be a price, and of that I have no doubt. And then there's this test that we're all running blindly into.'

'We don't have a choice,' Thomas says. 'The clock ticks. Caution's become a luxury.'

I snort. If caution is a luxury for me, that's fine. I know what I'm willing to pay. Thomas and Carmel aren't a part of it, but they might get pulled in anyway.

'Look,' he says. 'The situation is dark. Maybe even pitch black, if you want to get really dramatic.' He smiles. 'But don't feel guilty about being excited to see her again. *I'm* excited to see her again.'

There's no doubt in his eyes. He's absolutely certain that the plan will go from A to B, and everything will work out with rainbows and pots of gold. It's like he's completely forgotten just how many people I got killed last fall.

We changed trains in Glasgow and finally disembarked at Loch Etive, a sprawling, stretching lake of blue that reflects the sky with eerie stillness. When we crossed it on the ferry to the north bank, I couldn't shake the awareness of the depth beneath the boat, the idea that the reflection of sky and clouds was masking an entire world of darkness, caves, and swimming things. I'm glad to be across, on solid ground. There's moss here, and moisture in the air, clearing my lungs. But even now I feel the lake over my shoulder, sitting still and sinister as the yawning jaws of a trap. I much prefer

Superior, with her waves and rages. She doesn't keep her violence a secret.

Jestine's got her phone out. She's been periodically checking for texts from Gideon, but isn't really expecting one. 'Mobile service in the north country is spotty,' she said. Now she clicks her phone closed and rolls her neck back and around, stretching after sleeping in what was roughly a Q shape for hours on the train. Her hair is down and loose on her shoulders. We're all dressed comfortably, in layers and athletic shoes, backpacks affixed, looking for all the world like hikers out walking the country, which I guess is fairly common. The only things that set us apart are our pinched, nervous expressions. There is a very strong, stranger-in-a-strange-land vibe passing between us. I'm used to finding my feet fast in new places. God knows I've moved around enough. Maybe planting roots in Thunder Bay has made me soft. Having to rely on Jestine for everything doesn't sit well either, but there's no other option. At least she's doing a decent job of keeping Thomas and Carmel's minds off of what lies ahead by telling colorful local stories. She talks of ancient heroes and loyal hounds, and tells us about the dude from Braveheart and where he held his meetings. By the time she pulls us into a pub for fries and burgers, I realize she's taken my mind off everything too.

'I'm glad you two have worked things out,' Jestine says, looking across the table at Carmel and Thomas. 'You make a very cute couple.'

Carmel smiles and adjusts her hair, pulled into a sporty ponytail. 'Nah,' she says, and nudges Thomas with her shoulder. 'He's too pretty for me.' Thomas grins, grabs her hand, and kisses it. Since they just got back together, I'm willing to let this PDA business slide.

Jestine grins and takes a deep breath. 'We may as well stay here for the night and start off in the morning. There are rooms for board upstairs and we've got a long hike tomorrow.' She raises her brows at Thomas and Carmel. 'How do you want to room? The two of you and the two of us? Or boys in one, girls in the other?'

'Boys in one,' I say quickly.

'Right. Back in a minute.' Jestine gets up to make the arrangements, leaving me with my gaping friends.

'Where'd that come from?' Carmel asks.

'Where'd what come from?'

As usual, playing dumb gets me nowhere.

'Is there something going on?' She gestures with her head toward Jestine. 'No,' she says, answering her own question. But she's looking at Jestine, measuring just how attractive she is.

'Of course there isn't,' I say.

'Of course there isn't,' Thomas echoes. 'Although,' he says, and narrows his eyes. 'Cas does have a weakness for girls who can kick his ass.'

I laugh and throw a fry at him. 'Jestine did not kick my ass. And besides, like Carmel can't kick yours?' We smile and go back to eating with the mood shades lighter. But when Jestine returns to the table, I avoid looking at her, just to make a point.

My eyes are open in the dark. There isn't any real light in the room, only soft, cold blues streaming in from the window. Thomas is snoring in his bed next to mine, but not sawing logs or anything. It wasn't him that woke me. Not a nightmare, either. There's no adrenaline in my blood, no twitchy feeling in my back or legs. Whispering. I remember whispering, but I can't separate it from dream or waking sound. My eyes swivel to the window, out toward the lake. But that's not it. Of course it isn't. That lake isn't going to slither out of its banks and come up here after us, no matter how many things it has pulled under and drowned.

Probably just nerves. But even as I think so, my legs swing out of bed and I pull my jeans on, then slide the athame out from underneath the pillow. *Go with your gut* is the credo that has served me best, and my gut says there's a reason that I'm suddenly awake in the middle of the night. And I'm wide awake, stark fucking awake. The dry chill of the floor against my bare feet doesn't even make me flinch.

When I open the door of our room, the hallway is silent. That almost never happens; there's always a noise of some kind coming from somewhere, the creaking of the building against its foundation, the distant hum of a running refrigerator. But right now there's nothing, and it feels like a cloak.

There isn't enough light. No matter how wide I open my eyes, they can't take enough in to see much of anything, and I only vaguely remember the layout of the hall from walking up to our rooms. We took two left turns. Carmel and Jestine went farther back; the door to their room was around the corner. The athame shifts in my palm; the wood slides against my skin.

Someone screams and I bolt toward the sound. Carmel's calling me. Then all of a sudden she isn't. When her voice cuts off, my adrenaline spikes. I'm in their open doorway in two seconds, squinting against the light from Jestine's bedside lamp.

Carmel's out of bed, squeezed against the wall. Jestine's still in bed, but sitting straight up. Her eyes are fixed across the room, and her lips move rapidly in a Gaelic chant, her voice coming even and strong from her throat. There's a woman standing in the middle of the room in a long, white nightgown. A shock of white-blond hair spirals out over her shoulders and down her back. She's obviously dead, her skin more purple than white, and there are deep grooves in it, like wrinkles, except that she isn't old. It's shriveled, like she was left to rot in a bathtub.

'Carmel,' I say, and hold my hand out. She hears but doesn't react; maybe she's too shocked to move. Jestine's voice gets progressively louder and the ghost rises from the floor. The yellowed teeth are bared; she's getting more pissed by the second. When she starts to thrash, she sprays putrid water everywhere. Carmel squeaks and covers her face with her arm.

'Cas! I can't hold her much longer,' Jestine says, and the moment she does, the spell loses its grip and the ghost rushes the bed.

I don't think; I just throw the knife. It leaves my hand and runs into her chest with a meaty *thock,* like it just connected with the trunk of a tree. It drops her on the spot.

'What's going on?' Thomas asks, running into me from behind and shoving past to get to Carmel.

'Good question,' I say, and move farther into the room so I can close the door. Jestine leans over the edge of her bed and stares down at the body. Before I can say something soothing, she reaches out and shoves it, turning it face up, the athame's handle sticking squarely out of the chest.

'Isn't it supposed to…disintegrate or something?' she asks, cocking her head.

'Well, sometimes they explode,' I say, and she backs off fast. I shrug. 'He'd been disemboweled already, but when I put the athame into what was left, his gut sort of…blew up. Not into tiny bits or anything.'

'Eee.' Jestine makes a face.

'Cas,' Carmel says, and when I look at her, she shakes her head at me. I shut up, but really, if she expects delicacy then she probably shouldn't have come back. I walk to the ghost. The eyes aren't visible anymore; either they've disappeared, or they've fallen back into the skull. Despite the inherent grossness of the rotten, purple skin, and the way it shines like she was just lifted from the water, it isn't any worse than the other things I've seen. If this is what the Order calls a test, I've been worrying too much. I toe the ghost tentatively. It's just a corporeal shell now. It'll degrade in its own way, and if it doesn't, I suppose we could weigh it down and sink it into the lake.

'What happened?' I ask Jestine.

'It was strange,' she replies. 'I was asleep, and then I wasn't. There was something moving in the room. It was bent over Carmel's bed.' She nods at Carmel, still standing by the door, with Thomas's arm around her shoulders. 'So I started chanting.'

I look at Carmel to confirm, but she shrugs.

'When I woke up it was by my bed. Jestine was saying something.' She leans into Thomas. 'It was all pretty fast.'

'What was that chant?' Thomas asks.

'Just a Gaelic binding spell. I've known it since I was little.' She shrugs. 'It's not what I had planned on using. It was the first thing that popped into my head.'

'What do you mean it's not what you'd planned on using? Why were you planning to use something?' I ask.

'Well I wasn't; not really. I just knew this place was haunted. I didn't know for sure if the ghost would show up. Just said a few words as we crossed the threshold, to entice it, and then went to sleep and hoped.'

'Are you nuts?' Thomas shouts. I put my hand out, gesturing to keep his voice down. He presses his lips together and bugs his eyes out at me.

'You did this on purpose?' I ask Jestine.

'I thought it'd be good practice,' she replies. 'And I'll admit, I was curious. I've been taught about the athame being used, but of course I've never seen it.'

'Well the next time you get curious, you might think about telling your bunkmate,' Carmel snaps. Thomas kisses the top of her head and squeezes her tighter.

I stare down at the corpse. Wondering who she was. Wondering if she would have been a ghost I would have needed to kill. Jestine sits unaffected at the foot of the bed. I'd like to throttle her, yell until her ears pop about putting people in danger. Instead I reach down to pull the athame loose. When my fingers close around the handle, they hesitate, and my stomach does a small flip when I have to jerk at it to get the blade out of the bone.

The knife slides out, coated with a faint tinge of purplish blood. As soon as the tip of the blade is clear, the wound expands, curling the skin back in layers, tearing through the faux-fabric of the nightgown. It takes the skin down to the bone and turns the bone to black and then to dust; the entire scattering of muscle, sinew, cloth, and hair takes less than five seconds.

'Don't ever put my friends in danger again,' I say. Jestine locks eyes with me, defiant as usual. After a few seconds, she nods and apologizes to Carmel. But in those few seconds I saw what she was thinking. She was thinking I was a hypocrite to tell her that.

Chapter Twenty-one

We move the girls' things into our room, but after that, nobody goes back to sleep. Thomas and Carmel just sit together on his bed, snuggled up and not saying much. Jestine tucks herself into my bed, and I spend the last hours until dawn by the window, sitting in a chair and watching the black spot of the lake.

'That throw was brilliant,' Jestine says to me at one point, maybe trying to make peace, and I make some kind of affirmative noise in my throat, not ready to really talk to her yet. I think she could have fallen back asleep, but feels too guilty to let herself, seeing how shaken up Carmel is. As soon as there is enough light, we start getting ourselves together.

'We've already paid,' Jestine says, shoving her pajamas into her pack. 'I suppose we could just leave the keys at the bar and head out.'

'You're sure we'll make it to the Order by tonight?'

Carmel asks, peering out at the expanse of mist and trees. There's a whole lot of darkness and nothing else out there, and it looks like it might go on forever.

'That's the plan,' Jestine replies, and we shoulder our backpacks.

We go down the stairs, making as little noise as possible. But I suppose that's not necessary, considering the ruckus we made at three in the morning. I expected all the lights to come on and for the innkeeper to bang down the door and rush in holding a baseball bat. Except they don't play baseball in this country. So maybe they would have been holding a cricket bat, or just a big stick, I don't know.

At the bottom of the steps, I turn and hold my hand out for both sets of keys. I'll just leave them near the cash register.

'I hope nothing got broken last night.'

The voice is so unexpected that Thomas slips down the last few stairs and Carmel and Jestine have to catch him. It's the owner of the inn, a stout, dark-gray-haired woman in a chambray shirt. She's behind the bar, staring at us while she dries glasses with a white towel.

I go to the bar and hold the keys out. 'No,' I say. 'Nothing got broken. I'm sorry if we woke you. Our friend had a nightmare and everyone sort of overreacted.'

'Overreacted,' she says, and cocks her brow. When

she takes the keys, she grabs them, practically snatches them out of my hand. Her voice is a low, rough grumble; she's got a thick brogue, and the toothpick sticking out of one corner of her mouth doesn't make it any easier to understand. 'I ought to charge you another night's stay,' she says. 'For the extra efforts we'll be taking from now on.'

'Extra efforts?' I ask.

'Every Scottish Inn needs a haunting,' she says, putting down one glass and starting on another. 'A story for the tourists. A few roaming footsteps in empty hallways at night.' She levels her eyes at me. 'I expect I'll have to be finding a way to do it myself, from now on.'

'I'm sorry,' I say, and I mean it. My teeth grit at the urge to turn and glare at Jestine, but it wouldn't do any good. She'd just blink back innocently, not seeing anything wrong. I don't like the idea of following her through unfamiliar country. Not when she's clever enough to trick me into breaking my own rules.

'What the hell was that about?' Thomas asks once we're outside. 'How did the innkeeper know?'

Nobody answers. I have no idea. This place is strange. People look at you in one slow wink, and they have a link to magic, like they're all Merlin's second cousins once removed. The owner of the inn was an ordinary woman, but talking to her felt like talking to a hobbit. Now, outside, even the chill in the air feels off, and the dark lines of the trees seem too dark. But there isn't anything to do but follow Jestine, and she takes us down the roughly paved road, where we fill our water bottles in a fountain and then turn off, onto a pebble and gravel path through the woods.

Once we're moving and the sun comes up higher, finally visible through the peaks of the trees, things seem better. The hiking isn't hard, just a well-groomed trail and a few rolling hills. People pass us in small groups, on their way back to the Loch and beyond. They all look cheerful, weathered, and normal, outfitted in REI and khaki caps. Birds and small mammals skit through the underbrush and branches, and Jestine points out of a few of the more colorful ones. By the time we stop for a lunch of pre-packed fruit and cereal bars, even Carmel's color has gone back to normal.

'Another few hours on this trail, and then we should leave the path and head through the forest.'

'What do you mean?' I ask.

'We should be on the trail for half a day, and then we should see the mark,' Jestine replies.

'What's the mark?'

She shrugs, and the rest of us exchange a look. Carmel asks whether she means the Order, but I know she doesn't. She doesn't know what the mark is.

'You said you'd been here before,' I say, and her eyes widen innocently. 'You said you knew the way.'

'I said no such thing. I've been to the Order before, but I don't know exactly how to get there, and certainly not on foot.' She tears into a granola bar. The crunching sounds like breaking bones.

I think back. She didn't actually say it. Gideon said she knew the way. But he probably meant because she was told, not because she'd ever done it.

'How can you have been there and not know where it is? Weren't you practically raised there?' I ask.

'I was raised by my parents,' she says, giving me the arched eyebrow. 'I've been to the compound from time to time. But when I went, it was blindfolded.'

Thomas and I look at each other, just to confirm the craziness.

'It's tradition,' says Jestine, seeing the look. 'Not all of us break with it, you know.' I don't have to ask what that's supposed to mean.

'You messed up back at the inn, Jestine.'

'Did I? She was dead, and the athame sent her.' She shrugs. 'It's very simple, really.'

'It's not simple,' I say. 'That ghost probably never harmed a living person in its entire afterlife.'

'So? It doesn't belong here. It's dead. And don't look

at me like that, like I'm brainwashed. Your morality isn't the only morality in the world. Just because it's yours doesn't mean it's right.'

'But don't you wonder about where they might be being sent to?' Thomas asks, in an attempt to keep the conversation reasonable. Because I'm about ready to give her the finger. Or stick my tongue out.

'The athame sends them where they need to be,' she replies.

'Who told you that? The Order?'

Jestine and I lock eyes. She's going to look away first. Even if my eyeballs have to completely dry out.

'Wait a minute,' Carmel says. 'Back on point, are you saying that nobody knows where we're going?' She looks around; our blank faces serve as confirmation. 'And we're supposed to leave the groomed and maintained trail to go through unmarked forest?'

'There is a mark,' Jestine says calmly.

'What, like a flag or something? Unless there's a string of them leading through the trees, I'm not comforted.' She looks at me. 'You saw out your window this morning. These trees go on for miles. And we don't even have a compass. People die this way.'

She's right. People die this way. More frequently than we like to think about. But Gideon knows we're coming. If we don't show up on schedule, he'll send someone looking for us. And besides, in my gut I don't believe that we *can* get lost. Looking at Jestine, I don't think she believes we can either. But how do I explain that to Carmel?

'Thomas, you ever in the Boy Scouts?' I ask, and he squints at me. Of course he wasn't. 'Listen, if you want, you can just follow the path back to the inn.'

Thomas tenses at the suggestion, but Carmel crosses her arms over her chest. 'I'm not going anywhere,' she says stubbornly. 'I just thought it was worth mentioning that this is stupid and we're probably going to die.'

'Noted,' I say, and Jestine smiles. The smile puts me at ease. She doesn't hold grudges; you can disagree with her and not become an enemy. I've wanted to strangle her for half the time I've known her, but I like that.

'We should go soon,' she says. 'So we don't lose the light.'

After another hour and who knows how many more miles, Jestine starts to slow. Every once in a while she stops and looks around the woods in all directions. She thinks we've gone far enough. Now she's getting nervous that the marker won't be there. When she pulls up at the crest of a small hill, we all take our backpacks off and sit down while she stares. Despite good shoes and being in relatively good shape, we're all tired. Carmel is rubbing the backs of her knees while Thomas rubs his shoulder. They're both slightly pale, and clammy.

'There it is,' Jestine says, in a tone that implies she always knew it would be. She turns back to us, triumphant, a wicked gleam in her eyes. Down the path in the trees lining the trail I see it: a black ribbon, tied around a trunk, fifteen feet off the ground.

'We leave the trail there,' she tells us. 'And on the other side is the Order. Gideon said it would only be two hours through the woods. Just a few more miles.'

'We can do that,' I say to Thomas and Carmel, and they stand up, looking at the ribbon and trying to overcome their trepidation.

'Maybe the forest floor will be softer at least,' Thomas says.

Jestine smiles. 'That's right. Come on.'

CHAPTER TWENTY-TWO

'It's old-growth forest,' Jestine says, after the scenery changes gradually from meadow and pine to deciduous trees and fallen trunks overrun with moss.

'It's beautiful,' says Carmel, and she's right. Trees stretch tall over our heads, and our feet whisper through a blanket of low ferns and moss. Everything in sight is green or gray. Where the soil peeks through, it's black as pitch. Light filters down through the leaves, bouncing and refracting off their smooth surfaces, painting everything crisp and completely clear. The only sounds come from us, obscene interlopers crunching through with scratchy canvas backpacks and blundering feet.

'Look,' says Thomas. 'There's a sign.'

I glance up. A black, wooden sign has been tacked to one of the trunks. Written in white paint is the phrase:

The world has many beautiful places.

'Sort of weird,' he says, and we shrug.

'It seems humble. Like they know this forest is

beautiful, but not the *most* beautiful,' comments Carmel. Jestine smiles at this, but as we pass the sign, something starts to itch in the back of my brain. Images start flipping through my memory, disconnected, made-up images of things I've never actually seen, like pictures in a book.

'I know this place,' I say softly, at the exact moment that Thomas points and says, 'There's another one.'

This time the sign reads:

Consider the love of your family.

'That's a little random,' says Carmel.

'It's not random at all, if you know where we are,' I say, and all three of them eye me tensely. I don't know what Gideon was thinking, sending us here. When I see him at the Order, I might just wring his neck. I breathe in deep, and listen; a stark lot of nothing hits my ears. No birdsongs, no scurrying of chipmunk or squirrel legs. Not even the sound of wind. The breeze is choked off by the density of the trees. Beneath the layer of clear air, my nose barely detects it, mixed in with the loam and decay of vegetation. The place is laced with death. It's someplace that I've only heard about from charlatans like Daisy Bristol, a place that's been relegated to a campfire story.

It's the Suicide Forest. I'm walking through the Suicide Forest with two witches, and a knife that flashes to the dead like a damn lighthouse.

'Suicide Forest?' Thomas squeaks. 'What do you mean 'suicide forest'?' Which of course triggers an outburst of similarly alarmed questions from Carmel, and even a few from Jestine.

'I mean just what it sounds like,' I reply, staring dismally at the useless painted sign that does virtually nothing to change people's minds. 'This is where people come to die. Or, more accurately, this is where people come to kill themselves. They come from all over the place. To OD, or slit their wrists, or hang.'

'That's terrible,' Carmel says. She hugs herself and moves closer to Thomas, who sidles closer to her too, looking green enough to match the moss. 'Are you sure?'

'Pretty much.'

'Well, it's horrible. And all they have here is these lame signs? There should be...patrols or...help, or something.'

'I imagine there are patrols,' Jestine says. 'Only they're mainly for collecting bodies, not for preventing the suicides.'

'What do you mean, you imagine?' I ask. 'Don't tell me you didn't know what we were walking into. If I knew about this halfway around the world, you had to know about it in your own backyard.'

'Well, of course I've heard of it,' she says. 'From girls at school and the like. I never thought it existed really. It was like the story of the babysitter who answers the phone and the calls have been coming from inside the house. It's like the Boogeyman.'

Thomas shakes his head, but there's no reason to not believe her. The Suicide Forest isn't something the police would want publicized. More people would just come to kill themselves.

'I don't want to cross it,' Carmel declares. 'It just… doesn't feel right. We have to go around.'

'There is no way around,' Jestine says. But of course there has to be. The Suicide Forest can't be bordered by nothingness. 'We have to cross. If we don't, we might get lost, and you were right when you said there were miles and miles of forest to die in. I don't fancy winding up one more body in the woods.'

The phrase hits home for Thomas and Carmel, and their eyes flicker to the ground and trees around them. I'm going to be the deciding vote. If I want to try to find a way around, Jestine will come with us. Maybe I should. But I won't. Because that ghost back at the inn wasn't the test that the Order had planned. This is. And we've come this far.

'Just stay together,' I say, and the hope on Carmel's face vanishes. 'It probably won't be anything worse than a few dead bodies. Just keep on your toes.'

We switch formation to me in the front and Jestine in

the back, with Thomas and Carmel in the middle. As we pass by the second sign, I can't help but feel like we're walking into a black hole. But that's a feeling I should probably get used to.

Ten tense minutes pass before we catch our first glimpse. Carmel gasps, but it's just a pile of scattered bones, a ribcage and most of an arm, taken over by moss.

'It's OK,' Thomas whispers while I keep an eye on it to make sure it isn't going to reassemble.

'It's not,' Carmel whispers back. 'It's worse. I don't know why it's worse, but it is.'

She's right. The beauty of the forest has been stripped. There's nothing here but misery and silence. It seems impossible that anyone would want to spend their last moments here, and I wonder whether the woods lure them in with false breezes and sunlight, wearing a mask of peace, the whole damned system of roots and hanging branches preying on people like a spider.

'We'll be through before long,' Jestine says. 'It can't be much more than a mile now. Just keep heading northeast.'

'She's right,' I say, stepping over a fallen log. 'A half hour more and we'll be out.' Another body pops up in my peripheral vision, something fresher, still clothed and in one piece. It's hanging against the trunk of the tree. I can just see the side of it, and I keep my eyes trained forward even while I watch for movement, for the broken neck to jerk suddenly in our direction. Nothing. We pass by and it's just another body. Just a lost soul.

The march goes on, and we try to keep our footsteps quiet while at the same time wanting to run. There are bodies upon bodies in these woods, some in piles and some scattered in separate pieces. Someone in a suit and tie lay down against a fallen log and lies there still, his jaw yawning open and his eye sockets black. I want to reach back and take Carmel's hand. We should find a way to anchor to each other.

'Tell me again why you're going through all this,' Jestine says from the back. 'Gideon has told me some, and then Thomas told me more. But tell me again. Why all this trouble, for a dead girl?'

'That dead girl saved our lives,' I reply.

'So I hear. But that just means you light a candle and give her a nod every now and then. It doesn't mean you cross an ocean and walk through the forest of the dead just to find a way to the other side to pull her back out again. She did it on purpose, didn't she?'

I glance around. There are no bodies visible, for the moment. 'Not like these,' I say. 'She did what she had to. And she wound up someplace she doesn't belong.'

'Where ever she is, it is what she has made it,' Jestine says. 'You know that, don't you? You know that where she is, it's not what most people think of as Heaven or Hell. Just outside. Outside of everything. Outside of rules and logic, and laws. It has no value, good or bad. Right or wrong.'

I walk faster, even though my legs feel reliable as cooked noodles. 'How do you know?' I ask, and she laughs breathlessly.

'I don't. It's just what I've been taught; what I've been told.'

I glance over my shoulder at Thomas, who shrugs.

'Every doctrine has its own theory,' he says. 'Maybe they're all right. Maybe none are. Whatever, I'm no philosopher.'

'Well what would Morfran say?'

'He'd say we're all idiots for walking through the Suicide Forest. Are we still going the right way?'

'Yeah,' I say, but as soon as he asks, I'm no longer sure. The light is funny here, and I can't track the sun. It feels like we've been walking a straight line, but a line can curve all the way back on itself if you walk it far enough. And we've been walking for a long time.

'So,' Jestine says after a few minutes of tense silence. 'You were all friends with this dead girl?'

'Yes,' Carmel says. Her tone is clipped. She'd like

273

Jestine to shut up. Not because she's offended, but because she'd rather all our attention be on the trees and corpses. But so far, they're just corpses. Acre after acre of decomposing bodies. It's unsettling, but not dangerous.

'And maybe more than friends?'

'Do you have an issue with this, Jestine?' Carmel asks.

'No,' Jestine replies. 'Not really. It's just that I wonder what's the point? Even if you don't die trying, and you somehow manage to get her back – It's not as though she and Cas can settle down and raise a family.'

'Can we just shut up and get through the death woods?' I snap, and keep my eyes straight ahead. What are we talking about this for, when there are people hanging from branches like goddamn Christmas tree ornaments? Concentrating on the present moment seems more important than waxing theoretical.

Jestine doesn't shut up. She keeps on chattering, just not to me. Instead she talks to Thomas, quietly, small talk of Morfran and magic. Maybe she does it to prove that I'm not the boss of her. But I think she's doing it to mask her growing nervousness. Because we've been walking for far too long, and there's no end in sight. Still, our legs keep moving forward, and the unified thought is that it can't be much farther. Maybe if we think it hard enough, it'll turn out to be true.

We have to have gone another half mile before Carmel finally whispers, 'We're not going the right way. We should have been there by now.'

I wish she hadn't said anything. There's a light sheen of panic sweat on my forehead. For at least the last five minutes, I've been thinking the same thing. We've gone way too far. Either Jestine was wrong when she told us the distance, or the Suicide Forest is stretching its dimensions. The pulse in my throat says it's the latter, that we've walked into it and it isn't letting go. After all, it could be that no one intends to kill themselves here. They just do it after the woods drive them insane.

'Stop,' Carmel says, and grabs the back of my shirt. 'We're going in circles.'

'We aren't going in circles,' I say. 'We might be completely screwed, but I know that much. I've been walking in a straight line, and the last time I checked, both of my legs were the same length.'

'Look,' she says. Her arm shoots out over my shoulder, pointing into the trees. Off to our left, a corpse hangs against a trunk, strung up by black nylon rope. It's wearing a canvas vest and a tattered brown t-shirt. One of its feet is missing.

'We've seen it before. It's the same one. I remember. We're going around in circles. I don't know how, but we are.'

'Shit.' She's right. I remember that one too. But I have no idea how we've managed to double back on ourselves.

'That's not possible,' says Thomas. 'We would've felt it, if we'd curved around that far.'

'I'm not walking this again.' Carmel shakes her head. Her eyes are wild, ringed with white. 'We have to try another way. Another direction.'

'There's only one way to the Order,' Jestine interjects, and Carmel wheels on her.

'Well maybe we're not getting to the Order!' Her voice quiets. 'Maybe we were never supposed to.'

'Don't panic,' is all I can think to say. It's all that's important. I don't understand how these trees are stretching. I don't understand how I was put so far off track that I've wound up back at the beginning. But I do know that if any one of us panics now, that'll be it. Whoever runs first will let the fear out of everyone else, like a gunshot, and we will run. We'll be lost and maybe separated before we even know what we're doing.

'Oh, shit.'

'What?' I ask, looking at Thomas. His eyes are big as eggs behind his glasses. He's looking off over my shoulder.

I turn around. The corpse is still there, hanging from the tree, the lower jaw half dropping off and the skin sagging. My eyes scan the scenery and nothing moves.

The corpse just hangs. Only – I blink a second – it's bigger. Except that it isn't bigger. It's closer.

'It moved,' Carmel whispers, and grabs on to my sleeve. 'It wasn't there before. It was there.' She points. 'It was farther away; I'm sure of it.'

'Maybe not,' says Jestine. 'Maybe it's just your eyes playing tricks on you.' Sure. It's a reasonable explanation, and one that doesn't make me want to piss myself and run screaming. We've been in this forest for too long, that's all. Reality is starting to bend.

Something behind us moves, shuffling through the leaves and snapping twigs. We spin on instinct; it's the first noise the trees have made since we walked into them. Whatever it is it's not close enough to see. A few of the ferns attached to a large ash seem like they might be wavering, but I can't tell if they really are, or if my head's making it up.

'Turn around!'

Thomas's shout makes my scalp tighten as I spin. The body has moved again. It's at least three trees closer, and this time it's hanging toward us. The bleary, decomposing eyes regard us with something that's almost interest. Behind us, the trees whisper again, but I don't turn to look. I know what would happen. The next time I turn back, those whitened eyes might be inches from my face.

'Circle up,' I say, my voice as in control as I can manage. Our time is limited. The movement in the trees is all around now, and it isn't stopping. All of the corpses we passed before are on their way. They must've been stalking us the whole time, and I don't like to think of their heads turning to stare after our backs as we went.

'Keep your eyes open,' I tell them when I feel their shoulders press against mine. 'We'll go as fast as we can, but be careful. Don't stumble.' On my back left, I feel Carmel bend down and hear her pick up what must be a thick stick off the ground. 'The good news is we haven't gone in a circle. So we'll be out of here before long.'

'Some fucking good news,' Carmel snaps sarcastically, and despite everything I crack a smile. Whenever she gets scared, she gets so pissed.

We start off, moving as a unit, hesitant at first, and then faster. But not fast enough to look like we're in a hurry. These things would like nothing better than to chase us.

'There's another one,' says Thomas, but I keep my eyes on the bleary-eyed dude. 'Shit, there's another.'

'And two more on my side,' Jestine adds. 'It's too fast to track. They just appear, in the corner of my eye.'

As we go, I finally have to look ahead, taking my gaze off of Johnny Milk-eyes. I hope someone else picks him up, but when I see the other three corpses, two hanging in the trees before us and one resting against a far-off trunk, I know that we just don't have enough eyes.

'This isn't going to work,' Jestine says.

'How far is it to the edge of the woods?' Carmel asks. 'Could we run?'

'They'd just pick us off, one by one. I don't want to turn my back on them,' says Thomas.

But turning our backs is inevitable. The question is how to do it. Do I try to cut a path? Or do we all go together? The trio of dead things ahead of us stares at me with black sockets. Their expressionless faces are like a dare. I've never seen corpses look so *eager*, like dogs waiting to be taken off their leashes.

Carmel screams; there's a sharp whack from the stick she wields and a skeleton hits the ground beside us. The circle breaks as she backpedals. She hits it again, bringing her club down across its spine and cracking it. It isn't until I see the corpse behind Thomas and feel the spongy grip of a dead hand around my throat that I realize our mistake. We all dropped our guard. We all turned away.

I twist out of the fingers looking to break my windpipe and bring my elbow up blind to knock it back. The athame is in my hand in an instant; the blade drives into the corpse behind me and it sounds like it falls to pieces. When I cleave into the skeleton that Carmel dropped, it liquefies and sinks into the ground.

Two down, twenty-five to go. Looking into the trees, bodies are everywhere. They don't seem to move, they don't run up; they just *are* and every time we look away, they're closer. Carmel's doing this constant groaning, growling thing, swinging her club at everything that gets near. I can hear Jestine and Thomas, two chants in different languages, and I have no idea what they're doing. My knife slides through the black hole of an eye socket and the corpse disintegrates in a cloud of what looks like granular soil.

'There are too many,' Carmel shouts. Fighting them off is a pipe dream.

'Run!' I shout, but Jestine and Thomas don't budge. Thomas's voice rattles in my ears. The dialect reminds me of Morfran, of the Obeahman. It's pure voodoo. Ten feet ahead of him, a half-rotten body draped over a low branch suddenly collapses. In the next second it's nothing but a pile of writhing maggots.

'Not bad, Thomas,' I say, and when he glances over his shoulder, another corpse is in front of him, too fast to see. It sinks its teeth deep into the meat of his neck and he shrieks.

Jestine growls something in Gaelic and sweeps her

arm across her chest; the corpse lets go of Thomas and falls, twitching.

'Run!' she shouts, and this time we do, our legs crashing through fallen leaves and ferns. I stay in the front as much as I can, slicing into anything that shows up in our path. To my left, Carmel is channeling her inner Warrior Princess, using the club to pretty good effect with one arm. The other arm has hold of Thomas. Blood darkens the entire top half of his shirt. He needs help. He can't keep running. But there's new light ahead and a break in the trees. We're almost out.

'Cas! Watch it!'

My head turns at Jestine's warning, just in time to see the bleary eyes right where I feared they would be. Two inches from my face, and I'm tackled underneath him.

The weight is unexpected. It's like being steamrolled. And despite the strength in him, his arms are rubbery and soft; my nose is too close to his neck. I can hear his teeth snapping in my ear, and the skin around the knot of the rope is swollen and black, like an overinflated tire. During the roll to the ground, the athame got pinned at a bad angle. I can't get it up into his gut and I can just barely keep it tilted out of mine. When I push his head away with my other hand he jerks and bites down on my fingers. Mossy teeth grind right down to the bone and on reflex I curl my grip around his jaw. My fingers push through something soft and grainy. His rotting tongue.

'Keep running!' Jestine shouts, and then her foot connects with the corpse's ribcage. It doesn't roll him off, but in that split second, I can maneuver the knife. When he settles back down again, the blade slides right up under his sternum, and he dissipates in a cloud of the worst smelling stuff I've ever come across.

'You all right?' Jestine asks. I nod as she pulls me to my feet, but after feeling the tongue and smelling that decaying swamp gas, I might throw up. We stagger and run. The trees open up on a clear day and a green meadow, where Carmel is kneeling over a collapsed Thomas. On the other side of the clearing, Gideon stands with two others in front of a long, black car.

CHAPTER TWENTY-THREE

It's like having a nightmare and falling out of bed. We topple out of the Suicide Forest, haggard and bloody and half on our knees. And we wind up on four inches of soft grass, squinting against warm sunlight, staring into calm, condescendingly soothing faces.

The athame is still in my hand; I look back to the trees, expecting to see a row of pale faces in between the trunks, staring after us like prisoners from inside their cage. But it's just trees, and leaves, and moss. The instant that we left their boundary, they retreated, to return to the place where they hung, or lay in piles.

'It appears you were right, Mr Palmer,' someone says. 'He made it.' I look over toward the car. The man speaking is slightly shorter and younger, than Gideon. I can't tell how much younger exactly. The hair on his head is blond, streaked with gray, so that somehow the whole slick mess winds up looking silver. He's in a black button-up and dark slacks. At least he isn't in a brown robe, swinging a censer.

'Don't worry,' he says, walking toward us. 'They won't cross into the meadow.'

The nonchalant tone irks me, and Carmel grabs my arm just as I'm about to tell this clown where he can shove his meadow.

'He's still bleeding,' she says. I look down at Thomas. He's breathing OK, and the blood coming up between Carmel's pressing fingers is a slow leak, not an arterial spurt. I think most of his exhaustion is from that whammy of a curse he pulled in the woods, rather than the corpse-bite, but I wouldn't in a million years tell that to Carmel right now. She's ready to breathe fire.

Beside us, the man has his hands on both of Jestine's shoulders, looking at her fondly. 'You did well,' he says, and she lowers her head briefly. 'Not a scratch on you.'

'He needs a doctor,' I hiss, and when Mr Jackass doesn't respond, Jestine says it again.

'He's still bleeding. Is Dr Clements here?'

'He is,' he says, but doesn't look like he's in a huge hurry about it. When he smiles, I'm reminded of a snake's stretch, just before it eats the mouse. 'Don't worry. The compound isn't far. We'll tend to your witch friend. And to you.' His eyes drop to my split-open fingers, and I swear I see the corners of his mouth twitch.

'My name is Colin Burke.' He's got the nerve to hold his hand out to me. Carmel slaps it away, leaving a streak of red across his palm.

'I don't care what your name is,' she hisses. 'And I don't care who you are. If you don't get him some help, I will burn your place down.' Go Carmel. Burke doesn't seem too perturbed, but Gideon finally pipes up, telling her to give Thomas over. He helps him to his feet and supports him on the way to the car, avoiding my eyes while he does it.

'Put something down over the seat,' Burke says, and I'm *this close* to laying him out. But Thomas needs help, so I shut up and walk to the car.

The drive is quick, along a road that's part paved and part dirt path, cutting through the trees on the other side of the meadow, but the guy driving definitely doesn't hurry. He hasn't said anything to anyone, and I'd suspect that he's just a driver if it wasn't for the feeling that no one here is 'just' anything. I glance at Jestine. She's pulled a cloth out of her backpack for Carmel to press to Thomas's neck. Concern wrinkles her forehead.

We crest a small hill and start to slow. Tucked into a small, green valley is what must be the Order. It looks like one of those snooty, exclusive, Aspen-type resorts, just a compound of a few red wooden buildings and solar panels, and entire walls made of smoked glass windows. It has to be worth several million dollars, but it's still less conspicuous than a gray stone fortress or a monastery. Thomas must feel my wonder, because he struggles up from Carmel's lap to peer out the window. The bleeding has mostly stopped. He'll be OK, as long as he doesn't get an infection from dead incisors.

'Welcome,' some dude says to us as he opens the car door when it pulls up to the main building. He's young and groomed, in a black suit, looking like he fell out of GQ. He and the driver might be twins. It's sort of disconcerting, like Fembots in reverse. I bet the cook looks like this too.

'Robert, please alert Dr Clements,' says Burke. 'Tell him he has some stitching to do.' Robert leaves for the doctor and Burke turns to me. 'Junior members,' he explains. 'They learn the Order through observation, and do their time in service.'

'Makes sense,' I say, and shrug. It's also completely creepy, but I think he knows that.

As I look around, it feels like I've been splashed with cold water. I don't know what I expected, but it wasn't this. I thought...I guess I thought I'd show up to find just more Gideons. Old men in comfy sweaters, clamoring around me like grandfathers. Instead I find Burke, and the instant animosity runs both ways between us in a static current. Gideon, on the other hand, still won't look at me. He's ashamed, and he should be. We all got out in one piece, but we didn't have to.

'Ah, Dr Clements.' Now there's what I was expecting. A gray-haired, bearded man in a burgundy sweater and khakis. He walks straight to Thomas and gently pulls up the red-stained cloth, revealing a ragged, crescent-shaped cut. My stomach flips as images of Will and Chase, and imagined images of my dad, flash behind my eyes. Damn bite wounds.

'It'll need to be washed and stitched,' he says. 'With an herb pack it should heal well, with hardly a scar.' He puts the cloth back over the wound, and Thomas holds it down. 'Dr Marvin Clements,' he says, and shakes his hand. When he shakes my hand, he turns it over and scrutinizes my fingers. 'Those could do with stitches as well.'

'It's fine,' I say.

'Wash it at least,' he says. 'It's putrid.' He turns and takes Thomas by the arm to lead him inside. I go too, and Carmel's right behind. Jestine stays with Burke, and I'm unsurprised.

After Thomas is treated and my hand is scrubbed out with iodine, we're shown to a set of rooms arranged

287

around a common area. I grab a nervous shower and rewrap my hand. I don't trust one inch of this place, and leaving Thomas and Carmel alone for even twenty minutes makes me tense.

The room where they put me is large, decked out with a small fireplace and big bed with expensive-looking blankets. It reminds me of a hunting lodge I saw in a movie once. The only thing missing are the stuffed heads on the walls.

'I think if this place had stuffed heads, they'd be human,' Thomas quips. He and Carmel walk in holding hands.

'No lie.' I grin. There are windows cut into the wall, and skylights along the arch of the ceiling. There have to be about a million windows covering the whole compound, but it doesn't make it feel open, or illuminated. It makes it feel watched.

Gideon knocks on the open door, and Thomas turns too fast; he winces and presses his hand to his fresh bandage.

'Sorry, lad,' Gideon says, and pats his shoulder. 'Dr Clements makes an excellent henbane poultice. The pain will be out of it in an hour.' He nods at Carmel, waiting for an introduction.

'Gideon, Carmel – Carmel, Gideon,' I say.

'So you're Gideon,' she says, eyes narrowed. 'Was it

too much trouble to take the car and meet the ferry at Loch whatever the hell it was?' She turns away in disgust without waiting for an answer.

'I can't believe you sent us there,' I say, and he meets my eyes without flinching. He's solemn, and maybe regretful, but he's no longer ashamed, if in fact he ever was.

'I warned you,' he replies. 'Make up your mind, Theseus. You're either a child, or you're not.'

Damn him and his points.

'I never wanted you to come here. I wanted to keep my promise to your parents, and keep you out of danger. But you are your father's son. You always put yourself there. Hell-bent on ruin.'

His voice is fond, bordering on sentimental. And he's right. This was my decision. It all has been, right down to picking up the athame when I was fourteen.

'Colin wants to see you,' he says, and puts his hand on Thomas's shoulder to indicate that it has to be alone. He'd probably put his other hand on Carmel's shoulder too if he didn't mind having it bitten off. Either way, he won't leave them alone. So I guess I don't have to worry, for now.

A woman leads me through the hallways and up the staircase to where Burke waits. She's the first woman

I've seen, and it's sort of a relief to know that there are women, even if this one is slightly creepy. She's about fifty, with a stylish ash-blond bob. When we met outside the room they gave me, she smiled and nodded with the practiced, disaffected politeness of a society matron. We pass rooms with wide, open double doors, and there's a burning fireplace in every one. In one of them on my left, there's a group of people sitting in a circle. As we pass, they all turn their heads to watch. And I mean they all do. Together, like at the same time.

'Uh, what are they doing?' I ask.

'Praying,' she smiles. I want to ask to what, but I'm scared that she'd say they were praying to the athame. It's hard to think of Jestine being raised by these people. Every one of them is creepy. Even Dr Clements, when he washed and wrapped my hand, he looked at the blood like it was the Holy Grail. He'll probably burn the bandages in a brazier of sage or something.

'Here we are,' says my escort. Then she just stands there, beside the door, even though I make gestures to imply that she can leave. Freaks.

When I go into the room, Colin Burke is standing near yet another fireplace. He's got his fingers pressed together at the tips in that most dishonest of gestures, and the flames flicker red-orange across his cheekbones.

All at once I think of Faust.

'So, you're Theseus Lowood,' he says, and smiles.

'So, you're Colin Burke,' I say. Then I shrug. 'Actually, I've never heard of you.'

'Well.' He walks away from the fire to stand beside a tall leather chair. 'Some people keep their secrets better than others.'

Oh. So that's how it is.

I put my thumb and forefinger to my chin thoughtfully. 'I've heard that name before. Burke. An English serial killer, wasn't he?' I turn my palm up. 'Any relation?'

Behind the mild smile, he's gnashing his teeth. Good. And yet, in the back of my head I'm thinking that I shouldn't make an enemy of this guy. That I came here for his help. Then again, the front of my head is telling me that nothing I could do could make him more of an enemy.

Burke spreads his hands and smiles. It's a disconcertingly disarming gesture. Warm, and just this close to genuine.

'We're very pleased to have you here, Theseus Cassio Lowood,' he says. 'We have desired your return, for a long time.' He smiles again, even warmer. 'The warrior returns home.'

All this faux flattery. It's not enough to make me

forget he's a dick. Admittedly, though, he's sort of a charismatic dick.

'Pleased?' I ask. 'Then you must not know why I'm here.'

Burke looks down, almost regretfully, and his eyes flicker up, as gray as his hair. 'You've had a hard day of travel. We can talk about that later. Over dinner perhaps. I've arranged a welcome meal, to give the other members a chance to meet you. They're all curious.'

'Listen,' I say, 'That's – that's really nice of you and everything. But I don't have time—'

'I know why you're here,' he says sharply. 'Take my advice. Come to dinner. And let the others try to convince you not to die.'

There's a whole lot of smartass piled up on my tongue. But I manage to keep it down.

'Whatever you say,' I smile. 'You're the host.'

Walking with Thomas, Carmel, and Gideon to the dining room, I keep my eyes on the walls. There really are heads on the walls, elk and bear and some kind of goat. They make me think of Gideon's joke back at his place, about the eyes moving in the pictures around my house.

'Why are we doing this?' Carmel asks, staring at the goat head. 'I don't trust this place. And all these slaughtered animals are threatening to turn me vegan.'

Gideon smiles at that. 'We're doing this so that Colin can play the part of reasonable leader. He wants to kill you, Theseus.' The casual way he says it makes me sort of twitch. 'He wants to kill you and reclaim the athame for Jestine. Melt it down and re-forge it with her blood. In his mind, it'll be purified.'

'Then shouldn't we be running away?' Carmel asks. 'And why is he feeding him then?'

'Not everyone in the Order is convinced. They respect the old ways, and that includes the original warrior bloodline. They'll stand with you, if you swear to uphold the old tradition.'

'And if I won't?'

Gideon says nothing. We've reached the dining room, which isn't really any bigger than the other rooms. There is, of course, a fireplace in it, and a chandelier glints below the high ceiling, reflecting the yellow flame. There are at least a dozen people sitting at a table, being waited on by some more of the Fembot-like junior members. Jestine is nowhere to be seen. She's probably hidden away under guard, like a treasure. When we walk in, everyone stands. Burke is among them and manages to look like he's seated at the head, even though the table is round.

The man closest to me holds out his hand and smiles.

I shake it and he introduces himself as Ian Hindley. He's got thinning brown hair and a mustache. His smile seems genuine, and I wonder if he's a sympathizer. As I go along, shaking hands and hearing names, I can't tell which of them want to see me dead now from which of them will just want to later.

I'm seated beside Burke, and the food arrives almost immediately. Steak medallions and some kind of blackberry sauce. All of a sudden I'm inundated with small talk. Someone even asks me about school. I thought I would be too tense to eat. But when I look down, my plate is empty.

Their conversation is so nice, so pleasant, that I don't notice right away when it turns to tradition. The subject comes on slow and easy in my ears. Their words about the morality of the athame, and the intent of its creation, vibrate through like the buzzing of bees. It's interesting. It's another perspective. It's reasonable. If I swear to it, they'll stand behind me. If I swear to it, Anna stays in Hell.

My eyes start to wander around the table, across their laughing and smiling faces, over their eerily similar clothes. Gideon is talking amiably with them. So is Thomas, and even Carmel, their eyes lightly glazed. To my right, Burke sits, and the weight of his stare hasn't left my profile.

'They think they've got me,' I say, turning to him. 'But you know better, don't you?'

All at once the table falls silent. Like they hadn't really been having their own conversations at all.

Burke makes a pretty good show of looking around with regret.

'I had hoped that meeting the Order, and hearing your purpose, would keep you from making this mistake,' he says.

'Don't do it,' says a feminine voice, and I look across the table to see the ash-haired woman who walked with me earlier, whose name I now know to be Mary Ann Cotton. 'Don't profane yourself, or the Biodag Dubh.'

Oh, Mary Ann. Me and the Beedak Doo are just fine.

'This is a nice little cult you've got here, Burke,' I say.

'We are a sacred Order,' he corrects me.

'No. You're a cult. A buttoned-up, prissy British cult, but you're still a cult.' I turn to the rest of them and draw the athame out of my pocket, out of its sheath, letting them see the firelight reflect along the blade. 'This is mine,' I say over the top of their creepy sighs. 'It was my father's before me, and his father's before that. You want it back? I want a door to the other side, to free someone who doesn't belong there.'

It's so quiet that I can hear Gideon and Thomas push up their glasses. Then Burke says, 'We can't just take the athame back,' and when Dr Clements protests, making one last plea for the old bloodline, he holds up his hand and squashes it. 'The Biodag Dubh will forever serve your blood. Until that blood is extinguished.'

In the corner of my eye, I see Carmel's hand grip her chair, always ready to bludgeon something.

'This isn't the way,' Gideon says. 'You can't just murder the warrior.'

'You have no right to speak, Mr Palmer,' says a member with close-cut black hair. He's the youngest, probably the newest. 'You haven't been of the Order for decades.'

'Be that as it may,' Gideon goes on. 'You can't tell me that none of the rest of you don't feel the same. The bloodline has existed for thousands of years. And you're going to snuff it out, just because Colin says so?'

There's a ripple effect of people looking back and forth at each other, Thomas, Carmel, and me included.

'He's right,' says Dr Clements. 'Our will doesn't matter.'

'So what do you suggest?' Burke asks. 'That we open the door and allow a dead murderess back into the world? Do you think that's in accordance with the will of the athame?'

'Let the athame choose,' Clements says suddenly, like inspiration has struck. He looks around the table. 'Open the door and let Jestine go with him. Let them both go. The warrior who returns is the worthy bearer of the Biodag Dubh.'

'And what if neither of them returns?' someone asks. 'Then the athame will be lost!'

'What if he pulls the dead girl back?' asks someone else. 'She can't remain here. It can't be allowed.'

Thomas, Carmel, and I exchange glances. The resistance came from Burke's staunchest supporters, but the rest of the table seems to be with Dr Clements. Burke looks ready to chew glass, but in the next second, his face breaks into the warm, slightly embarrassed smile of a corrected man.

'Then that is what will be,' he says. 'If Theseus Cassio is willing to pay the price.'

Here we go.

'What's it going to cost?'

'Cost?' He smiles. 'Plenty. But we'll get to that in a moment.' Incredibly, he calls for coffee. 'When the athame was created, those who created it knew how to open a door to the other side. But those magics have been lost for centuries. For tens of centuries. Now the only way to open the door resides in your hand.'

I look down at the blade.

'The door can only be opened through the Biodag Dubh. You see, you've had the key the whole time. You just didn't know how to turn the lock.'

I'm getting tired of people talking about the knife like it isn't a knife. Like it's a gate, or a key, or a pair of ruby slippers.

'Just tell me what it's going to cost,' I say.

'The price,' he says, and smiles. 'The price is your life's blood, leaking out of your gut.'

Somewhere around me, Thomas and Carmel gasp. Burke looks regretful, but I don't believe it for a minute.

'If you insist,' he says. 'We can perform the ritual tomorrow evening.'

CHAPTER TWENTY-FOUR

My life's blood, leaking out of my guts. Oh, is that all? That's what I should have said. I shouldn't have let him see the fear shiver through me. I shouldn't have even clenched my jaw. It gave him too much satisfaction, knowing I was scared, and that I wasn't going to turn back. Because I'm not. Not even with Thomas and Carmel giving me their bug eyes.

'Come on,' I say. 'I knew from the beginning that it might end up like this. That I might have to walk a fine line between breathing and not breathing, if I was going to save her. We all did.'

'It's different when it's just a possibility,' Carmel says.

'It's still just a possibility. Have some faith.' My mouth is dry. Who am I trying to convince? They're going to practically gut me tomorrow, to open the door. To Hell. And once I bleed it open, they're going to shove me and Jestine through.

'Have some faith,' Carmel repeats, and nudges

Thomas to say something, but he won't. He's been behind me on this. All the way.

'This might not be such a great idea,' he whispers.

'Thomas.'

'Look, I didn't tell you everything my grandpa told me,' he says. 'They're not backing you. All of his friends, the voodooists, they're not looking out for you.' He glances at Carmel. 'They're looking out for us.'

Some kind of disgusted, disappointed sound comes out of my nose and throat, but it isn't real. It's not surprising. They made their position about bringing Anna back pretty clear from the start.

'They think it's out of their jurisdiction,' Thomas goes on. 'That it's the Order's business.'

'You don't have to explain it,' I say. Besides, that's just an excuse. No one but us wants Anna in the world. When I pull her out of Hell, it's going to be into a room of people who want to send her right back. She'd better be ready to fight. In my mind I see her, exploding into the room like a dark cloud, and lifting Colin Burke by his puppy scruff.

'We can find some other way to help Anna,' Carmel says. 'Don't make me call your mother.'

I half smile. My mother. Before I left for London she made me promise to remember that I'm her son. And I am. I'm the son she raised to fight, and do the right thing. Anna is trapped in the Obeahman's torture chamber. And that can't be left alone.

'Will you guys go find Gideon?' I ask them. 'I want you to – will you do something for me?'

The looks on their faces say they hope I'll still change my mind, but they nod.

'I want you to be there, for the ritual. I want you to be part of it.' As someone in my corner. Maybe just as witnesses.

They turn back down the hall, and Carmel tells me one more time to think about it; that I have a choice. But it's not a real choice. So they go, and I turn around to pace the halls of this fireplace-infested druid brain-washing summer camp. As I turn a corner to a long, red hall, Jestine's voice rings out.

'Oi, Cas, wait up.' She jogs to me. Her face is slack and serious. Without the confident smirk, she's changed entirely. 'They told me what you said,' she says, slightly flushed. 'What you decided.'

'What they decided,' I correct her. She looks at me evenly, waiting, but I don't know what for. Tomorrow night she and I are going completely off the map, to the other side, and only one of us is supposed to come back. 'You know what it means, don't you?'

'I don't think it means what you think it means,' she replies.

'Jesus,' I snap, turning away. 'I don't have time for riddles. And neither do you.'

'You can't be angry with me,' she says. The old smirk returns as she keeps pace. 'Not four hours ago I saved your best mate's life. If it hadn't been for me, that corpse would have chewed through his carotid faster than you could blink.'

'Thomas told me I shouldn't trust you. But I didn't think you were anything to worry about. Still don't.' She bristles at that, like I knew she would. Even if she knows it's a lie.

'None of this was my choice, right? You of all people should know what that's like.'

She's fidgeting while she walks. For all her tough talk, she must be terrified. Her hair hangs down her shoulders in damp, wavy strings. She must've had a shower. When it's wet it all looks dark gold. The red blends in, hidden.

'Stop looking at me like that,' she snaps. 'Like I'm going to try to kill you tomorrow.'

'You're not?' I ask. 'I sort of thought that was the point.'

Her eyes narrow. 'Does it make you nervous? Wondering who would win?' There's steel in her jaw and for a second I think I'm looking at a genuine crazy person. But then she shakes her head, and her frustrated expression looks a whole lot like Carmel's. 'Have you ever considered that I might have a plan?'

'I never considered that you didn't,' I reply. But what she calls a plan I call an agenda. 'Have you ever considered that it might be just a tiny bit unfair? What with me bleeding all my guts out.'

'Ha,' she scoffs. 'You think you're the only one? Blood is a one-passenger ticket.'

I stop walking.

'Jesus, Jestine. Say no.'

She smiles and shrugs, like being stuck like a pig happens to her every other Thursday. 'If you go, I go.'

We stand in silence. They mean for one of us to make it back with the athame. But what if neither of us brings it back? Part of me wonders if I could just lose the athame there forever, and they'd be without it; without a way to open the gate and without a purpose. Maybe then they would just disappear and get their hooks out of Jestine. But even as I wonder, the other part of me hisses that the athame is mine, that stupid blood-tie singing in my ears, and if the Order has its hooks into Jestine, the athame itself has its hooks into me.

Without a word, we start to walk together down the long hall. I'm so pent up and irritated with this place; I want to kick down the closed doors and break up a prayer circle, maybe juggle the athame with a couple of candles just to see the horrified looks on their faces and hear their screams of 'Sacrilege!'

'This is going to sound weird,' Jestine says. 'But can I hang out with you guys tonight? I'm not going to get much sleep, and' – she glances around guiltily – 'this place is giving me the creeps right now.'

When I walk in with Jestine, Thomas and Carmel are surprised, but they don't seem hostile. They're probably both pretty thankful that Thomas still has his whole carotid. Gideon is in the common area with them, sitting in a wingback chair. He'd been staring into the fire before we came in and doesn't really look focused now that we're here. The light from the fire digs into all of the creases of his face. For the first time since I've been here, he looks his age.

'Did you talk to the Order about being in the ritual?' I ask.

'Yes,' Carmel replies. 'They'll make sure we're ready. But I don't know how much good I'll do. I've been a little busy for extra witchcraft lessons.'

'Witch or not, you've got blood,' Gideon pipes up. 'And when the Order readies the door tomorrow, it's going to be the strongest spell anyone has attempted in perhaps the last fifty years. Every one of us will have to pay in, not just Theseus and Jestine.'

'You're going,' Thomas says to me, sort of dazedly. 'I guess I hadn't thought of that. I thought we'd just pull her back. That you'd stay here. That we'd be there.'

I smile. 'Get that guilty look off your face. A corpse just tried to eat you. You've done enough.' It doesn't do any good though; I can see it behind his eyes. He's still trying to think of more.

They all look at me. There's fear in them, but not terror. And there's no reservation. Part of me wants to smack them upside their heads, call them lemmings and adrenaline junkies. But that isn't it. Not a single one of them would be here if not for me, and I don't know whether that's right or wrong. All I know is that I'm grateful. It's almost impossible to think that less than a year ago, I might've been alone.

Gideon said it would be a good idea to get some sleep, but none of us really listened. Not even him. He spent most of the night in the same wingback chair, dozing uneasily, on and off, jerking awake every time the fire crackled too loudly. The rest of us lay where we could without leaving the room, on one of the sofas, or curled up in a chair. The night passed quietly, all of us staying in our own heads. I think I passed out for a few hours around three or four in the morning. When I woke up it felt like the very next moment, except the fire was dead and pale, misty light was drifting in through the line of windows near the ceiling.

'We should eat something,' Jestine suggests. 'I'll be too nervous later on, and I don't fancy being bled dry on an empty stomach.' She stretches, and the joints of her neck crack in a long string of pops. 'Not a comfy chair. So, do you want to go find the kitchen?'

'The chef might not be there this early,' Gideon says.

'Chef?' Carmel exclaims. 'I could not give a shit about a chef. I'm going to find the most expensive thing in that kitchen, eat one bite, and throw the rest on the floor. Then I'm going to break some plates.'

'Carmel,' Thomas starts. He stops when she fixes her eyes on him, and I know he's reading her mind. 'Don't waste the food, at least,' he mumbles finally, and smiles.

'You three go ahead,' says Gideon, taking me by the arm. 'We'll catch up shortly.'

They nod and head for the door. When they turn into the hall, I hear Carmel mutter about how much she hates this place, and that she hopes Anna can somehow get it to implode like she did with the Victorian. It makes me smile. Then Gideon clears his throat.

'What is it?' I ask.

'It's the things that Colin didn't tell you. Things that you might not have considered.' He shrugs. 'Maybe just the useless hunches of an old man.'

'Dad always trusted your hunches,' I say. 'You always seemed to help him out.'

'Right until I couldn't,' he says. I guess it shouldn't surprise me that he still carries that around, even though what happened wasn't his fault. He'll feel the same way about me if I don't make it back. Maybe Thomas and Carmel will too, and it won't be their fault either.

'It's about Anna,' he says suddenly. 'Something that I've been pondering.'

'What is it?' I ask, and he doesn't reply. 'Come on, Gideon. You're the one who kept me back.'

He takes a deep breath and rubs his fingers along his forehead. He's trying to decide how, or where, to start. He's going to tell me again that I shouldn't be doing this, that she's where she should be, and I'm going to tell him again that I am doing it, and he should butt out.

'I don't think that Anna is in the right place,' he says. 'Or at least, not exactly.'

'What do you mean, exactly? Do you think she belongs on the other side, in Hell, or not?'

Gideon shakes his head, a frustrated gesture. 'The only thing anyone knows about the other side is that they know nothing. Listen. Anna opened a door to the other side and dragged the Obeahman down. To where? You said it seemed like they were trapped there, together.

'What if you were right? What if they're trapped there, like a cork in a bottleneck?'

'What if they are,' I whisper, even though I know.

'Then you might need to consider what you would choose,' Gideon replies. 'If there is a way to separate them, will you pull her back, or send her on?'

Send her on. To what? To some other dark place? Maybe someplace worse? There aren't any solid answers. Nobody knows. It's like the punch line from a bad spook story. What happened to the guy with the hook for a hand? *Nobody knows.*

'Do you think she deserves to be where she is?' I ask. 'And I'm asking you. Not a book or a philosophy, or the Order.'

'I don't know what decides these things,' he says. 'If there's judgment from a higher power, or just the guilt trapped inside the spirit. We don't get to decide.'

Jesus, Gideon. That's not what I asked. I'm about ready to tell him I expected a better answer when he says, 'But from what you've told me, this girl has had her share of torment. If I were cast as her judge, I couldn't condemn her to more.'

'Thank you, Gideon,' I say, and he bites his tongue on the rest. None of us knows what's going to happen tonight. There's a weird sensation of unreality, laced with denial, like it's never going to happen, it's so far away, when the time remaining is measurable in hours. How can it be that in that small space of time, I could see her again? I could touch her. I could pull her out of the dark.

Or send her into the light.

Shut up. Don't complicate things.

We walk side by side to the kitchen. Carmel has stayed true to her word and has broken at least one dish. I nod at her, and she blushes. She knows it's petty, and that it doesn't make an ounce of difference to the Order if she breaks twelve entire place settings. But these people make her feel powerless.

When we eat it's surprising just how much we manage to put away. Gideon whips up some hollandaise and assembles some wicked eggs Benedict with a heaping side of sausage. Jestine broils six of the biggest, reddest grapefruits I've ever seen, with honey and sugar.

'We should keep as many eyes trained on the Order as we can,' says Thomas between bites. 'I don't trust them as far as I can throw them. Carmel and I can keep tabs while we help prepare the ritual.'

'Make sure to put in a call to your grandfather as well,' says Gideon, and Thomas looks up, surprised.

'Do you know my grandfather?'

'Only by reputation,' Gideon replies.

'He already knows,' says Thomas, looking down.

'He'll have the entire voodoo network on standby. They'll be watching our backs from their side of the world.'

The entire voodoo network. I chew my food quietly. It would have been nice to have Morfran in my corner. It would have been like having a hurricane up my sleeve.

In observation of Carmel's rebellion, we left the kitchen a complete disaster. After we got ourselves cleaned up, Gideon took Thomas and Carmel to meet with the Order members. Jestine and I decided to walk the grounds, to nose around and maybe just to kill time.

'They'll be coming for one or the other of us before long,' I say as we walk the edge of the tree line, listening to the trickling whisper of a stream not far off.

'For what?' Jestine asks.

'Well, to instruct us on the ritual,' I reply, and she shakes her head.

'Don't expect too much, Cas. You're just the instrument, remember?' She snags a twig off a low-hanging branch and pokes me in the chest with it.

'So they're just going to shove us through blind and hope we're good at winging it?' I shrug. 'That's either stupid, or really flattering.'

Jestine smiles and stops walking. 'Are you scared?'

'Of you?' I ask, and she grins. There's early adrenaline

coursing through both of us, springy tension in our muscles, tiny, silver fish darting through my capillaries. When she swings her twig at my head, I see it coming a mile away and trip her up with my toe. Her response is a crisp elbow at my head and a laugh, but her moves are serious. She's practiced and fluid; well trained. She's got counters I haven't seen before, and when she catches me in the gut I wince, even though she's pulling her punches. But I still knock her backward and block more than she lands. The athame is still in my pocket. This isn't half of what I can do. Without it, though, we're almost an even match. When we stop our pulses are up and the adrenaline twitch is gone. Good. It's annoying when it doesn't have anywhere to go, like waking up from a nightmare.

'You don't have much of a problem hitting girls,' she says.

'You don't have much of a problem hitting boys,' I reply. 'But this isn't real. Tonight will be. If you leave me on the other side, I'm as good as dead.'

She nods. 'The Order of the Biodag Dubh was entrusted with a duty. You corrupt it by bringing back a dead murderess.'

'She's not a murderess anymore. She never really was. It was a curse.' What's so hard to understand about that? But what did I expect? You can't rinse the cult off a person in only a couple of days. 'What do you know about this anyway? And I mean really know. What have you seen? Anything? Or do you just swallow what you're told?'

She glares at me resentfully, like I'm being unfair. But she's probably going to try to kill me, and kill me *righteously*, so eff you very much.

'I know plenty.' She smiles. 'You might take me for a mindless drone, but I learn. I listen. I investigate. Far more than you do. Do you even know how the athame functions?'

'I stab. Things go away.'

She laughs and mutters something under her breath. I think I catch the phrase 'blunt instrument.' Emphasis on the 'blunt.'

'The athame and the other side are linked,' she says. 'It comes from there. That is how it functions.'

'You mean it comes from Hell,' I say. In my pocket, the athame shifts, like its ears were pricked at the subject.

'Hell. Abbadon. Acheron. Hades. The other side. Those are just names that people call the place where dead things go.' Jestine shakes her head. Her shoulders slump with sudden exhaustion. 'We don't have much time,' she says. 'And you're still looking at me like I'm going to steal your lunch money. I don't want you dead,

Cas. I'd never want that. I just don't understand why you want the things that you do.'

Maybe it's the minor scuffle we just had, but her fatigue is contagious. I wish she wasn't mixed up in this. Despite everything, I like her. But you know what they say about wishing in one hand. She moves closer, and her fingers trace the line of my jaw. I take them away, but gently.

'Tell me about her, at least,' she says.

'What do you want to know?' I ask, and look off into the trees.

'Anything,' she shrugs. 'What's made her so special? What made you so special to her, that she'd send herself into oblivion for you?'

'I don't know,' I say. Why did I say that? I do know. I knew it the moment I heard Anna's name, and the first time she spoke. I knew when I walked out of her house with my insides still on the inside. It was admiration, and understanding. I'd never known anything like it, and neither had she.

'Well, tell me what she looked like then,' Jestine says. 'If we're going to bleed to death looking for her, I'd like to know who we're looking for.'

I reach into my pocket for my wallet and fish out the newspaper photo of Anna when she was alive. I hand it to Jestine.

'She's pretty,' she comments after a few moments. Pretty. That's what everyone says. My mom said it, and so did Carmel. But when they said it, it sounded like a lament, like it was a shame that such beauty was lost. When Jestine said it, it sounded derisive, like it was the only nice thing she could think of to say. Or maybe I'm just being defensive. Whatever it is, I hold my hand out for the picture and put it back in my wallet.

'It doesn't do her justice,' I say. 'She's fierce. Stronger than any of us.'

Jestine shrugs, a 'whatever' move. My hackles rise another few inches. But it doesn't matter. In a few hours, she'll see Anna for herself. She'll see her dressed in blood, her hair floating like it's suspended in water, eyes black and shining. And when she does, she won't be able to catch her breath.

Chapter Twenty-five

J estine was wrong. The Order did show up to take one of us. They took her, just before sunset. Two women walked up without a word. They weren't much older than us, both with stark black hair left loose and hanging. Jestine introduced them as Hardy and Wright. I guess junior members go by their last names. Either that or their parents are jerks.

Gideon came for me not much later. He found me wandering under the lampposts along the paved footpath. Good thing, too. The adrenaline had set in again, and I was this close to doing wind sprints. He led me back to the compound and through the buildings to his room, where rows of white candles had burnt down to nubs, and three of the dummy athames rested on red velvet.

'So,' I say as he closes the door. 'What can you tell me about this ritual?'

'I can tell you that it begins soon,' he replies. Vague. It's like I'm talking to Morfran.

'Where are Carmel and Thomas?'

'They'll be along,' he says. A smile breaks the solemnity of his face. 'That girl,' he chuckles. 'She's a firecracker. I've never heard such a tongue. Normally I'd say she was insolent, but under the circumstances – it was rather lovely to see Colin's face turn that shade of red.' He cocks an eyebrow at me. 'Why didn't you pursue her?'

Carmel, antagonizing Burke all day long. I wish I could've seen it.

'Thomas beat me to it,' I reply, and grin.

Our smiles fade slowly, and I stare at the shrinking candles. The flames float on the wicks, so small. It's strange to think that they can reduce the wax pillar to nothing. Gideon goes to his closet and slides the door wide. At first it looks like he's reaching for a bundle of red curtains, but when he lays them out on the bed, I see that they're actually ceremonial robes, just like the one he was wearing in Thomas's stolen photo.

'Ah,' I say. 'I was wondering when the robes and censers were going to show up.'

Gideon straightens both robes, pulling at the hoods and sleeves. I'm wearing an army-green t-shirt and jeans. It feels fine to me. The robes look like they weigh twenty pounds separately.

'Is wearing one of those going to help me with the

spell?' I ask. 'I mean, come on, you know most of the ceremony is just ceremony.'

'The ceremony is just ceremony,' he repeats, sort of like my mom does. 'No, it won't really help you. It's only tradition.'

'Then forget it,' I say, eyeballing the plain rope that ties around the waist. 'Tradition can shove it. And besides, Anna would laugh her ass off.'

His shoulders slump and I brace for impact. He's going to yell now, about how I never take things seriously, about how I never show respect. When he turns I step back, and he grabs me by the shoulder.

'Theseus, if you walk out that door right now, they'll let you go.'

I look at him. His eyes are shining, almost shaking behind his wire glasses. They'll let me go, he said. Maybe they would and maybe they wouldn't. Burke would probably come after me with a candlestick if I tried, and the whole thing would turn into a life-size game of Clue. I tug free gently.

'Tell Mom,' I say, and then stop. My mind is blank. Her face floats in it for a second, and disappears. 'I don't know. Tell her something good.'

'Knock, knock,' Thomas says, and pokes his head in. When the rest of him follows and Carmel after that, I can't suppress a smile. They're both wearing long, red

317

robes, the hoods down in the back and the sleeves hanging over their hands.

'You guys look like Christmas monks,' I say. The toes of Thomas's Converses poke out at the bottom. 'You know you don't have to wear those.'

'We didn't want to, but Colin had a bird.' Carmel rolls her eyes. 'They're really heavy. And sort of itchy.'

Behind us, Gideon takes his robe off of the hanger and puts it on. He tightens the waist and straightens the hood on his back. Then he takes one of the dummy knives from the velvet and tucks it into the rope at his hip.

'You'll each need one,' he says to Thomas and Carmel. 'They've already been sharpened.'

They exchange a look, but neither one turns green when they go over and take a knife.

'I talked to my grandfather,' says Thomas. 'He says we're idiots.'

'We?'

'Well, mostly you.' We smile. I might be an idiot, but Morfran will be watching. If Thomas needs protection, he can send it from across the ocean.

I clear my throat. 'Listen, I – I don't know what kind of shape we're going to be in when we get back. If they try to do something to Anna—'

'I'm pretty sure Anna could rend the Order into bits,'

Thomas says. 'But just in case, I know some tricks to slow them down.'

Carmel smiles. 'I should've brought my bat.' A strange look comes on to her face.

'Has anyone considered how we're getting Anna back to Thunder Bay?' she asks. 'I mean, I'm pretty sure her passport has expired.'

I laugh, and so do the others, even Gideon.

'You two had better go along,' Gideon says, and motions out the door. 'We'll be right behind.'

They nod and touch my arm as they pass.

'Do I need to ask you to make sure they're safe, if – ?' I ask Gideon after they're gone.

'No,' he replies. He puts his hand on my shoulder, heavily. 'I swear that you don't.'

In the space of a day, this place has aged a century. Electricity has been exchanged for candlelight. It flickers along the walls of the halls and bounces across the stone surface of the floor. Business attire is gone too; every person we pass has robed up, and each time we go by they make this gesture of blessing and prayer. Or maybe it's a hex, depending on the person. I don't do anything in return. Only one hand gesture springs to mind, and it just isn't appropriate.

Gideon and I move through the maze of passages

and connected rooms until we stand in front of a set of tall oak double doors. Before I can ask where the Order keeps the battering ram, the doors open from the inside to reveal a stone staircase, twisting down into the dark.

'Torch,' Gideon says tersely, and one of the people near the door hand him one. The light reveals finely carved granite steps. I expected them to be dark and wet; primitive.

'Careful,' I say when Gideon starts down.

'I won't fall,' he replies. 'What do you think I grabbed the torch for?'

'It's not that. I was mostly thinking that you'd trip on the robe and break your neck.'

He grumbles something about being perfectly capable, but he steps carefully. I follow and do the same thing. Torch or no torch, the stairs are dizzying. There's no handrail and they twist tightly around and around until my sense of direction is shot and I have no idea how far we've descended. The air is progressively colder, and damper. It feels like we're walking down the throat of a whale.

When we reach the bottom, we have to curl around a wall, so the candlelight hits us suddenly as we walk into the large, circular space. Candles line the wall in three rows: one row of white pillars and one row of black. The center row is a pattern of both. They sit on shelves carved into the rock.

The robes are standing in the center in a semicircle that's waiting to close. Only the senior-most members of the Order are present, and I look at their faces, all old and anonymous, except for Thomas and Carmel. I wish they'd put the hoods down. They look weird with their hair obscured. Burke is of course standing at the center like a keystone. He doesn't make any show of warmth this time. His features are cut sharp in the candlelight, and that's just how I'll remember him. Looking like a jerk.

Thomas and Carmel are on the edge of the semicircle, Thomas trying not to look out of place and Carmel not giving a shit one way or the other. They give me nervous smiles, and I eyeball the Order members. At each one of their belts glitters a sharpened knife; I glance at Gideon. If this goes wrong, he'd better have some kind of trick up his sleeve, or he, Thomas, and Carmel will all be Julius Caesar'ed before he says two words.

Thomas locks eyes with me, and we glance up. The ceiling isn't visible. It's too high for the candlelight to reach. I look at Thomas again and his eyes widen. We hate this place. It feels like it's underneath everything. Underground. Underwater. A bad place to die.

No one has said anything since Gideon and I arrived.

I feel their eyes, though, on my face and flickering over the knife handle in my back pocket. They want me to take it out. They want to see it, to ooh and aah over it one more time. Well, forget it, assholes. I'm going through the gate, finding my girl, and coming back out again. Then we'll see what you have to say.

My hands have started to shake; I clench them up tight. Behind us, footsteps echo down the stairway. Jestine is being led in by Hardy and Wright, but led is the wrong word. Escorted is better. To the Order, this show is all about her.

They let her go without a red robe too. Or maybe she refused it. When I look at her, there's still a persistent twinge in my gut saying she's not my enemy, and it's hard not to trust it after so long even if it seems crazy. She walks into the circle and her escorts retreat back up the stairs. The robed circle closes up behind her, leaving us alone in the center. She acknowledges the Order and then looks at me, tries to smirk, and falters. She's wearing a white tank and low-riding black pants. There are no visible talismans, or medallions, or jewelry. But I catch a whiff of rosemary. She's been anointed for protection. Around her leg is a strap that looks to contain a knife, and there's a similar one strapped to her other thigh. Somewhere, Lara Croft is wanting her look back.

'Can we really not change your mind?' Burke asks without an ounce of sincerity.

'Just get on with it,' I mutter. He smiles without showing his teeth. Some people can't make anything but dishonest faces.

'The circle has already been cast,' he says mildly. 'The gateway is clear. All that remains is to swing it wide. But first, you must choose your anchor.'

'My anchor?'

'The person who will serve as your link to this plane. Without them, you wouldn't be able to find your way back. You must each choose.'

My mind flickers to Gideon. Then I look left.

'Thomas,' I say.

His eyes widen. I think he's trying to look flattered but succeeds in just looking sick to his stomach.

'Colin Burke,' Jestine says beside me. No big surprise there.

Thomas swallows and steps forward. He draws the dummy athame from his belt and wraps his fist around the blade. When he pulls the edge against his palm, he manages to keep from flinching, even as the blood wells and spills out the side of his fist. He wipes the athame on his robe and slides it back into his belt, then dips his thumb into the blood pooling in his palm. It's warm when he smears a small crescent onto my forehead, just above my brow. I nod at him as he backs up. Beside him, Carmel's eyes are wide. They both thought I'd choose Gideon. I thought so too until I opened my mouth.

I turn; Burke and Jestine repeat the ritual. His blood is shining and crimson against her skin. When she turns to face me, I fight the urge to wipe it off. She swallows hard, and her eyes are bright. Adrenaline is releasing into our blood, making the world sharper, clearer, more immediate. It's not the same as when I hold the athame but it's close. At a nod from Burke, the rest of the Order pull their knives out. Carmel is only a half step behind them as they all drag the blades across their palms; her eyes narrow at the brief sting. Then all of them, Thomas and Burke included, turn their hands over, allowing the blood to drip onto the floor, spattering onto a mosaic of pale yellow asymmetrical tiles. When the droplets strike, the flames on the candles flare and energy like the waves over intense heat rushes to the center and reverberates outward. I can feel it, beneath my feet, changing the surface. Just how is hard to describe. It's like the ground beneath our shoes is becoming *less*. Like it's thinning out, or losing a dimension. We're standing on a surface that isn't a surface anymore.

'It's time, Cas,' Jestine says.

'Time,' I say.

'They've done their part, paving the way. But they can't open the door. That you have to do yourself.'

Magic is swimming through my head in a torrent. Looking around the circle, I can barely distinguish Carmel and Gideon from the others. Beneath the hoods, their features have blurred. Then I catch sight of Thomas, so clear that he might as well be sparkling, and my stomach drops down a few inches in my throat. My arm moves; I don't realize that I'm reaching for the athame until it's in my hand, until I'm looking down at it, the flames from the candles flickering orange on the blade.

'I have to go first,' says Jestine. She's standing square to me. The athame is pointed toward her stomach.

'No.' I pull back but she grabs my shoulder. I didn't know this is what they meant. I thought it would be Burke. I thought it would be a shallow cut on the arm. I don't know what I thought. I didn't think anything; I didn't want to. I back up another step.

'If you go, I go,' Jestine says from between clenched teeth. Before I can react, she grasps my hand where it holds the athame and plunges it deep into her side. I watch the blade sink in like a nightmare, slow but so easily, like it was sliding through water. When it comes out it shines a translucent red.

'Jestine!' I shout. The word dies loud in my ears. The

walls give off no echo. Her body folds up and she sinks to her knees. She's clutching at her side; only the smallest bit of blood breaks through her fingers, but I know it's worse than that.

Her life's blood.

As I watch, she loses a dimension, becomes less, like the air around us and the floor beneath our feet. She's gone, crossed over. What's left is hollowed out, nothing more than a place marker.

I look down at her, hypnotized, and turn the athame inward. When it breaks through my skin the world spins. It feels like my mind is being pulled out through a pinhole. I clench my jaw and press harder, thinking of Jestine, thinking of Anna. My knees hit the floor, and the light goes out.

CHAPTER TWENTY-SIX

There is nothing good here. There never has been. My cheek lies pressed against a surface that is neither hot nor cold, neither dull nor sharp. But it is hard. Everywhere my body touches it is about to shatter. This was a mistake. We don't belong here. Wherever it is, it is the lack of everything. No light, no darkness. No air or taste. It's nothing; a void.

I don't want to think anymore. My eyes might pop and run out of my head. I might break my skull against the bottom and listen to the empty pieces, wobbling like the discarded shell of an egg.

(Cas, open your eyes.)

My eyes are open. There isn't anything to see.

(You have to open your eyes. You have to breathe.)

This place is the thing behind madness. There is nothing good here. Off the map. If you eat frustration it chokes you. This place exists in the wake of a scream.

(Listen to my voice. Listen. I'm here. It's difficult, but

you have to *make* it. In your mind. Form it in your mind.)

Mind is unraveling. Can't make it stay together. Come all this way to drift off and break apart. There are things people need. Air. Water. Laughter. Strength. Breath.

Breathe.

'That's it,' says Jestine. 'Take it slow.' Her face materializes like fog in a mirror and the rest of the world follows suit, filling in like a paint-by-number. I'm lying on what feels like stone in a gravity chamber, heavy density against my skull, dug up against my shoulder blades. This must be how a caught fish feels, pulled up onto a dock, the wood pressing into its gills and eye when nothing has ever pressed against it before. Their gills throb to no use. My lungs pull to no use. Something is moving in and out of them, but it isn't air. There's no sensation of nourishment hitting my blood. I grab my chest.

'Don't panic about that. Just keep breathing. It doesn't matter if it's real or not. Let it feel familiar.' She grabs on to my arms; she feels so warm, warmer than anything I remember. I don't know how long we've been here. It feels like hours. It feels like a second. They could be the same thing.

'It's all about the mind,' she says. 'That's what we are.

Look.' She touches my stomach, and I wince, anticipating pain. Only there isn't any. The wound isn't there. It should be there. There should be a hole ripped in my t-shirt and blood should have spread out in a circle. The knife should be sticking out of me.

'No, you don't need that,' she says. I look down again. Where there was nothing, now there's a small tear and a dark patch of wetness. 'You don't need that,' she says again. 'That still exists. Over there. On the other side, our bodies are bleeding out. If we don't make it back before they're empty, we'll be dead.'

'How do we get back?'

'Look behind you.'

Behind me there is stone. I'm lying on my back. But I turn my head slightly.

Thomas. I can see him. And if I focus, the window widens to reveal the rest of the room. The Order's cuts are still open, dripping slowly to the floor. Our bodies are there, mine and Jestine's, curled up where they fell.

'We're on the other side of the mirror,' I say.

'In a manner of speaking. But really, we're still there. We're still alive. The only thing that came, physically, is the athame.'

I look down. It's in my hand, and there is no blood on the blade. I squeeze it, and the action brings emotion in a wave. The familiarity in this place of nothing almost makes me want to plunge it into my stomach again.

'You have to stand up now.' Jestine rises to her feet. She's shades brighter than everything else. She holds out her hand, and behind her head there is endless black sky. No stars. No edges.

'How do you know all this?' I ask, and struggle up without help. Wherever we are, there aren't any rules of perspective. It seems like I can see forever and yet only a few feet in every direction. And there's no light. At least not light how we would recognize it. Things simply are. And what they are is flat stone, cliff-carved walls of something that might be gray and might be black.

'The Order kept records of when they retrieved the metal for the athame. Most are lost and what's left is dodgy, but I studied every last bit.'

'Are you going to try to ditch me in here, Jestine?'

She glances down and to the side. I can't see anything behind her, but if I look back and see Thomas, then she must look back and see Burke. He's her anchor.

'If you die here then this is where you belong.'

'Does anything really belong here?'

'I'm not here to help you get the girl out. I have my own plan.'

I squeeze the athame tighter. At least Anna is 'the girl' now, and not 'the dead murderess.'

'How long do we have?' I ask.

'Until we have no more.' Jestine shrugs. 'It's hard to say. Time isn't the same here. Time isn't time here. There aren't any rules. I don't wear a watch, but if I did I'd be scared to look at it. The hands would probably be doing that weird out-of-control spin. How long do you think it's been, since you started to bleed?'

'Does it matter? I'd be wrong, wouldn't I?'

She smiles. 'Exactly.'

I look around. This place looks the same in all directions. Even stranger is the fact that despite knowing that I'm dying somewhere behind me, there is no sense of urgency. I might stand in the same place and look around passively for Anna until it's been too late for days, until my body on the other side had been sent home and buried. It's an act of will to make my legs move. Everything here is an act of will.

When I walk, the stone juts sharply into my feet like I'm not wearing any shoes. Apparently shoes of the mind have really shitty tread.

'This is pointless,' I say. 'She isn't anywhere. There isn't anywhere for her to be. It's an expanse.'

'If you're looking for her, then you'll turn a corner and there she'll be,' replies Jestine.

'There aren't any corners to turn.'

'There are corners everywhere.'

'I hate you.' I lift my brows at her and she smiles. She's looking too, eyes rolling from side to side desperately. I have to remind myself that she was chosen, and it's the Order's fault, not hers, that she's lying bleeding by my side. She's got to be scared. And she's turning out to be a better guide than I could have asked for.

A wall appears all at once in front of us, a black, porous stone wall that seeps water like the bedrock along the roads on the way to Thunder Bay. Turning my head, I see other walls too, to my left and right. They stretch out behind us in a line for miles, like we've been walking in a maze. Except that we hadn't been until just now. I twist my head more sharply to look back through the window at Thomas. He's still there, my anchor. Do we keep walking, or turn around? Is this the way? His face doesn't react to these questions. His eyes are trained on my body, watching the blood saturate my shirt.

We're passing by something, lying on the ground. It's a carcass, busily being worked on by bugs. The fur of whatever it was used to be white, but aside from the presence of four legs it could have been anything. A dog maybe, or a big cat. It might've been a small calf. We walk past without comment and I try to keep my eyes off of the movement beneath the hide. It doesn't matter. It's not what we're looking for.

'What's that say?' Jestine asks, and points to the wall ahead. It's not a wall really, but a low limestone formation, white and eroded, low enough to climb over. There's wet black paint on it that says MARINETTE OF THE DRY ARMS. Beside it is what looks like a rough sketch: the blackened bones of forearms and fingers and a thick black cross. I don't know what it means. But I suspect that Morfran would.

'We shouldn't go this way,' I say.

'There's really only one way to go.' Jestine shrugs.

Ahead the wall changes, from porous wet rock back to colorless stone. As we get closer, I blink and it turns translucent, like thick, dusty crystal or glass. There's a pale mass at the center, something frozen or trapped. I wipe across the stone with my hand, feeling the granular dust slide against my palm. It reveals a pair of eyes, wide and yellowed and full of hate. I clear the glass lower as my hand drags down, and see that the front of his white shirt still bears the bloodstains of his wife. His widow's peak of hair is wild and suspended in the rock. It's Peter Carver. The first ghost I ever killed.

'What is it?' Jestine asks.

'Just a scarecrow,' I reply.

'Yours or hers?'

'Mine.' I stare into his frozen face and remember the way he chased me, the way he scrambled after me across the floor, his stomach sliding and legs flopping uselessly. A crack forms in the glass.

'Don't fear it,' Jestine says. 'He's just a scarecrow, like you said. Your scarecrow.'

The crack is a tiny hairline fracture, but it's getting longer. As I watch, it races upward, crackling across the bloodstain on his shirt like a lightning bolt.

'Focus,' Jestine hisses. 'Before you let it out of the rock.'

'I can't,' I say. 'I don't know what you mean. We just have to go. We have to keep going.' I walk away. My heavy legs move as fast as I can manage. I turn a corner and then another. It feels like running and it's stupid. The last thing we need is to be lost. The last thing we need is to not pay attention and the path to turn into a cave. My legs slow. There are no scraping sounds behind us. Peter Carver isn't dragging himself along in our footsteps. For all I know, I might've imagined the fissure in the rock to begin with.

'I don't think anything happened,' I say, but she doesn't reply. 'Jestine?' I look around. She isn't here. Without thinking, I go back the way I came. I shouldn't have run. Leaving her in front of Carver, thinking she was the one who had to do something about it. What the hell is the matter with me?

'Jestine!' I call out, and wish that my voice would

ring off the stones rather than fall flat. No sound comes back, not mine or her answering yell. I turn a corner, then another. She isn't there. And neither is Peter Carver. They're both gone.

'It was here,' I say to no one. It was. It's just that coming back the way I came didn't work. None of the walls look the way they did when I passed by the first time.

'Jestine!'

Nothing. Why didn't she tell me we couldn't separate? Why didn't she follow me? My stomach hurts. I put my hand against it and feel warm wetness. The wound is coming through.

I don't need that. I left that behind. I need to focus. To find Anna, and Jestine.

A few deep breaths and my hand comes away dry. Wind passes over my cheeks, the first sensation of that kind since I've been here. It brings noise with it. A manic, girlish giggle that sounds nothing like Jestine or Anna. I hate this place. Even the wind is nuts. Footsteps patter behind me, but nothing's there when I turn. What am I doing here? It feels like forgetting. There's pressure against my shoulder; I'm leaning against the cliffside. When the wind brings the laughter again, I close my eyes until I feel her hair brush against my cheek.

She's sunk half in and half out of the rock. Her eyes are bloodless, but she looks a whole lot like Cait Hecht.

'Emily Danagger,' I whisper, and she smiles without humor as she melts backward. The instant she's gone her footsteps sound behind me, running closer. It sends me stumbling forward. I twist through rock formations that look like spined fossils and trip over stones that weren't there before I hit them. Just another scarecrow, I keep thinking, but I don't know how long I run before the wind changes from a giggle to harsh, unintelligible muttering. It gives me such an urge to clamp my hands over my ears that at first I don't notice the other thing that it carries: a strong smell of sweet smoke. The same smoke that spat down over my bed last fall. The same smoke my father smelled right before he died. It's the Obeahman. He's here. He's close.

All at once my legs feel pounds lighter. The athame sings in my hand. What was it Jestine said? If I'm looking for her, I'll turn a corner and she'll be there. But what about him? Should I be so eager? What can he do to me anyway, in this place?

It happens just like she said it would. One corner of stone and there he is, at the end of the maze of walls, as if it was leading me to him.

The Obeahman. The athame spins deftly between my fingers. I've been waiting for this. And I didn't know that until right now. Looking at him, at his hunched back, clothed in the same long, dark green jacket, the same rotting dreadlocks hanging over his shoulders, my stomach twists like an eel. Murderer. MURDERER. You ate my father in a house in Baton Rouge. You stole the power of the knife and took in every ghost I meant to send away.

But even as my brain screams these things, my body stays hidden behind the stone wall in a half-crouch. I wish I'd asked Jestine what could happen to us here. Is it like they say in dreams? That when you die in them, you die for real? I slide closer to the edge, letting a sliver of eye show around the corner. If it's possible, the Obeahman is bigger than I remember. His legs seem longer, and there are more bends to his back. It's like seeing him through a funhouse mirror, elongated and unnatural. He still hasn't seen me, hasn't smelled me or heard me. He's just bent over a low, flat stone, his arms working like a spider at a web, and I could swear that each arm has grown an extra joint.

I remember the spell using the Lappish drum, and how frightened Anna seemed. She said this was his world.

The Obeahman pulls hard at something. He tugs and jerks; it looks like white string, the kind a butcher uses to tie up a roast. When he pulls the string again he raises his arm, and I count four distinct joints.

Rushing in would be a mistake. I need to know more. Looking around the maze walls, there's a set of rough-cut steps to my right. I didn't notice them when I passed. Probably because they hadn't been there. I climb up silently, and when I reach the top I drop down on my hands and creep to the edge. I have to dig my fingers in to keep from throwing myself over it.

It's Anna on the rock. He's got her lying there as on a mortuary slab. Her body is wrapped round and round with white string, stained dark with blood in places. The jerking motion I watched him do with his arms was from sewing her mouth and eyes shut.

I can't look, but my eyes won't close as he ties his knots and slices through the string with his fingers. When he straightens and surveys his work, one hand cradles her head like she's a doll. He bends close to her face, maybe to whisper, or to kiss her on the cheek. Then his jointed arm snaps back into the air, and I see that his fingers have sharpened into points before he shoves them deep down into her gut.

'No!' The scream rips out of me as her body contracts, her head whipping back and forth, her eyes sewn shut against tears, mouth sewn shut against noise.

The Obeahman twists his face upward. The look of shock is unmistakable, even though his eyes are sewn shut too, crisscrossed slits laced through with black string. The crosses of black seem to hover over his face in a psychedelic scribble and the eyes behind them bulge and bleed. It wasn't like that before, when he was just a ghost. What is he now?

I flash the knife and he roars with a sound that only machines make; it has no discernible emotion, so I can't tell if he's afraid, or enraged, or just insane. The sight of the knife backs him off though, and he turns and disappears into the rocks.

I don't waste any time, scrambling off the rock like a crab, afraid to let Anna out of my sight, not wanting this place to swallow her up like it did Jestine. My landing has no grace, hard and mostly on my hip and shoulder. It hurts, a lot, and there's a tender spot in my gut that feels like a bad bruise. 'Anna, it's me.' I don't know what else to say. My voice doesn't seem to be easing her mind. She's still thrashing, and her fingers twitch at her sides, stiff as a bundle of sticks. Then she slumps back and lies flat.

I glance around, and take a deep breath. There's no scent or sign of the Obeahman, and the passageway where he disappeared into the rock is gone. Good. I hope he gets lost as shit. But somehow I don't think he will. This place feels like his place, like he's cozy here as a dog in its own backyard.

'Anna.' My fingers trace lightly over the string and I consider the athame. If she thrashes again, I could end up cutting her. Dark, almost black blood is spreading around the wound he made in her stomach, staining the string and the white fabric of her dress. It makes it hard for me to swallow, or think. 'Anna, don't – ' I almost said, *Anna, don't die*, but that's stupid. She was dead when I met her. Focus, Cas.

And then, almost like I wished it, the string unwinds. It snakes back off of her body, like it was never there at all, and the blood goes with it. Even the string zigzagged across her eyelids and lips slides free and disappears, leaving no holes behind. Her eyes open and focus on me warily. She pushes up onto her elbows and pulls in a breath through her mouth. Her eyes stare ahead. They aren't panicked. They aren't tormented. They're vacant, and don't seem to see me at all.Her name. I should say her name. I should say something, but there's something different about her, something disconnected. This feels like the first time I saw her, coming down the stairs in a dripping red dress. I was in awe. I couldn't blink. But I wasn't afraid. This time I am; I'm afraid that she won't be the same. That she won't understand me or know who I am. And maybe part of me is afraid that if I move too quickly, those granite fingers of hers will shoot out and squeeze the words from my throat.

The corner of her mouth twitches.

'You're not real,' she says.

'You're not either,' I say. Anna's eyes blink once, and swivel my way. The instant before I look into them there's a flash of panic, but as her eyes travel up from my stomach and over my chest, there's so much skepticism in them and so much quiet hope that all I can think is, there's my girl, there's my girl, there's my girl. Her eyes stop at my chin and one of her hands lifts, hovering over my shirt.

'If this is a trick,' she says, and starts to smile, 'I'm going to be very, very angry.'

'Anna.' I shove the athame into its sheath in my pocket and reach out to pull her off the slab but her arms wrap around me and squeeze. I draw her head down to my shoulder and just stand; neither of us wants to let go.

She has no temperature. The rules of this place have taken that away, and I wish for the press of her cold skin, the way I remember. I suppose I should just be glad that she still has the right number of joints.

'I guess I don't care if you're real,' she says against my shoulder.

'I'm real,' I whisper into her hair. 'You told me to come.' Her fingers dig into my back, pulling at my shirt. Her body sort of jerks in my arms, and at first I think she's going to be sick. But then she draws back to look at me.

'Wait,' she says. 'Why are you here?' Her eyes scan me wildly and her balled-up fists feel like stones on my ribs. She's panicking. She thinks I might be dead.

'I'm not dead,' I say. 'I promise.'

Anna climbs down off the rock, cocking her head suspiciously. 'Then how? Nothing's here that isn't dead.'

'There are two things, actually,' I say, squeezing her hand. 'Me, and this other, annoying girl that we have to find.'

'What?' Anna smiles.

'It doesn't matter. What matters is we're leaving.' Except I don't really know how we do that. There isn't a line tied around my waist for me to tug on and be pulled back. We need Jestine.

Anna's eyes are bright, and her fingertips trace my shoulders, still waiting for me to disappear. 'You shouldn't have come,' she says, like a scolding, but she can't quite make it stick.

'You told me to,' I say. 'You said you couldn't stay.'

She blinks at me. 'Did I?' she asks. 'It doesn't seem so bad, right now.'

I almost laugh. Right now it doesn't. When she's free of burns, and cuts, and not strung through with butcher's twine, it doesn't seem so bad.

'You have to go back, Cassio,' Anna whispers. 'He won't let go of me.' Through her bright eyes I can see what this place has done to her. She seems smaller somehow. There's happiness on her face to see me, but she doesn't really believe that I can get her out.

'It's not his choice,' I say.

'Always his choice,' she corrects. 'Always his pleasure.'

I hold her tighter. Over six months she's been here, but what does that mean? Time doesn't exist. Even I've been here too long. It seems like I walked that maze with Jestine for an hour, and then an hour more without her. Not true. Nowhere near true.

'How did this happen?' I ask. 'How did he beat you?'

She draws away and tugs at the strap of her white dress with one hand. The other stays firmly attached to me, and I don't let go of her either.

'I fight and lose, again and again, over and over, until forever.' Her eyes lose focus, over my shoulder and I wonder what she sees. If I looked in the same direction, I might not see the same thing. Her eyes sharpen. 'Prometheus on the rock. Do you know that story? Every day he's punished for giving mortals fire by being strapped to a rock and having his liver eaten out by an eagle. I always thought it was a poor punishment. That he'd just get used to the pain, and the eagle would have to think of some new torture. But you don't. And he does.'

'I'm so sorry, Anna,' I say, but the words bounce off. She's not complaining. In her mind there's been no crime. She thinks that this is retribution. That this is justice.

She studies my face. 'How long has it been? I don't remember you right. The memory is from too far away, like I knew you when I was alive.' She smiles. 'I think I've forgotten what the world is.'

'You'll remember.'

She shakes her head. 'He won't let go of me.' The movement is strange. It doesn't fit; it hangs on her lopsided and it makes me wonder just how much damage has been done.

I pull her gently to her feet. 'We have to go. We have to find my friend, Jestine. We – ' I cringe as sharp pain hits my gut. Then it's gone and I can breathe again.

'Cas.' Anna's staring at the front of my shirt. I don't need to look down to know that the blood is starting to show. I'm not sure whether that means I'm not focusing hard enough on forgetting it, or that time is short. But I'd rather not take chances.

'What did you do?' she asks. She presses her hand against my stomach. 'Never mind. We just have to find Jestine, and then we can get out of here.'

Something taps my shoulder. When I turn, there's Jestine, looking as pleased with herself as ever.

There are cuts and lacerations on most of her fingertips and knuckles. Blood streaks are smeared across her cheeks and forehead like war paint, probably from wiping her torn-up hands against her face.

'Where have you been?' I ask. 'What happened?'

'I've been solving our problems,' she says, and digs her hand into her pocket. The move makes her grimace, but when she pulls her hand back out, she's absolutely beaming. When she unfurls her fingers, I see rough chips of shining silver in her palm.

'Two pockets full,' she says. 'I found a vein. Of the metal. The same metal that's in the blade of the Biodag Dubh.' She puts it back, out of view. Two pockets full. Plenty for the Order to forge a new athame. Something inside me quivers, some quiet, growling, jealous thing. 'Now the Order will have its proper warrior. They'll leave you and yours alone.'

I wouldn't count on it, I want to say, but she nods at my shirt.

'Wound's starting to show. I can feel mine too. I think that's our cue to leave.' Her eyes shift toward Anna, and they regard each other levelly. Jestine smirks. 'She looks like her picture.'

I put my arm around Anna protectively. 'Let's just get her out of here.'

'No,' says Anna, and when she speaks, the Obeahman

roars, a high, mechanical screech that rings out from everywhere, like he's directly above, or beneath us.

Jestine cringes and pulls out a short knife and what looks like a chisel. Both have chips and dents out of them. I guess they're what she used to get the metal out of the rock.

'What's that then?' she asks, makeshift weapons at the ready.

'The Obeahman,' I explain. 'The ghost that Anna dragged down here last fall.'

'No ghost,' Anna says loudly. 'He's not a ghost anymore. Not here. Here he's a monster. A nightmare. And he won't let go of me.'

'You keep saying that,' I say.

'Where he goes, I go.' She closes her eyes, frustrated. 'I can't explain it. It's like I'm one of them now. One of his. Twenty-five murderous dead. Four moaning innocents. We wear him like chains.' Brittle, pale fingers slide down her arms and wipe at the fabric of her skirt. It's a traumatized, cleansing gesture. But when she sees Jestine watching, her hands return to her side.

'He's tied to her,' Jestine says. 'If we pull her through, he comes along for the ride.' She sighs. 'So what do we do? You're not going to be in much shape to send him back when we get home. I suppose the Order could hold him, maybe bind him or banish him for a while.'

'No,' Anna insists. 'He's past that.'

My ears have mostly shut off as they go back and forth. Twenty-five murderous dead. They're all here, locked inside him. Every one that I killed. The greasy-haired hitchhiker. Even Peter Carver. That's why I saw him in the rock, and why Emily Danagger chased me through the cliffs. None of them went where they were supposed to. He was lying in wait like a shark, mouth open, waiting to swallow them whole.

'Anna,' I hear myself say. 'Four moaning innocents. What do you mean by that? Who are they?'

Her eyes move to mine. There's regret in them. She hadn't meant to say it. But she did.

'Two boys you know,' she says slowly. 'One man you don't.' Her eyes lower. Will and Chase. The jogger in the park.

'That's three. Who's the fourth?' I ask even though I know. I need to hear it. She looks back up and takes a deep breath.

'You look so much like him,' she says.

My fists clench, and when I yell it's at the top of my lungs, so the sound will carry far enough in this place for that bastard to hear.

CHAPTER TWENTY-SEVEN

'Hey,' Jestine says. She takes me by the shoulders and shakes once. I shrug her off. 'Now's not the time to be doing anything stupid.'

The hell it isn't. I pace across the damned rock, clenching my teeth every time my foot strikes the hardness of the surface. It sends vibrations of pain all the way up to my knees. What do I have? The knife in my hand. The rage in my throat. This body, bleeding out in another dimension. I turn to Anna. Her eyes trail across the landscape, wondering at the way the rock seems to hint at shades of red and electricity. It's picking up on my intentions. The edges are getting sharper.

'Can we beat him?'

Her lips part in surprise, but something moves in her irises too. Something quick, and dark, that I remember. It makes my pulse go faster.

Jestine shoves me in the shoulder. 'No, we can't bloody beat him! Not here. She couldn't beat him, and from what I understand, she's some big badass ghost.' She glances at Anna, who stands quietly, dark hair hanging down her sides. 'Course I can't see that now. But even if we could, we don't have time. Can't you feel that? Can't you hear it? Colin says that my breathing is slowing. What does Thomas say?'

'Thomas doesn't say anything,' I reply. And it's true. I haven't heard a peep from him since we crossed over. If I looked back now, I could see him, but I don't. Jestine's breathing is slowing. Mine must be too. But time is different here. Over here we might have hours. And I'm not leaving until this is finished.

'What is this?' I ask Jestine, holding the knife up before her eyes.

'Have you lost your mind?' She knocks it away like it was a threat. 'We're out of time.'

'Just tell me,' I say, and hold it back up again. 'It's here, where it came from. So over here is it just a knife? Or can I still use it?'

Jestine looks past the blade, into my eyes. I don't waver, and she looks away first.

'I don't know what it is,' she says. 'But it's tied to the magic of the Order. It's always more than just a knife.'

'I can feel it too,' says Anna. 'It doesn't hum like before but – he could feel it. That's why he ran.'

'Is he afraid of it?'

'No.' She shakes her head. 'Not afraid. Maybe not even surprised. Maybe just excited.'

Cas? Can you hear me? Time's up. Get back here.

Not now, Thomas. Not yet.

'Jestine,' I say. 'Don't take any chances. Go back. Anna and I will follow, if we can.'

'Cas,' she says, but I step back and take Anna by the hand.

'I can't leave here until he's done,' I say to them both. 'Until he's alone and torn apart. I can't let him keep them any longer. Not Will, or Chase, or that poor jogger from the park. Not my dad.' The corner of my mouth curls and I look at Anna. 'Not even that asshole Peter Carver. I'm going to cut them loose. And you too.'

'One more time,' she says, and when her eyes snap to mine, she's the girl I remember. Her hand presses my stomach. Yes, I know. We have to hurry.

'Fuck it all,' says Jestine. 'You stay, I stay. You can use me anyway. I've got chisels, and magic.' She wipes at her forehead with the back of her wrist. 'But let's get on with it.' She nods at Anna. 'You'd better come in handy. Something tells me we won't have time to be saving damsels in distress.'

Anna's brows knit. 'Damsels? You get sliced open, burned, and dashed against the rocks about a thousand times or so. Then we'll see who the damsel is.'

Jestine lets her head fall back and laughs madly; it rings through the dead air without an echo.

'Facing him one on one would be trouble. I don't even know if he can kill us here, but hand to hand he could incapacitate us, pull our spines out like he was deboning a fish. And that'd be enough. We'd lie here until our bodies bled out on the floor of the deep well. Then he'd have us.' Jestine crosses her arms.

'It should be together then,' Anna says. 'Can you fight?'

Jestine nods in my direction. 'I can take Cas on pretty easily.'

'Is that supposed to impress me?' Anna asks, inclining her head, and Jestine laughs.

'Cas, your girl's got quite a tongue.' She steps closer and narrows her eyes. 'And she seems suspiciously, suddenly sane.'

'It's the purpose,' Anna replies. 'There is no purpose here. No reason. It's disconnected. If I had to describe this place in one word, that would be it. The purpose makes me all right.'

She glances at me. Jestine doesn't know her well enough to recognize the shadow in that glance, but I do. She's not all right. But she's going through the motions and wearing the masks. There'll be more time, later on, to mend her, and make her forget. I tell myself that. But if I'm truthful, I have no idea what can be done to wash it away.

Cas. You've got to come back now.

No, Thomas. Not now. My eyes scan the bleak, expansive landscape. It looks flat, with just a slight slope here and there. The lack of distance and perspective makes my head spin. But it lies. It all lies. He's out there somewhere, and he's got plenty of places to hide.

'He's not going to come to us,' I say. 'I think he knows what I want.'

'Well, we can't just stand around,' Jestine says. She blinks fast and her head moves in a quick, jerky twitch. Burke must be in her ear.

'He might come,' says Anna. 'If we let him hunt us.'

'Sounds fun,' Jestine mutters sarcastically. She looks at me. 'I suppose solitary prey is more appealing than a herd. If I scream, come running.' She takes a deep breath and turns to go.

'Don't,' I say. 'If you lose sight of us, you might lose us completely. This place can take you.'

She grins over her shoulder. 'This place takes you where you want. We'll be seeking him, and he'll be seeking us, and then we'll double back on each other. You're always lost here, Cas. One way or another.'

I smirk. I didn't lose her before. She disappeared on

purpose, so she'd have time to find her damn vein of metal. Fine. I should have known.

'Don't take chances,' I tell her. 'If you have to go back, then go back.'

'Don't get dramatic,' she scoffs. 'I'm your friend but I'm not dying for you. I'm not Thomas. I'm not *her*.' Her footsteps fall flat on the rocks as she walks away, whistling a tune that sounds like Elmer Fudd's when he's after rabbits. When Anna and I look at each other, I know that behind us, Jestine has disappeared.

Walking through Hell with Anna, it feels like I should blurt out every damn thing I've wanted to say to her for the last six months. It feels like we're on borrowed time, even though I'm here to bring her home. I never really counted on seeing her again. It was just a dream. A quest, like a knight after the Holy Grail. But I'm here now, with a hole in my stomach that's starting to throb, trying to lure my father's killer out into the open. The surreality of this moment is probably making my brain bleed in nine places.

'I won't tell you that you shouldn't be doing this,' Anna. 'Trying to free your father. I know I would, if he were mine.'

'Is that what I'm trying to do? Free him?'

'Isn't it?'

I guess it is. I'm trying to free all of them. Will and Chase – they'd have been stuck here forever if I hadn't come looking for Anna, and the thought makes my insides twist. And my dad. I thought Anna had done it six months ago, when she dragged the Obeahman down here.

Something moves in the corner of our vision, and we both jump. But it's not him. It's something in the distance, hanging from the branches of a lonely tree. We keep on walking, walking without walking, because we can't really tell by looking whether we've made any progress. The landscape just shifts and changes; rock formations crop up and disappear. It's like being on an enormous treadmill. Now we look down over a canyon of sorts, cut down deep into the stone. There's what appears to be a black, oil-slicked river cutting through the bottom.

'Do you – have you ever talked to him? My dad, I mean?'

Anna shakes her head gently. 'He's just a shadow here, Cassio. They all are.'

'But do you think he knows where he is? Has he known the whole time?'

'I don't know what they know,' she says. But she looks away. She doesn't know. But she thinks he does.

Ahead, the canyon looms closer, too quickly for the

pace at which we're moving. I hate this place. It'd drive a physics professor batshit crazy in the span of three seconds. Where is he? Where is Jestine? The pain in my side is heavy, and it's starting to get harder to walk. If Jestine's breathing had slowed already, she might not even be here anymore. I guess I hope she isn't. By my side, Anna tenses as she scans the landscape. But there's still nothing there.

'Listen,' I say. 'After this is over, assuming I'm still alive to go back, I want to take you with me. I came here for you, and so did Thomas and Carmel. We want you to come back.' I swallow. 'I want you to come back. But it's your choice.'

'I'll still be dead, Cassio.'

'So will I be, someday. It doesn't matter.' I touch her shoulder and we stop so I can look into her eyes. 'It doesn't.'

She blinks, long and slow, her lashes black against her cheeks.

'All right,' she says, and I exhale all over. 'I'll come back.'

The Obeahman's scream cuts through the still and vibrations resonate up through our feet.

'There he is.'

CHAPTER TWENTY-EIGHT

The walking, distant stick figure at the bottom of the canyon could be anyone. But it isn't. It's my father's murderer, my father's jailer. He got the better of me once, with a curse that almost killed me. It'll be different this time. This time I'll make it stick.

His footsteps sound in our ears, too loud for being so far away. As he moves closer, our position changes; the cliffs shift in the space of a blink. We'd been looking down. Now he's straight ahead.

'What's wrong with his arms and legs?' I ask.

'Borrowed joints. Borrowed strength.' Anna's eyes are steel; she doesn't blink at his approach.

The extra joints make him ungainly. Before his gait was stiff, almost dragging. Now his legs jerk like they're attached at wrong angles. He walks closer to the wall and grins as he grasps on to it with his hands, heaving himself up onto the side of the rock face, defying gravity. When he pivots and skitters forward faster, on all fours,

I take a step back in spite of myself.

'Showoff,' I say, meaning it to come out mocking, but it sounded high and nervous, close to a squeak. It's like Anna said. He is whatever he wants to be here. He can probably twist his head all the way around. I wish I could tell my dad how well I'm following his advice about always being afraid.

'I'll slow him down, try to hold him,' says Anna, and her hair turns black and starts to lift. The white recedes from her eyes and dark veins stretch beneath her skin. The dress goes red in a slow, deliberate soak.

The Obeahman has come down from the wall and walks briskly on disjointed legs. His stitched-over eyes are trained on me. He doesn't want Anna anymore. He has her. I'm the last loose end.

'He'll break my arms first,' Anna says.

'What?'

'I'm just telling you,' she replies like it's a matter of course. 'I'm going to try to hold his arms, so he'll break mine. I can't beat him. Don't rely on me. I don't know if you can.' She looks at me and her expression reads easy. Regret. Empty wishes for more time or better chances.

I wish Thomas and Carmel were here. Only I don't. I just wish there was a plan, or a trap, like last time. It would be nice to have some kind of advantage, aside from the one clenched in my fist. Anna steps forward.

'Aren't you afraid?' I ask.

'I've done this before,' she replies. She actually manages a smile. Then she's gone, closing the distance, her movements quicker than I remember. She throws a punch and his teeth rake a red gash into her forearm. She doesn't wince, or scream. The way she's fighting is robotic. She knows she's going to lose and she's used to it. She doesn't even feel the pain.

'Don't just stand there! Help her!' Jestine yells at me as she streaks past to jump into the fray. I have no idea where she came from. It's like she popped out of the rock. But it doesn't matter; she doesn't hesitate. She dodges one of his arms and jams the end of her chisel into his shoulder. Anna has hold of his head, but it isn't a good hold.

My legs are frozen. Between the two of them I don't know what to do, where to attack. None of their movements have any effect. We should have gone. Gotten out when we could. Inside my head, Thomas is talking to me, his voice urgent. I can't pay attention or look back. Instead I watch as the Obeahman snaps Anna's arm like a twig, shoves her, and sends her rolling. Jestine he just shrugs off like an annoyance not to be bothered with. Not once has he taken his gaze off me. I stare where his eyes should be, watching the movement of the black stitches and the slow trickle of blood. I fear him. I've always feared him. He jerks his head once when he unhinges his jaw. He'll be on me in seconds to tear pieces out of me like he did with the others, and my dad and I will stay here forever.

Black tendrils of hair rise up about his shoulders in the instant before Anna's arm snakes around the front of him and takes hold of his jaw, her fist folding over his teeth and squeezing down. The Obeahman screeches, his black tongue lashing as she wrenches him around, grimacing.

'Stay away from him,' she growls, and smashes his body against the rock. The force is enough to send pebbles skittering. She does it again, and again, bashing him against the stone. I hear joints popping.

I hear Jestine say, 'Bloody hell,' in a breathless voice.

The Obeahman is like an angry animal. His fingertips sharpen down to points and he slices through her chest and shoulders, shredding muscle until her arm falls and his feet find purchase on the ground. Still Anna doesn't stop, jerking her shoulder, pounding his head into the rock so hard that any moment it must burst like a watermelon. But it doesn't. And the only blood running down his chin is from the cuts his teeth are leaving in her palm as she holds his jaw. She goes down on one knee and her grip finally fails. He claws across her back and she slumps down into the dirt.

Impossible, I think as he strides calmly toward me with Anna's blood dripping from his fingertips. I want to kill him more than anything, for her, for my dad. But it feels impossible. He's closer now. Close enough so I can smell his smoke.

Jestine scrambles up off of the ground; she rises up behind him, screams, '*Leithlisigh!*' and strikes her hand down onto the back of his head. He falls forward, but not before catching her with his arm and slamming her down, so hard, onto the rock. I scream her name but the sound of her bones cracking is louder than my voice.

I dart forward and drag her out from under his arm. There's blood on her teeth, and leaking from the corner of her mouth. Her legs trail behind, bouncing across the ground like rubber.

'That's it,' she groans. 'That's all.' She lifts her head and we look back at the Obeahman. Whatever her spell was, it still has him doubled over. And something else: there are shadows around him now, and the effect is almost like watching him move too fast to see. Sometimes there's an extra arm visible, or a head that isn't his. I think I see the County 12 Hiker, still in a white t-shirt and leather jacket. Then it's gone. But that's what it is. He's separating.

'What did you do?' I look down at Jestine. There's sweat beaded on her forehead and her skin has turned bluish. Anna has managed to get to her feet and kneels beside us.

'It's a curse,' Jestine says, sputtering blood down her chin. 'He's destabilized now. I thought I could do more but—' she coughs. 'I'm done. I'm dying. And I don't want to die here.' There's so much surprise in her voice. I want to do something, to keep her warm or to stop the bleeding. But there's nothing I can do. The inside of her probably looks like someone took a sledgehammer to it.

'Go back,' I say, and she nods. She twists up onto her shoulder and when she looks down at the ground, I know it's not stone that she's seeing, but Colin Burke. She glances once at Anna, sees black veins, and smiles. She glances at me, one more time, and winks. Then her brow knits and her eyes close. It seems that she falls down, and through, and then she's gone, like she never was.

Behind us, the Obeahman still writhes, his hands pressed against his head, trying to hold himself together. I look at Anna's broken arm, at her cuts, draining blood down into her dress.

'Don't get hurt anymore,' I tell her.

'It won't matter, after,' she says, but she stays kneeling where she is when I turn away.

The athame is at home in my hand. I don't expect anything. I don't know what's going to happen. I just know that I'm going to cut him, and find out.

As I get close, the smell of him fills my nostrils, the sickening smoke, and beneath that, the sour scent of stale, dead things. It's on the tip of my tongue to say something, to whip out one last, end-of-your-ass quip, but I don't. Instead I bring my foot up into his stomach, rocking him back just enough so I can push the athame deep into his chest.

It doesn't do anything. He screams but he's been screaming. I pull the knife out and make another cut, but when I do his fingers lock around my arm and squeeze. The bones grind beneath the skin as he lifts me with him, rising to stand. Shadows of spirit are still blinking in and out of existence in the air. I peer closer, searching for my dad's face. I stop looking when the Obeahman's teeth sink into my muscle. My arm flexes and contracts instinctually, but it's butterfly wings against a bulldozer. He jerks his head and most of my shoulder rips loose and goes with it.

I panic. All my limbs strike out at once and I make desperate grabs for the athame with my good arm. When I get it I just slice the air. I want him away. I don't want to watch him swallow pieces of me.

One of the cuts severs an arm. Not his but someone else's, one of the trapped ghosts, but it's the Obeahman who screams as that body is twisted and torn free, pulling up and out through the hole in his chest. We sort of fall away from each other, staring up at the shade of Will Rosenberg's familiar face as it twists skyward. For one mad instant he looks my way, and I wonder what he sees and if he understands. His mouth opens, but I'll never know if he wanted to speak. The shadow of him blinks out, gone into nothing. Gone wherever Will was supposed to go before the Obeahman got his hooks in.

'I knew it, you fucker,' I say, something nonsensical like that. I didn't know anything. I had no clue, but now I do, and I cut the air around him, and over him, the blade sweeping through and cutting down into his shoulders and head, staring up at spirits as they jerk free and fly. Sometimes two at a time. His scream is in my ears but I'm looking for my dad. I don't want to miss the sight of him. And I want him to see me. When I roll and dodge it's on autopilot; just a matter of time before I mess up. The distraction of a glimpse of black tail is enough to slow me down, and the Obeahman's fist connects with my sternum like a battering ram, crushing my chest. Then there's only air, and pain, and the hard, stone ground.

Anna is screaming. I open my eyes. She's fighting him. She's losing, but she's doing what she can to hold him back. She should let him come. There's too much blood in my throat for me to talk. I can't tell her anything. It's nothing but sputter and spray. Jestine is dead. And I am dead. It's over.

But I could go back. I could do what Jestine did, and die with Thomas and Carmel and Gideon there. The room would still have the warmth of lit candles. My head half turns, thinking of it. If I turn just an inch more, I'll be able to see Thomas, see the whole room, and if I press until the glass shatters I'll be back there.

'Cassio, get out!'

Anna, I can't breathe. She's still fighting, one-armed, refusing to fall. How many ghosts did I cut loose in those seconds? Three? Maybe five? Was one of them my dad? I couldn't tell. I wonder how much it counts, that I did my best. I wonder if he knows that I'm here.

CAS!

My body jerks. I felt that one. Right between my eyes: Thomas's voice firing across my synapses.

Come back! You've got to come back! There isn't blood left in you. Your heart is slowing! The blood is slowing! We're stopping it, do you hear me? I'm stopping it!

There's no blood left in me. Funny, Thomas. Because there's a hell of a lot of it still pumping into my lungs. Gallons of it, filling me like a sinking ship. Except that…there isn't. Not really. And I'm lucid, despite not having taken a decent breath for what seems like an hour.

I look at Anna, using her broken arm now like she doesn't care if it tears off completely. Because she doesn't care. It doesn't matter. None of it matters, not the ragged remains of my shoulder, or my crushed chest. The Obeahman kicks one of Anna's legs sideways at the knee and she tumbles.

I push myself up onto my elbows and spit blood onto the stone. The pain is dulled, still strong but no longer intense. It feels...inconsequential. I bend my knees, get my legs under me, and stand up. When I look down at my good arm, I smile. Did you see that, Dad? The athame never left my fist.

The Obeahman sees me rise, but I barely notice. I'm too busy watching the ghosts try to break free of his body, tracking their movements to see where they emerge the most. The vibrations of the knife are singing up through my wrist. Get in. Get out. Cut.

When I dive forward he's unprepared. The first cut catches a ghost trailing out of his left leg. I kick out and put him on one knee, then get to my feet and cut across his bent back, severing another spirit before jumping away. Two more twist and spin out of his chest, and he screams, music in my ears. A four-jointed arm swings for my head; I duck and cut down beneath his ribs, then once more behind his head. No time to think, no time to look. Just get them out. Set them free.

Two more. Then one more. My dad's voice is in my ear. Every piece of advice he ever gave me flashes through my mind and makes me faster, makes me better. This is what I was meant to do, what I've waited for, trained for.

'It doesn't feel like I thought it would,' I say, wondering if he can hear me, if he'll know what I mean. It doesn't feel like I thought it would. I thought there would be rage. But there's only elation. He and Anna are with me. The blade flashes and the Obeahman can't stop us. Every time a ghost flies the Obeahman gets angrier, more frustrated. He tries to plug the hole in his chest, pressing his fingers down into the wound. The ghosts only tear it wider.

Anna fights with me, pulling him to the ground. I cut and count and watch them fly. The last of them leave him in a storm; they erupt from his chest, forcing the wound wide. He lays on the stone, split nearly in half, empty of everything but himself.

It all happened so fast. My eyes scan the blankness that should be sky, but there's no one there. My dad's not there. I missed him, in the middle of all of it. All that remains is the son of a bitch who took him away in the first place.

I step forward and kneel. Then, without really knowing why, I drag the athame across the stitches of his eyes.

The lids snap open. His eyes are still in there, but they're rotten and black. The irises have turned an unnatural yellow, almost iridescent, a snake's eyes. They swivel toward me and fix me with a look of disbelief.

'Go to wherever your Hell is,' I say. 'You should have gone there ten years ago.'

'Cas,' Anna says, and takes my hand. We stand up and back away. The Obeahman watches, his pupils maddening pinpoints against the yellow iris. The wound in his chest is no longer growing larger, but the edges are drying out, and as we stand, the dryness spreads, turning his flesh and clothing to an ashy brown, before caving in. I look into his eyes until the decay takes them over. For a second he lies there like a cement statue against the rock, and then he collapses, and the pieces of him scatter in all directions, until they disappear.

CHAPTER TWENTY-NINE

I never saw my dad.

After I realized that the blood didn't matter, it all went so fast. I just cut and cut and didn't think. And they all left. Around us now, everything feels empty.

'It's not empty,' Anna says, even though I'm pretty sure I didn't say anything out loud. 'You set him free. You let him move on.' She puts her hand on my shoulder and I look down at the athame. The blade shines bright, brighter than anything else here.

'He's moved on,' I say. But part of me hoped he would stick around. Even if it was just long enough for me to see him. Maybe to tell him – I don't know what. Maybe just to tell him that we were OK.

Anna wraps her arms around my waist and rests her chin on my shoulder. She doesn't say anything comforting. She doesn't tell me something that she doesn't know for certain. She's just here. And that's enough.

When I take my eyes off of the athame, everything is different. With the Obeahman gone, the landscape is changing. It wrinkles and reforms around us. Looking up, the dark, bruised void is brighter. It looks clearer, and I can almost make out the faint twinkling of stars. The rocks are gone too, and so are the cliffs. There are no more sharp edges. There are no edges at all. We're standing together in the middle of something beginning.

'We should go,' I whisper. 'Before Thomas gives me a nosebleed.'

Anna smiles. The dark goddess is gone, receded back under the skin. She's just Anna, looking at me curiously in her plain white dress.

'What's going to happen now?' she asks.

'Something better,' I reply, and take her hand. She looks beautiful here. Her eyes sparkle, and the sunlight warms the color of her hair to a shining, chocolate brown.

'How do we get back?' she asks. I don't reply. Instead I stare over her shoulder, at the changing landscape. I don't know if I'll be able to remember what it was like to see this. If I'll be able to remember what it was like to watch creation. Maybe it'll all fade, like a dream after waking.

The world behind her rises out of the mist, only there was never any mist. It comes upon us, up and around us, like watercolor spilling across a blank page. Sunlight beams down on uncut green grass, grass that I could fall down on and sleep for hours. Maybe days. Farther off are trees, and on the edge of that, there's the Victorian, Anna's Victorian, standing white and tall and unbroken. It never looked like this when she lived there. It never, ever looked like this. So bright and straight in the sun. Not even when it was newly built.

'Cas? Is it Thomas? Do we have to hurry?' She looks into my eyes, starts to follow them. I grab both of her hands.

'Don't,' I say. 'Don't look.'

She doesn't. Her eyes widen and she listens, trusting me, afraid of what she might see if she does. But I can't hide the feel of the breeze as it moves through our clothes. I can't muffle the sound of warm things, of birds singing and insects buzzing in the flowers near the house. So she looks. Her hair falls over her shoulder, and I expect to feel her fingers pull loose from mine any second. This is her place. Her other side. The blemish of the Obeahman is gone. She belongs here.

'No.'

'What?'

'I don't belong here.' She squeezes my hands, tighter than before. 'Let's go back.'

I smile. She crossed over death to call me. I crossed

370

through Hell to find her.

'Anna!'

We both look toward the sound of my voice. There's a silhouette in the open doorway of the Victorian.

'Cas?' she asks uncertainly, and the figure steps out into the light. It's me. It's impossibly, completely me. Anna smiles and tugs at my hands. A small laugh escapes her throat.

'Come on,' he calls. 'I thought you wanted to go for a walk.'

She hesitates. When she half turns back and sees me, the real me, she looks confused, and squeezes her eyes shut.

'Let's go,' she says. 'This place lies. For a minute I – I didn't remember where we were. I didn't remember you were here.' She looks back toward the Victorian again, and when she speaks, her voice is far off, almost there already. 'For I minute I thought I was home.'

'Come on,' the other me calls again. 'Before we have to go meet Thomas and Carmel.'

I look back over my shoulder. The candlelit room is still there. I can see Thomas, kneeling on the ground, his hands working frantically. I don't have much time. But everything is happening too fast.

If I let go of Anna's hands, she'll forget me. She'll forget everything except what lies across that field. It will all be gone. Her murder, and her curse. She'll forever live out the life she should have had. The one we might have had together, if everything had been different. This place lies. But it's a good lie.

'Anna,' I say. She turns back to me, but her eyes are wide and conflicted. I smile, and let one of her hands go to slide my fingers into her hair. 'I have to go.'

'What?' she asks, but I don't answer. Instead I kiss her, one time, and try to tell her in that single gesture everything that she'll forget as soon as she turns away. I tell her I love her. I tell her I'll miss her. And then I let her go.

CHAPTER THIRTY

There's the sound of something shattering, and the feeling of being slammed into something, all without moving. My eyes crack open and see a room filled with candlelight and red robes. There isn't much sensation in my body that isn't straight pain. Thomas, Gideon, and Carmel are on me immediately. I hear their voices as three distinct squawks. Someone is applying pressure to my stomach. Other members of the Order stand around looking useless, but when Gideon barks, there are a few red flutters. At least some of them have run off to do something. I stare up at the ceiling that is too high to see, but I know it's there. I don't have to look to the right or left to know that I came back alone.

This situation is vaguely familiar. I'm lying in a bed with an IV stuck in my arm and stitches in my guts, both internal and external. My back is propped up by four or five pillows and a tray of uneaten food rests on the bedside table. At least there's no green Jell-O on it.

They say I was out for a week, and that my survival was touch and go for most of that. Carmel says that I pushed the limit on blood transfusions, and that I'm incredibly lucky that the Order has basically a fully functioning ER built into their basement. When I woke up, I was surprised by the head of auburn and silver hair zonked out by my bed. Gideon flew my mom into Glasgow.

There's a knock at the door, and Thomas, Carmel, and my mom walk in. Mom immediately gestures to the tray of food.

'You'd better eat that,' she says.

'I'm taking it easy on my stomach,' I protest. 'Come on. It just had a knife in it.'

Not funny, her narrowed eyes say to me. OK, Mom. I pick up the bowl of applesauce and slurp it down, just to make her smile, which she does, reluctantly.

'So, we've decided that we'll all stay on until you're well enough to travel,' says Carmel, taking a seat on the foot of the bed. 'We'll fly back together, just in time for school to start.'

'Whoop-de-do, Carmel,' Thomas says, spiraling his finger in the air. He gives me a look. 'She's so damn excited to be a senior. Like she didn't run the whole school already. Personally, I'm in no rush. Maybe we can take one more swing through the Suicide Forest on the way out, just for kicks.'

'You're hilarious,' Carmel says sarcastically, and shoves him.

One more knock at the door, and Gideon comes in with his hands in his pockets and sits down in the chair. I notice the uncomfortable look traded between him and my mom. I don't know if things will ever be the same for them after this. But I'll do my best to explain that it wasn't Gideon's fault.

'I just got off the phone with Colin Burke,' Gideon tells us. 'Jestine is apparently doing very well. She's up and about already.'

Jestine didn't die. The wounds she received at the hands of the Obeahman were no more fatal than mine were. And she came back earlier than I did, so she didn't lose quite as much blood. She was also apparently more careful about where she took her wound, because she didn't do as much internal damage to herself as I did either. Maybe someday I'll get her to come clean with all of her secrets. Or maybe not. Life's more interesting with gray areas.

Silence lingers in the room. I've been conscious now for three days, but they keep pussyfooting around, and haven't asked too many questions about what happened over there. But they're dying to know. I won't mind telling them. It's just sort of fun to wait and wonder which one is going to burst first.

I look around at their uncomfortably curious faces. None of them do anything but give a closed-lip smile.

'Well, I'm going to see about dinner for the rest of us,' my mom says, and crosses her arms. 'You're still on mushy food for a while, Cas.' She claps Thomas on the shoulder as she leaves. No doubt she knows that I chose him to be my anchor. If she was fond of him before, she might just adopt him now.

'Did you at least see her?' Thomas asks, and I smile. Finally.

'Yeah. I saw her.'

'What...what happened? Was it the Obeahman?' He asks so hesitantly. Carmel's eyes are bugged out, watching me for signs of stress, ready to jump on Thomas and stop the questions. It's sort of silly, but I appreciate their worry.

'It was the Obeahman,' I say. 'You were right, Gideon. They were trapped there together.' He nods, and his eyes go dark. He didn't really want to be right, I suppose. 'But he's finished now. I finished him. And I freed the others. All of the others he took into himself over the years. All those ghosts. And Will and Chase.' I nod at Carmel. 'And my dad.' Gideon closes his eyes.

'Don't tell Mom yet,' I say to him. 'I will tell her. But – I didn't see him or anything. I didn't talk to him. It's hard to explain.'

'Don't worry,' he says. 'Tell her in your own time.'

'What about Anna?' Thomas asks. 'Was she all right? Did you free her too?'

I smile. 'I hope I did,' I reply. 'I think I did. I think she'll be all right now. I think she'll be happy.'

'I'm glad,' Carmel says. 'But are you going to be OK?' She puts her hand on my knee and squeezes it through the sheets. I nod. I'll be fine.

'What about the Order?' I ask Gideon. 'Jestine brought metal back with her, to forge another athame. Did they tell you that?'

'They alluded to it.' Gideon nods. 'She always was a clever girl.'

'Another athame?' says Thomas. 'Can they do that?'

'I'm not sure. They seem to think so.'

'So what,' Carmel groans, sounding exhausted. 'Does that mean we're going to have to take out the entire Order? Not that I'd mind, but seriously?'

'If they wanted me dead, they had a prime opportunity to do it,' I say. 'I was basically dead on that floor. They could have just left me. Denied me care.' I look at Gideon, and he nods agreement. 'I don't think I have anything to worry about from them. They'll have their athame. And their instrument,' I add bitterly. 'They'll stay off my back.'

'They got what they wanted,' Gideon agrees. 'And they appear to have gone. We're the only ones left here. The Order departed the moment Jestine was well enough to be moved.' I notice that Gideon refers to the Order as if he wasn't a member. Good. He reclines in the chair and folds his hands on his chest. 'It would seem, Theseus, that your way is clear.'

I smile, and remember my last moments with Anna. I remember the way she kissed me, and that I could feel her smile, barely restrained in her cheeks. I remember that her lips were so unbelievably warm.

Thomas and Carmel stand by my bed, looking down on me with bruises and scarred necks. Maybe somewhere my dad is looking on too. Maybe while being batted at by a hair-pulling black cat. My smile stretches wider.

My way is clear.

ACKNOWLEDGMENTS

Girl of Nightmares owes a lot to my editor, Melissa Frain. As far as editors go, she is the bomb diggity. So thank you, Mel, for having a great eye, and being crazy supportive. Thank you also to my agent, Adriann Ranta, who continues to navigate the publishing waters for me and tell me what's what. Thank you to Seth Lerner and the artist Nekro, for another amazing cover. And thank you to the entire team at Tor Teen, for doing all the things it takes to make a book a book.

Also, the world needs readers, so thank you to all of them, and the reviewers, teachers, librarians and bloggers who continue to spread the love of books.

A quick shout out to my parents, in particular my dad this time, who never doubts and drives sales in places like Minot, North Dakota. Thanks, Dad!

And finally, the usual suspects: Ryan VanderVenter, Missy Goldsmith, Susan Murray, and Dylan Zoerb, for luck.

ABOUT THE AUTHOR

Kendare Blake is an import from South Korea who was raised in the United States. She received a Bachelor's degree in Business from Ithaca College and a Master's degree in Writing from Middlesex University in London. She brakes for animals, the largest of which was a deer, which sadly didn't make it, and the smallest of which was a mouse, which did, but it took forever. Amongst her likes are Greek Mythology, rare red meat and veganism. She also enjoys girls who can think with the boys like Ayn Rand, and boys who scare the morality into people, like Bret Easton Ellis.

F R A C T U R E D

T E R I   T E R R Y

The sequel to the astonishing

S L A T E D

Kyla can't forget Ben.

And she is starting to remember other things: like her birthday, and that Nico helped prepare her for Slating, so that part of her could survive it.

She thinks he is on her side, and tells him she has recovered some of her memories.

But will he help her find out what happened to Ben?

978 1 40831 948 2 £6.99 pbk
978 1 40831 949 9 £6.98 eBook

ORCHARD BOOKS
www.orchardbooks.co.uk